p r a i s e

"*All Good Children* is suffused with compassion, outrage, despair, and dreams that die at birth. Dayna Ingram has crafted every fiber of this rich tapestry with the utmost care. And—like the reader—all are held in exquisite tension."
LEA DALEY, author of *FutureDyke*

"Dayna Ingram has a gift for imagining rich and disturbing worlds. Although The Over are fantastical, the rest of the world seems brutally realistic. I was hooked from the first fire-and-brimstone chapter, and was kept clinging on until the very last page. *Eat Your Heart Out* is one of my favourite books (who can resist lesbians and zombies?), and *All Good Children* definitely lives up to those expectations. Disturbing and enthralling, *All Good Children* is the queer post-apocalyptic we've been waiting for."
DANIKA LEIGH ELLIS for *The Lesbrary*

"A postmodern fable of desperation and justice that draws you in, daring you not to turn away before you turn the page."
SALEM WEST, author of *Hoosier Daddy*

"With *All Good Children*, Dayna Ingram captures the global horror of an inter-species planetary takeover in a different and subtle way, by intimately focusing on how one family suffers, and endures. Being complicit to suffering may be a greater nightmare than the chilling creatures she's created. Countering them, we find a great example of feisty humanity in one angry young teenage girl."
JIM PROVENZANO, Lambda Literary Award-winning author of *Every Time I Think of You*

# ALL
# GOOD
# CHILDREN

## DAYNA
## INGRAM

LETHE PRESS
MAPLE SHADE, NEW JERSEY

Published by LETHE PRESS
118 Heritage Ave, Maple Shade, NJ 08052
lethepressbooks.com

ISBN: 1-59021-589-3 / 978-1-59021-589-0

LIBRARY OF CONGRESS CATALOGING-IN-PUBLICATION DATA
Names: Ingram, Dayna, author.
Title: All good children / Dayna Ingram.
Description: Maple Shade, NJ : Lethe Press, [2016]
Identifiers: LCCN 2016001794| ISBN 1590215893 (pbk. : alk. paper) | ISBN
9781590215890
Subjects: LCSH: Lesbians--Fiction. | GSAFD: Science fiction.
Classification: LCC PS3609.N4686 A79 2016 | DDC 813/.6--dc23
LC record available at http://lccn.loc.gov/2016001794

✤

Cover and interior design
by INKSPIRAL DESIGN

FOR MY MOTHER

# PROLOGUE
## TWENTY-SIX
## YEARS EARLIER

THROUGH THE BARS ON HIS kitchen window, Dominick Silamo watches Pretoria's greatest suburb burn. It is a large window and the house is built into the hillside; he can see the whole of the downtown shopping center and the roadblocks trailing off into the smoke-filled horizon. Molotovs and pipe bombs have exploded shops and houses, cars and military vehicles. The smoke is dark and fathomless, and somewhere deep inside it creatures beat their wings like *izulu*, hunting. Although mythology insists fire is the only means of destroying *izulu*, the impossible birds-of-prey defy this, swooping and diving through the smoke as the fire consumes all that lies below them.

Silamo rinses his hands in the sink. He just had this faucet installed two months ago; stainless steel and modern, a symbol of the type of household his family would create here. The faucet handles are diamond-shaped cut glass. The refrigerator is new, too, and the cabinets are refinished, polished mahogany. Marble countertops were meant to be installed next week. He hadn't decided about the kitchen floorboards yet; they are scuffed and splintering in loose spots near the table. He was waiting until next week to look at tile samples for possible replacement.

The fires haven't yet reached the hillside; the small cul-de-sac is safe from them for now. The street has not, however, been able to avoid looters and opportunists. He hears alarms sounding off in his neighbors' identical two-story houses. No one has tried to break into his home. He is the chief of police. Things will have to grow a little more dire before they dare to explore his place.

He cannot think—does not want to think—how things could grow more dire. There are *izulu* in the air, straight out of storybooks and into their city, perhaps not summoning bolts of lightning but still as deadly. They swoop down into the streets and skewer citizens with their talons, lifting them up and up and up and then dropping them down and down and down. Bullets do not stop them; they are indifferent to bullets. No one has gotten close enough to try a knife, least of all him. Some folklore enthusiast thought of fire, and now here is Silamo, sweating in his unfinished kitchen, taking a break from packing the last of his bags.

Silamo selects a mug from the rack above the window and fills it with water. His gulps are greedy and loud. He wipes his forehead with the back of his wrist. Though the fires seem confined to the commercial centers, the heat has risen with the ash-black smoke. Silamo has stripped to a white sleeveless undershirt, nearly translucent with his sweat, and porous cotton slacks cinched with a plain belt. In his front pocket he carries his badge and identification, a small roll of large bills and his wedding band. In the living room next to the couch are three duffel bags filled primarily with underwear and socks, a bit more money, a compass and a road map of South Africa. The keys to his Jeep are on the table by the front door. He is almost ready to go but he must do this one last thing.

He saw them coming up the abandoned street while packing the final duffel bag upstairs. The Lieutenant General of the National Defense Force and two of the *izulu*. Just walking, strolling even, slow and steady strides with the smoke curling like a beckoning finger behind them. Lieutenant General Zuma led the way; the creatures kept pace behind him. Silamo's heart stopped then sped up. As they drew closer, he found himself studying the lieutenant general's uniform: pressed olive green suit adorned with silver and red military medals that gleamed in the sun; stiff octagon of a hat stamped snug over a sweating forehead. The suit was fitted, it moved with Zuma's body, sighed when he sighed, tensed when he tensed, sweated when he sweated. Silamo couldn't process it. He needed a drink of water.

There is a knock on the door. They actually knock. Silamo stands in his kitchen, mug of water in one hand, the other pressed against his fleshy stomach. He wonders what will happen if he pretends not to be home, but they must know already he is here or they would not have walked all this way. He sets the mug on the lip of the counter and moves for the other room but the mug has been precariously placed and it topples. As he exits the kitchen, he hears it thud and crack simultaneously against the floorboards, and he reflexively issues a stern hiss—"Shh!"

Silamo places both palms against the heavy front door, whispers a quick prayer, pulls back the bolt locks and opens the door.

The *izulu* enter first.

They tower over him, a man his mother always lovingly referred to as a giant, her little giant. They tower over him and make him feel like a child again, plaintive cries for his mommy tickling the back of his throat. Nine feet maybe, they have to duck under the doorframe and hunch slightly so as not to graze the ceiling. Their faces are the most striking, bald as they are against the coarse feathers that sheathe their bodies. The skin is pale and appears riddled with gooseflesh, something you want to touch but don't want to touch. It crinkles around the eyes and smoothes around the protrusion of the beak. These two have similar but different beaks, and Silamo wonders, while he can still muster enough unclouded thought to wonder, if the beaks of all *izulu* are different. The one on the left is serrated along its under edge and pointed at the tip, its nostrils placed about halfway down the shaft. The one on the right is sharp-edged but smooth with a tip that hooks downward. The color of the left is as peach pale as the bald head, the color of the right melds from pale to coal black at its hooked end. Their eyes are different too, though Silamo doesn't linger too long on them; the left's are red, the right's are a jaundiced yellow.

They push through the doorframe and Silamo backs up into the living room, ankles nudging his wife's old knitting rocker. He watches them walk into the space, an awkward shuffle on their taloned feet, so unused to such movements. What they really want to do is fly. What they really want to do is pierce his shoulders with those talons and lift him into the skies and fly and fly and fly until he grows too heavy. But what they do inside his home is shuffle to either side of the living room's arched threshold and turn their disturbing faces toward Lt. Gen. Zuma.

Zuma walks between the sentries with his hands clasped casually behind his back, his dark face filled with a toothy grin. His own eyes are rheumy with age, the green irises once vibrant, faded after forty years of military service. He has seen so much, Silamo knows; a hero as Silamo himself was growing up, yearning for someone to emulate. Silamo recalls meeting him for the first time at a fundraising event four years ago, the summer he became Chief of Police. He was so struck by the upright brilliance of the man then—how straight and tall he stood, even so close to retirement age; how magnificently he smiled, with his entire face, at each guest and shook every hand—that only after several liters of strong beer could Silamo even approach him. He remembers looking into the old lieutenant general's eyes and being jealous of the wisdom reflected in them; now all he sees in the man's eyes is a cool denial and a willingness to forget.

"Chief Silamo. I trust we have not come at a bad time."

Standing between the *izulu*, the living room becomes small, suffocating. Silamo feels his throat closing around the acrid meat-rot stench of the beasts. "Little bit, actually," he says. "Little bit of one, yes."

The lieutenant general's grin stretches his jaw line as he laughs. "Forgive me, then. This interruption won't last long. I am correct in assuming you are still active chief of police here, yes?"

The *izulu* to Zuma's left unfurls a hand from its folded wing and scratches its hooked beak. Silamo has seen these hands; surprised at first, yes, because the carrion-eaters these creatures so closely resemble in body do not possess hands, but the *izulu* they are at heart, of course, do. The skin is leathery and pale, like their faces, rippled like faded scar tissue; their wings seem stitched into the arms, he can see where these stitches begin and then are obscured by the dark feathers. Unlike the three-pronged talons of their feet, their hands are small and five-pronged, like fingers, though they are also talons. In the center of the hand—the palm—something crimson stains the paleness but Silamo can't see it clearly. The tip of what would be the *izulu's* index finger scratches at its beak, then disappears beneath its wing with a sound like a tent-flap closing.

Silamo remembers when he was last active as police chief, his first tactical maneuver when this all began, three weeks ago: to evacuate downtown Pretoria, primarily the university and administrative district, which were being hit the hardest with what early reports claimed were guerrilla attacks of unknown origin. Civilian witnesses swore to seeing bombs dropped, non-exploding bombs, they said, or silent exploders: one second a dark streak through the sky, soundless, and the next a body on the steps of the courthouse, or what was once a body, all the things that made it a body now splattered outside of it in a bloody sea. Silamo assembled a team and went in with his lofty goals of establishing perimeters, setting up road checks, rushing the injured to waiting mobile medical units. There were no injured, of course; the *izulu* left no injured.

The SANDF were still mobilizing air-strike units, so until then all Silamo was meant to do was get the civilians to safety and attempt to positively identify the bombers, the shooters, whomever. As the carnage seemed localized at the university, Silamo moved in on the campus with a small contingent of officers. They swept the place, clearing out students who had taken refuge under desks and inside closets, staff who had barricaded themselves in their offices with ineffectually stacked waste bins and orthopedic roller chairs. There was no damage inside the buildings, no terrorist waiting with bombs or guns. The remnants of the attack were smeared along the main building's steps, the sidewalk, the streets for three blocks in every direction. Bodies moldering in the afternoon sun, attracting flies and rodents with the collective allure of decay.

His officers met no resistance inside the university nor throughout their respective sweeps of the three-square-block radius. Silamo made the call to load up the civilians and take them out of the strike zone. He was ready to report to the SANDF that there would be no need for an air unit; whoever had perpetuated these attacks was gone now, damage done. Van doors slammed closed around him as he stood next to his vehicle, trying not to look at the bodies in the streets, or to breathe too deeply through his nose. He would have to call in a cleaner, and of course the coroner would have to examine what was left of the bodies, to determine cause of death. What sorts of bombs were these? What sort of people launched an attack in this manner?

He waited beside his vehicle while the others evacuated, smoking a cigarette. His wife was always trying to get him to quit, for Heaven's sake. He felt the things he'd seen today warranted at least one cigarette, maybe two.

As he opened the car door and stamped out the cigarette stub, he caught movement in the shadows of a bank across the street. He waited a moment, squinting into the darkness of the alley. There, he saw it again. His hand moved to the pistol at his waist, and he closed his door and started across the street. From behind him, a woman's voice shouted, "Help me!"

He turned and saw a slender woman crawling on her elbows from beneath a truck parked four cars down from his. She appeared unhurt but she was shaking badly and her face was red and puffy from crying, her hair and light blue pantsuit dirty from having hidden under the truck for so long.

"You, there!" He called to her. She was trying to stand up, using the truck to brace herself, continuing to shout for help. He strode toward her, saying, "I'm here. I'll help you."

One second it was not there, and the next it was. It was on her in a blink; he could not even say if he had blinked, but there it was, like an apparition. She was stooped, her hands groping the hood of the truck as she struggled to stand. Then the talons were in her, stabbing just beneath the shoulder blades. The massive thing was something Silamo was unable to comprehend; six feet away from it and he couldn't describe it as anything other than the mythological *izulu*, though it was a vulture, a mutated bird of prey, as he would later tell it, and a devil, a demon, a bad dream.

It could have disappeared with the woman as quickly as it appeared on top of her, but it lingered. It pushed its wings against the air and pulled her from the truck, from the safety of the ground. Silamo felt the wind move around him with the movement of the thing's wings, a span that doubled its size. It hovered over the truck, looking down at Silamo; Silamo was certain it looked down at him. Its orange eyes saw him. It beat its wings slowly, purposefully, and it let the woman in its grasp squirm and scream, and it made no sound, no sound but the wind. It was Christ-like, Silamo will remember thinking later: the spread of its wings, the sun glaring behind it, its extreme calm and severe intention as it hovered there, seeing Silamo, making sure Silamo saw it.

Another non-blink and it was gone. Only then did Silamo bring up his pistol. Only then could he move; only then could he feel the warm trickle of urine down his thigh.

That was three weeks ago. He knew he should have died. The thing should have grabbed him. It let him live, which frightened him. Because it was purposeful, calculating. They wanted him to know they were back so that he could report it to the SANDF. A civilian, a mass of civilians, could be discredited, ignored, accused of madness or attempting to incite panic. But he was chief of police. Someone would listen to him. Someone important would listen, and they would know: the *izulu* had declared another war.

Back in the house, Lt. Gen. Zuma's bemused remark pulls Silamo into the present: "My apologies if the question is too difficult."

Silamo's chest aches with the breath he only just now realizes he has yet to release. Painfully, he exhales. Forcing himself to look at Zuma, he concedes, "Yes, I'm still the chief. What can I do for you?"

"How about a cup of tea?"

"Yes. Yes, of course. All right."

Silamo steps backwards through the kitchen archway, and Zuma finally catches on. "Oh my," he says, "I forgot. Do they bother you that much? Very well, they'll stay here."

The *izulu* remain as sentries in the living room while Zuma follows Silamo—who still does not turn his back on the lieutenant general—into the kitchen. Zuma's boots click across the hardwood. Silamo remembers himself enough to pull out a chair for him. His own heel knocks into the dropped mug and crunches the chipped-off ceramic handle.

Zuma looks down, then back up, that disarming smile still stitched on. "Not too careful today, are we?"

The back of Silamo's neck begins to sweat. He attempts to smile but then drops it. Bending down to retrieve the ceramic pieces, he says, "My mind has been on other things."

Zuma sits at the corner of the table, resting his hands, wrist over wrist, across the top, and crossing his right leg over his left thigh. His back is straight, his eyes steady, his smile constant. He does not remove his hat. His eyes shift over Silamo's shoulder and he points a lazy finger. "Incredible view."

Silamo places the mug shards in the sink and looks out the same window. The smoke has thickened and is rising higher. Sounds from the street are rising too: screams and cries, angry shouts, car alarms, things breaking. The smell of sulfur is beginning to seep into the house as well. *Fire and brimstone*, Silamo thinks. He feels uneasy with his back to Zuma so he grabs two fresh mugs and turns around.

"What type of tea, then?"

It seems the most absurd question anyone could ask in the midst of a war, but if Zuma insists on these sorts of pleasantries, Silamo is determined to play along.

"Rooibos. Always been my favorite. You have it?"

Zuma's eyes, and his smile, never leave Silamo as he fills the kettle with water and starts the gas burners. He places two tea bags in the mugs, pulls out a chair for himself across the table from Zuma and sits. He is careful to keep his hands on the tabletop so the lieutenant general can see he has no secrets. If he turns his head even slightly to the left he can see both *izulu* through the archway. He focuses on Zuma.

"I stopped by headquarters before coming here," Zuma says. "It's completely barricaded. Are there officers inside?"

"Some. It was their choice. Others I've sent to Jozi to assist with military operations. As per your orders."

"Going to ground." Zuma shakes his head. The lip of his hat shadows his eyes. "Unwise. Do they think to wait it out, as if this were a common storm?"

"There do not seem to be many wise decisions left to us, Lieutenant General."

"You are right. What can we do? Fight. Flight. Those are the rock and the hard place, as far as I see it. Neither offers salvation. Strange no one has yet chosen surrender."

"Strange?" Silamo folds his fingers together so as not to make fists. His knuckles whiten with the strain. "You would have us surrender? What does that mean to them, other than death?"

"What does it mean to whom?"

"Them." His eyes flick left without seeing much more than amorphous shadows. "The *izulu*."

Zuma's eyes linger on the creatures before turning back to Silamo. His smile appears even more bemused. "*Izulu*, you say? That's delightful. Our people have many names for them. Demon is most common. When they first rose—what was it? twenty years ago?—the popular term was vampire, which is closer. Vulture, of course, works best as far as resemblance. I think it's regional, the names. Certain ones stick better than others. I must admit 'izulu' is new to me."

Silamo struggles for a nonchalant shrug. "What do you call them?"

"They prefer to be called 'the Over.' It derives from Nietzsche's übermensch. Over men. You've heard of this? They have a mild preoccupation with our human philosophies." Zuma chuckles.

Silamo has trouble catching a breath long enough to ask, "How do you know this?" When Zuma only smiles into the question, Silamo suggests, naïvely—but, god, how he longs to be naïve—"Do you control them?"

Zuma outright laughs; his mouth opens and his shoulders move with the boisterous sound, but his eyes remain steady and fixed on Silamo. It makes the hairs along Silamo's arms stand up.

The laugh is cut off by the sharp cry of the tea kettle. Zuma says, "I'm quite parched."

Silamo makes no move to get up from the table. He is afraid his muscles will prove too weak for the task. He wipes sweat from his brows with his fingers, and slides his hands into his lap under the table.

"Allow me," Zuma says.

He rises and goes to the stove. Silamo listens to him pour the tea and open the tins on the counter, searching for sugar cubes. The lieutenant general begins to whistle. A light smell of herbal sweetness fills the room.

Zuma places a steaming mug in front of Silamo and retakes his seat at the other end of the table. He stops whistling and sips from the mug, making a satisfied sound as he puts the mug back down.

In the silence, something large and nearby explodes outside. Neither man flinches; they are staring at each other. One of the house's old floorboards begins to moan, and Silamo says, "So you *have* surrendered."

"You misunderstand," Zuma says. "I have not given up; I've defected. And you will, too, by the end of this conversation."

While Zuma talks, Silamo eases a small blade out of its sheath on the underside of his belt. He holds it against his thigh. "Convince me, then."

Finally, Zuma abandons his false smile. "You know this is not a war, don't you? You have always been a smart man, a prudent man. Pretoria, Jozi, the whole of Gauteng—this isn't even a *battle*, not to them. It's practice, a rehearsal; it's training, it's recruitment, it's preparation for the Big Show. Not far off, that. You know what Australia was? A failsafe. They'll always have Australia. That sounds like a song, doesn't it? Is it a song?"

Silamo's sweat runs cold along his skin. Suddenly, he feels calm. Zuma is insane, he thinks. An insane man who has given up. A man of high rank, which makes things difficult. But not lost.

"Perhaps a movie," Silamo says.

Zuma slaps his palm on the table, shaking the mugs a little. "A movie! That's what we're missing. That is something that would take the fear out of it, isn't it? To memorialize in film the colossal failure that was the War for Australia. The entire continent a nuclear wasteland, unfit for human habitation. *Exactly* how the Over planned it."

"You seem excited."

"That's a side effect of the mind control." Zuma twists his back toward Silamo, and Silamo's arm goes rigid, his fist tightening around the blade. But then Zuma removes his hat and bends his head forward enough for Silamo to see the large hole at the base of his neck. A glossy membranous film covers the wound's two-inch diameter, the skin around it an irritated pink. Silamo's mouth slacks open and he has to work hard to close it.

Zuma twists back around. "How does it look? I haven't seen it myself. It's a mite fresh."

Silamo struggles to work up saliva. "You let them do this to you? I would have died. I would have fought them. I would have died fighting them."

"Is that why you packed those three bags at the door?" Zuma's smile returns. "Full of weapons with which to fight your enemy? I know you are running, and that is smart, Chief Silamo. In fact, I want you to run. The Over want you to run. But they would prefer if you took a select group of citizens with you."

"I'll do nothing for them."

"Will you listen? Listen to yourself. Only when backed into a wall do you find your strength, your bravery. I'm hefting you over that wall. I'm giving you the tools to—"

"—to be mind-fucked?"

"—to climb over. Mind-fucked? You're killing me, Silamo. May I call you Dominick? Formalities seem silly at this point, do they not?" Zuma sips at his tea again, although by this time it has cooled enough to gulp. "I misspoke. Mind control isn't exactly correct. I admit, I wanted to shock you. I see it worked. But no, it's not that exactly, it's...a pathway.

A communications link. This way, they can speak to me. I can know them, the way only a handful of us are beginning to know them. It's, well, it's a form of trust. They trust me. They trust me to be their Liaison, to begin negotiations of their treaty."

"I don't believe this."

"No need to take it on faith, dear Dominick. They'll be more than happy to show you. They've already shown me so much. They've shown me the future, Dominick, and it certainly isn't here. No, we must sacrifice our holdings here, for the survival of our species. That's what they're offering us, after all, survival. Not only that, but—listen, the treaty will be signed, I've no doubts. Our president has already signed it. All the leaders will. And when we explain it—you and I and all the other Liaisons—to the citizens, the world will understand. They'll see it is not so great a sacrifice, the things the Over ask of us. A few will die, certainly, but look out your window, Dominick—look at the city burning, the people burning it. Can we survive much more of this? Can we?"

"I know you have a knife on you."

Silamo plays Zuma's bluff. "Yeah, and a sharp-shooter outside with you in his sights. I have nothing, Zuma. I have nothing."

"The Over tell me it's clutched in your right hand, and when I turned my back to you a moment ago, you nearly raised it to throw at my neck. Let's not play games anymore, Dominick, shall we?"

"Do not use my name," Silamo growls. He brings the knife up to the table and rests his knuckles against the edge. "I'll kill myself before I let them take me."

"Don't be so dramatic." Zuma laughs and throws up his arms, shaking his head at nothing. He fits his hat back onto his head, looks into the living room and hooks a thumb at Silamo. "This guy." He looks back at Silamo. "Are you shaking? I am trying to tell you, Chief Silamo, that there is no need for shaking. No need for fear. Listen. All I need for you to do is evacuate the people on this list." From his breast pocket, he produces two sheets of folded paper and slides them across the table to Silamo, who does not reach for them. "You'll have to take them to Jozi and use the rivers to the Indian Ocean. There'll be a naval ship waiting at Durban. The Over will not attack you; it's not them I'm worried about. But our citizens are panicking. They no longer fear our human consequences, if ever they truly did.

"The names on this list, these men and women are important. They're vital to the Over's treaty negotiations. Failure of this mission is not an option. That is why you need to be made a Liaison, Silamo. Total trust."

"I think you had it right, Zuma. It is mind control. A touch of madness hasn't helped your case so much either. No man with any honor would strike a deal with demons."

"It's a good deal," Zuma says. "Ninety percent of the world's current population will be spared. And that's a worst-case scenario—if the negotiations take longer than expected, if certain world leaders try their nukes again, or chemical warfare. But with full cooperation, we may only lose one or two percent. A token number, in the grand scheme. As I said, they've shown me the future. It's a controlled future, certainly, but it allows us to keep many of our familiar freedoms. It isn't communism. There will be systems in place so the Over will get what they need, and what they need is us. Humans. We are life to them. *Life*. Let me show you."

Zuma rises once again, and Silamo rises with him, knocking his chair back in his haste. He presses the edge of the blade to his throat and says again, "I'll kill myself. I want no part of them. I'll kill myself, I swear it."

"Dominick." Zuma frowns, and for a moment his eyes appear genuinely sad. "You disappoint me. Very well. If you cannot find it in your heart to care about the billions of lives you will save by joining the Over, I think you can find some compassion for your wife and daughter."

"They're dead," Silamo says. "They died in one of the first riots. There is nothing you can threaten me with, Zuma. My only choice is death now."

"Die now." Zuma picks up the list of names and holds it out to Silamo. "Or die later. Die a coward or a hero. The people on this list are counting on you. You are their salvation. Surely you can sacrifice your own life for something greater than spite?"

Silamo's eyes blink to the *izulu*—the Over—standing in the living room. They haven't moved, but their heads are tilted identically, as if they are listening though they have no ears. The floorboards creak again.

Silamo lowers the knife and sets it on the table. He takes the list of names from Zuma. "All right. I'll do it. This one last mission. Only...only not here. The fires, the bombs, they're getting closer. We'll go somewhere safer. Then I'll do it."

Zuma clamps a heavy hand on Silamo's damp shoulder. Silamo fails to turn his grimace into a smile, but Zuma smiles wide enough for both of them. "Good man," he says. He stretches an arm out in front of them. "After you."

Silamo's body tenses as he walks beneath the archway into the living room. The sentries watch him; his mind flashes a memory of watching a movie with his daughter only—what? last summer? earlier? In it, a young boy on a quest must pass through a guard of giant golden sphinxes, whose eyes are closed. As he walks, their eyes open and they fire lasers at him. He makes it through, but only just. Silamo closes his own eyes as he walks past the *izulu*; if they do laser him to death, he prefers not to see it coming.

He doesn't open his eyes until his foot bumps into one of the duffel bags. He looks down at it. No need for it now, not for him. He stuffs two fingers into his pocket and fishes out his wedding band. He drops it onto the duffel bag as he moves to the front door.

Outside, the wind has picked up and the world feels as if it exists inside an oven. Everything is closer, pressing in: the shouting, the crying, the breaking, the burning. Maybe Zuma, despite his insanity, does have a point. If the treaty can stop this violence, can save billions, as Zuma claims it can, maybe it is worth it. Maybe it is worth giving up the world.

Zuma walks out of the house, closing the door behind him. He adjusts his hat to best shield his eyes from the glare of the sun, straightens his unruffled shirt front, and marches to Silamo's side. "A car is waiting for us at the bottom of the hill, if it hasn't been bombed yet." His white teeth burn through Silamo. "Shall we?"

"The Over." Silamo looks back at the house. "Aren't they coming?"

"Oh my, I thought I'd explained clearly. Being a Liaison to the Over requires total trust. You broke that before you even began. They couldn't just let that slide. It wouldn't be fair."

From inside the house, a child's scream rips open Silamo's gut. He shouts for her, "Heaven!"

The heel of Zuma's hand crashes into Silamo's nose. The world blinks out and gravity rushes away from him. Pressure mounts inside his head, and he is squinting at the sky, the sun an evil eye burning out his sins. Zuma's dark head bends into his field of vision. He can feel the blood streaming from his nose into his mouth, down the back of his dry throat. He can hear his wife crying, and the sound of something else, some vital thing being pulled apart.

"Pity," Zuma says, a drop of spittle falling onto Silamo's eyelid. "You were my first choice for this mission. Remember that god-awful charity gala? We had some laughs. I had hoped to spare you. Well." Zuma lifts his heavy boot above Silamo's face. "I'll find someone else."

# ONE
## JORDAN

THOSE SLENDER WRISTS. Bare and smooth, she must moisturize. There's that game the other kids play at school, curling index fingers around wrists to touch the thumb, and moving up and up and up. The farther they can move up, the more babies the person will eventually birth. The science of junior high reflecting the spells we learned in grade school using only a well-placed buttercup to discern how boy crazy you might be. I could wrap my fingers around those wrists and all four tips would touch my thumb. She would have ten children, maybe, a household or two, a village. But the elbow might put a stop to that, and the muscles that come after, though they're hard to see beneath her blazer. Blue like her eyes. I wonder what she'll tell us and what her voice will sound like when she speaks.

I am upstairs in my room. I used to share with Jeremy, until last summer when he successfully traded up for a second-hand baby grand piano and I was relegated to the attic. Dad put my mattress on top of a group of boxes full of memories he swears we'll never need to check on, but just in case, we'll save on a box spring. My sheets are pink with pale yellow flowers and they match my pillowcase and my comforter. I didn't pick them out. Jason has sheets patterned with antique muscle cars, and Jeremy has plain black, and I have yellow flowers swimming in a pink expanse, and my name is Jordeena (an old family name) but I haven't let anyone call me that since I was three. It's Jordan, please and thank you.

The woman pulls into the driveway. I placed a bet with myself that she would park on the street, but now her Mazda is boxing in our pickup and it's a possibility that this was calculated. I wonder if she knows that my parents would never run—well, maybe Mom but never Dad—and if they did, we have horses in the barn that can go places her Mazda only sees in its SUV dreams. She's wearing heels and a skirt that only pretends to fall past her knees. She probably wouldn't chase us. She'd make a call, that's all it would take, and wait disinterestedly for us to fall. Fall. It's almost Summer.

I pick through my dresser. Mom would kill me if she knew I was not dressed yet, but she's still at the hospital and Dad's in the field. We have a fox problem and our last good dog died last week. I think I'll dress down, fuck impressions.

A pair of Jason's old Wranglers, torn at the knees almost symmetrically, two sizes too big and I won't bother with a belt. Mom doesn't know about the stud in my bellybutton so I throw on a long black t-shirt. Seems to me that kind of thing should be no big deal, but she freaked when Jeremy pierced his ears last year and I'm not taking chances. Sneakers on, and one last peek out the window.

She's finger-combing her hair and checking her makeup in the Mazda's side mirror. Doesn't look like she's wearing much, some light lipstick, blush, subtle eyeshadow. She's pretty and I wish she weren't. Her hair's the same shade as mine, light brown if you look too quickly or from too far away, golden if you don't blink. The sleeve of her blazer slides down her arm as she combs, and the wrist stares up at me. Briefcase at her feet. I wish I'd been told what to expect.

Before I leave my room, I grab the beaded bracelet from my nightstand. We made them in art class yesterday, and it's garish and bright and doesn't go with what I'm wearing. If she admires it, I'll offer it to her.

The doorbell doesn't even have a chance to ring before Jeremy's piano starts up, and I can't tell if it's "Chopsticks" or something Mozart scribbled on a napkin before dessert. Jeremy likes to experiment, mixing scores like a human blender, and then convincing the uneducated that he composed them himself. I know why he's playing now, as rehearsed as anything, and I want to hit him. I hope he's wearing a tie and the silver cufflinks Mom bought him; I hope his shoes are polished and he hasn't shaved the inch and a half of pale yellow hair above his lip that he insists is a mustache. If he takes her hand and kisses it, I'll punch a wall or pee my pants, I haven't decided yet.

Downstairs, the smell of baking cookies wafts into the living room. If Mom managed to get Jason to bake, then I will pee my pants.

Jason comes into the room at a half-run, almost knocking into the couch. He's not wearing a suit but he has his nice pants on, the ones Dad picked up from the dry-cleaner yesterday, probably the first time he's ever set foot in one of those places. I wanted to go with him because I bet myself that the place smelled like dryer sheets. Jason's short-sleeved flannel shirt is tucked into his waistband, and he looks at his reflection in our only framed piece of "real" art (a print of Van Gogh's "Starry Night") and licks his hands and smooths back his dark hair. He shaved.

"Let me get the door," he says, walking right by me, never even looking.

I slouch on the sofa, propping my feet up on the coffee table and keeping my knees spread as far away from each other as possible. I wish I had some gum.

The front door opens in the foyer, around the corner from the living room, so I can't see them but I hear him being pleasant and it's weird. They're probably shaking hands as he welcomes her in. "You must be, oh and I'm, and come on in, and right this way, and make yourself comfortable."

She precedes him through the doorway and if his hand is not pressed against the small of her back I know he wishes it were. She stops in front of the bookcase and looks at me, smiling without showing her teeth. Jason steps around her and finally notices me, and I can see his anger in the way his eyes narrow and his fake smile falters and he pinches the pocket of his slacks, but he can't say anything in front of her. I don't stand up.

He speaks to her instead. "Mrs. Omalis, this is my sister Jordan."

"Pleasure to meet you," she says to me, and she sounds British but only a little. She turns to my brother and touches his arm when she says, "It's *Miss* Omalis."

His sheepish smile masks his hard-on. He directs her to my dad's chair next to the couch.

"My dad's out with the livestock right now," he tells her. "But he should be back any minute. Can I get you something to drink?"

"Yes, thank you, a glass of water?"

She says it like a question, like she's not sure we have plumbing out here, like she's never heard of a well. I'm surprised Jason didn't go straight for the brandy. Mom would've.

Before he leaves the room, he looks at me. "Jordan, you want to help me?"

"No," I say. I don't even look at him. I'll get it later, but right now, this is too much fun.

He leaves before he says something he can't take back.

There would be uncomfortable silence except Jeremy is still pounding away at his minor keys and there isn't a door thick enough in this house to drown it out. She looks in the direction of the stairs and her smile returns.

"Who's upstairs?"

I'm sure she already knows, so I cross my arms and look at my shoes. There's still dirt on the bottoms, probably manure too, but the cookie smell will cover it up. I kind of want a cookie, maybe Jason will bring a plate out with her water. I bet he does.

The sounds of her opening her briefcase draw my eyes away from my feet. She's pulling out a folder and a clipboard. She snaps the case shut and sets it back against the side of the chair. Dad bought that chair at a flea market before any of us were born, and Mom crocheted a blanket that hangs over its back and arms to hide the holes and tears. He rocked me to sleep in that chair, he let me stay up late and watch old movies. She takes out a pen and starts writing.

Without saying anything, I move to the other side of the couch, closer to her. She smells like tulip petals. Mom keeps a garden out behind the barn and this woman smells like Mom's hands do when it's rose season. Tulips and roses are two different flowers. How does she do it? One is her shampoo, and the other is her perfume. She's looking at me.

"What grade are you in, Jordan?"

It's probably too much if I roll my eyes, but I have no gum to chew obstinately so you work with what you've got.

She laughs a little, it sounds almost like she's humming, but it's a laugh. She marks something on her clipboard and without looking back up at me, says, "Do you want to tell your parents about your new jewelry, or shall I?"

My hand goes instinctively to my stomach. It's still a little sore. Of course she'd blackmail me, of course.

"Do they have to know?" I ask, giving her control, as if I had any of it to begin with.

"Perhaps not," she says, looking at me again. "What grade are you in?"

Her pupils are small but they undulate, her irises shimmering like the surfaces of pools. Her hair is so straight she must use an iron to keep it just so. I wish she made noise when she moved her arm, the sounds of her clothes creasing and crinkling; I wish I could hear it when she swallowed.

"Ninth," I say.

She marks it down. "Do you like it?"

I can hear Mom's voice in my ear telling me to be enthusiastic, to boast of my perfect attendance and test scores, and segue naturally into how I've always wanted to teach and help today's youth become the leaders of tomorrow. There are too many lies in that to untangle, and I don't see the real difference in being me or being the lie, so I'll let the rest of them experiment with becoming statistics and leave me out of it.

"It passes the time," I say, and I hope she knows what I mean. I want to see it in her eyes that she knows, but she blinks and turns back to her clipboard and makes another mark. Her eyeshadow is darker up close.

The piano stops, the back door slams. Two male voices waft in from the kitchen with the waning odor of the cookies I'm beginning to think don't really exist.

"Your father?" she asks, pointing through the doorway with her pen.

The front door opens and closes loudly and she walks into the room knowing what she'll find so her back is straighter and her smile is on.

"My mother," I say.

There hasn't been a day Mom's come home from the hospital in anything but her floral scrubs, yet here she is, shrugging off her coat with an unselfconscious smile to reveal an eggshell-blue blouse and just-below-the-knee black skirt. Plain brown leather belt, pumps. Tasteful. Where are those damn cookies?

The woman rises to her feet to greet her, and my mom steps forward, her coat thrown over one arm, the other extended.

"Hello, you must be Heaven Omalis," Mom says, and they shake, and she's still smiling away.

"Pleasure to meet you, Mrs. Fontaine. I've just been getting acquainted with your lovely daughter."

Growing up with two older brothers you'd think I'd be attuned to sarcasm, but all I catch is a look of disdain on Mom's face when she sees what I'm wearing. Omalis is still smiling.

"Have you? I'm sure she's been most accommodating." Ah, there's the sarcasm. "Please, sit."

Omalis smoothes out her skirt and sits in one graceful motion. Mom drapes her coat over the arm of the sofa and sits on the other end, spending several awkward seconds trying to figure out how to cross her legs. At the ankle, like a lady. Even I know that.

To me, she says, "Forget to do your laundry?"

Her hair is thin and it's the most unattractive thing about her. It just lies there on top of her head like it's waiting for you to tell it to do something, but then it would probably just ignore you anyway. It's brown and plain and doesn't at all go with her eyes, deep green, so emphatic you know they're saying something but you're the one who's not listening. She tried to get a perm once but the curls didn't take. I think she should shave her head and get a wig, one that suits her, maybe raven black and wispy, licorice red and full.

"We ran out of detergent," I tell her. There, excuse taken care of, back to the niceties.

"You have a very warm home, Mrs. Fontaine," Omalis says.

We both look at her. For a second, I think my mom is going to say something about turning down the thermostat, or something corny like, "Well, it *is* filled with love," but she clasps her hands in her lap and offers a pleasant thank you on the lips of the smile she's trying so hard not to look strained. I know she wants to bite her hangnails, but she keeps her hands folded in her lap.

Jason appears in the doorway from the back, a tray carefully balanced in his hands. He sets it on the table and apologizes for taking so long. A glass of water, a cup of tea, and lo and behold, a plate of cookies.

"Mom, the tea is for you," he says. "I know how you like to wind down after a long day at work."

"Thank you, dear," Mom says, taking the mug, surprised and delighted. Like she hasn't been training him all week.

"Dad just got in," he says to the room. "He wants me to apologize on his behalf; he felt it was only a courtesy to shower before he joins us."

My mom twitters like a circus bird on crack. I lean in for a cookie but she grabs my wrist and gently places my arm back in my lap. She looks at me sidelong so quickly I don't think anyone else catches it. When I was little we used to bake cookies together and it wasn't any fun unless there was a flour fight, and there always was, right at the end; we would bathe in it, and it would stain our skin and dry us out and then we'd put on our swimsuits and take a shower together, and she would smell like flour and baking soda and vanilla for days. Today, she smells like the mall's latest free sample.

"Jason," Mom says, "could you run upstairs and get your brother?"

Jason nods and walk-runs up the stairs. I run a finger under the bracelet on my left wrist and snap it against the skin. The beads knock together but Mom doesn't look, and Omalis is asking questions again.

"How long have you lived here?"

"Oh, what has it been now? Thirteen years, just a bit after Jordan was born." She puts her hand on my knee. It isn't warm. "Before that, we lived in Hazard, Kentucky, where Jay helped with his father's farm. But—you know men and their ambitions—Jay had to have a farm of his own, wanted to get into the cattle-ranching business, so here we are."

"It's a lovely place," Omalis says. The more she speaks the more uncertain I am of her accent, because the vowels are rounder than with the accents I hear on TV but the lilt is the same. "I wonder if I might be able to take a tour before I leave, hmm?"

She makes that sound, "hmm," come out of her like it just melted out, like it was in there all this time just slowly building up until it got the chance to spill over, and it's so buttery and soft, how can you deny it?

"Of course, my husband would love—"

"Perhaps Jason could show me around," she cuts in, "while we chat."

Mom falters only slightly, it's fairly impressive really, how only the veins in her neck constrict and her temple pulses once, and it passes. No involuntary eye twitch or hard swallow or sporadic fluttering of limbs. She's been practicing.

"Jason would adore that," she says. "He really knows his way around the farm. I think he enjoys helping his father around the stables more than just about anything else."

I think he'll enjoy eye-humping Miss Omalis as he lets her walk ahead of him through the stables, offering to saddle up Grady just so he can cop a feel as he helps her onto the horse's back.

My brothers clamber down the stairs like schoolboys on Christmas morning. Jason slows his pace when he hits the landing, Jeremy following at his heels. Jeremy is wearing a black sweater and black Dockers and a pair of Dad's loafers. He didn't shave, the fair whiskers hang loosely above his upper lip, and his hair is so gelled you could ice-skate on it. Mom pats the cushion between us and he sits down.

"Jason, grab some chairs from the dining room," Mom says.

"Oh no, Jason, don't bother with that," Omalis says, waving a hand that bends like a wilting flower over her slender wrist. Slender but strong, I see that, from this close up. "It really would be more expedient to simply interview each child individually, no need to wait for the entire family to be present."

"Jay will only be a moment—"

While Mom wages her gentle protest, I watch the front of Jason's pants, trying to see if his boner shriveled up when Miss Omalis referred to him as a child. The dress pants are too spacious to tell.

"I don't want to take up any more of your time than is necessary," Omalis continues. "Running a farm is very consuming work, I know. So I'll dispense with the pleasantries here and skip right to the formalities."

She uncrosses and re-crosses her legs, left over right this time, at the knee. She's not wearing pantyhose. The dimples in her naked knee wink at me as she rambles to my mother.

"We just need to make sure that you fully understand and appreciate what I'll be doing here today, and that we have your full compliance. I'll be conducting a short interview with each of your children, during which I will administer a brief oral psychological examination. I'm here to observe and record, not to assess, you understand. I will present my observations after I leave here and the final analysis will be made, at which time I will return here and let you know the decision. This process usually takes no longer than one week."

There is a pause in Omalis's preamble and I expect to hear Mom's voice, but when it doesn't come I look at her. Her eyes are closed and she's holding Jeremy's hand.

"Mrs. Fontaine," Omalis says. She leans over her clipboard, and her lilt drops an octave. If the space between her chair and my Mom's position on the sofa were not so wide, I think she'd take her hand. "It is very important, Mrs. Fontaine, that you realize my presence here is not a final judgment. It is simply a step, and it could very well lead nowhere."

This is supposed to be comforting but Mom doesn't let go of Jeremy's hand or open her eyes. Omalis is wearing lip gloss instead of lipstick and I bet it has a flavor, something fruity.

"I'll go first," Jason says in the silence. "For the interviews."

Omalis's smile is placating. "I think I'd like to save you for last."

He'll have wet dreams over that single sentence for weeks.

"Let's start with the youngest, shall we?" She says. "Work our way up, yes?"

Mom rises with Miss Omalis and finally drops Jeremy's hand. "The dining room is all set up, or the patio, there's a great view." She's trying.

"I think, actually, I'd like to see Jordan's room, if she wouldn't mind."

Mom's frown is almost comical. Before she has a chance to say anything, I plop my feet on the floor and shoot up, grabbing a handful of cookies as I make my way to the stairs. "Come on," I toss over my shoulder.

I hear my mother twitter nervously. "I'd ask you to pardon her as she was born in a barn, but it seems too obvious."

I like that Omalis doesn't laugh. Her footsteps follow me to the attic.

The attic stairs aren't steep but they're no picnic either, though obviously this woman is fit enough to climb them without breaking a sweat. I usually make it to the top slightly winded myself, but I hold back this time, forcing myself to release air in measured exhalations. I slump onto my bed immediately and watch her mount the last step, twisting on the landing to look at me. Her eyes trail over me and continue on to my nightstand, which is really an old cedar chest with who-knows-what inside, and to my dresser, magazines spilling out from beneath it, and to the clothes strewn across the floor, the stuffed animals on the cushion-less wooden rocking chair at the foot of my bed. I keep meaning to shove them in one of those boxes meshed together at the other end of the attic but I haven't gotten around to it yet.

"You can move that stuff," I tell her, indicating the rocking chair. "If you want to sit."

I fill my mouth with a cookie so she can't launch into her questions right away.

Miss Omalis goes to the chair, leans her briefcase against the wall, and sets her clipboard on the bed so she can carefully pick each animal up individually and place it neatly on the mattress, leaning each comfortably against the wall. I'm sure Mr. Blue Bunny and Mrs. Pink Walrus are very much obliged. I chew my cookie and watch her. She doesn't seem at all self-conscious; I'm waiting for her to pat Green Turtle's head or maybe give his chin a nice quick chuck.

Finally, she sits down, smooths out her skirt again, and picks up her clipboard. I expect her to push a finger against the bridge of her glasses until I remember she isn't wearing any, which is a shame really because they would suit her quite well, especially with that accent.

"Impressive collection," she says, eyeing her arrangement. "Do you have names for them?"

"Sure," I say. I don't, but she went through a lot of trouble. "That one is Sigmund, that's Mary Shelley, the one behind her is David Cassidy, that one's Puck, and the one on the end is Mrs. Lovett. The other three are just numbers, in the order I got them."

I'm sure she'll have fun psychoanalyzing all those name choices, even though I don't see the point to it anyway, like my fate wasn't sealed along with everyone else's long before we were even born, like I should really believe any of the things she said downstairs.

She smiles at my answer, only a half one, kind of lazy but it still crinkles the corners of her eyes. She scribbles something on her clipboard.

"How long have you lived in the attic?" She asks.

I shrug and reach behind me to fold my pillow, kicking my legs, dirty shoes and all, up onto the bed. Mom would love that. "I don't know, a year or something."

"Do you like it better?"

I rest my head against the folded pillow and stare over my knees at Miss Omalis. The final cookie bobs slowly up and down on my stomach. "Better than what?"

"It affords quite a bit more privacy," she says. "I should think any teenage girl would relish even a modicum of that rarity, in a house with two older brothers."

"Privacy to do what?" If I keep her talking maybe she'll run over time on this appointment and have to end it short; maybe she'll realize I'm just being ornery and give up.

"Oh, I don't know." She swipes a hand breezily through the air, painting a picture. "Journal, have your friends over, sleep in silence, think without interruption, pierce something."

"We didn't do it here," I say reflexively.

The corners of her mouth dimple. "It was only an example."

If she were my friend, I'd kick a stuffed animal at her, or call her something I didn't really mean, or flick her off. As it is, I avert my eyes from hers and bring my wrist up to my mouth, the one with the bracelet, and nibble at the beads. She still hasn't asked about it.

"Why can't you tell your mother?"

My belly laugh nearly topples the cookie off my stomach.

"She'll freak out?" She offers. It sounds like she hasn't used that phrase in probably a decade.

"I think so," I say.

"But that's why you did it in the first place, right?"

When I look at her, she's got that lazy smile on again, and I wish I were close enough to smell her shampoo.

"Teenage rebellion is taboo," I say.

Her smile widens but she doesn't show her teeth all the way and she doesn't laugh. I bet her laugh—her real, spontaneous laugh—is exactly like her voice, melodic and hymn-like, overly-rounded vowels and languid consonants.

"Where are you from?" I ask.

She stops smiling. "Is that important?"

"You have an accent," I say. Stupid. Duh, she knows that. "It's not British exactly, and it can't be Australian…."

Her fingers brush at a strand of hair that's fallen across her forehead. She doesn't tuck it behind her ear and it falls back across it again. "No, no," she says. "It's South African."

"Oh."

Outside, the bull bleats out a mating call or a call of warning, who knows which, and the chickens cluck in response. They must be at the side of the house if I can hear them from here; Mom will be furious with Dad for not penning the chickens and gating the cattle.

"What do you want to be?" she asks, breaking the silence with her subject change.

I would bite my tongue but I'm not causing myself pain over this ridiculous hoop show, so I shove the remaining cookie into my mouth instead.

She bends her arm over the clipboard. Her pen seems a little more eager now. "Hopes, dreams, aspirations? What do you want to do with your life? I'll wait until you've swallowed."

I chew as slowly as I can but as soon as the crumbs turn to mush turn to near liquid I have no choice but to swallow, or spit it out I guess but I've already gotten dirt from my shoes on the bed, no need to add to the stains.

Miss Omalis taps the pen against the clasp of her clipboard. She's on the verge of uncrossing and re-crossing her legs, and she's not taking her eyes off of me. I can't believe she is really asking me this, especially after what she's revealed, considering what she's.... Oh, fuck it, just say it.

"Is this what you always wanted to be?" I ask.

Her eyes don't leave mine and she doesn't miss a beat. "Yes. What do you want to be?"

"I don't believe you."

"You don't have to believe me. What do you want to be?"

"Which answer keeps me out of the Summer Program?"

She exhales, part gasp, part exaggerated sigh, and presses her thumb into the center of her forehead, closing her eyes. The tendon in her wrist tenses, stretching the skin, making the vein pulse. If she were wearing my bracelet, the beads would rattle against each other.

After a moment with her eyes closed, she opens them and slides her pen into the clasp of the clipboard. Twisting over the arm of the chair, she gathers up her briefcase and returns the clipboard to it, snapping it closed with an ominous finality.

She stands up. "Jordan."

If I were a poet, I could maybe say what emotions play across her face, what an eyebrow twitch means or how many moons are set free by the undulation of her pupils, the crinkles in her chin.

"Nothing can keep you out of the Program," she says. "I'm sorry."

I lie there and stare at the ceiling, listening to her footsteps recede down the stairs. I think about her with my brothers, going through the motions, jumping through the hoops, recording expected answers in appropriately marked boxes. They'll lie to her, and she'll lie to them, but she didn't lie to me. She didn't lie to me.

For some reason, that matters.

# TWO
## JUNE

IF YOU ASKED ME TODAY, I would tell you I hate my job. *Career,* Jay would correct me, but some days it is very difficult to look at it that way. A career is something you are stuck in—*have the opportunity to advance in,* oh, be quiet Jay. A career is a choice of a path that you will follow for the majority of your years, however tenuous a grasp you have on that time frame, and suppose you discover halfway down the path that you want to do something else, or simply do not want to continue doing what you're doing. It's just plain too late; you have to double-back, you might as well just continue on. See? Stuck.

A job, you can change. Jobs are fluid, they pass through people and people pass through them. Quitting carries much less stigma when applied to a job than to a career, and there is less self-loathing, of course. That small thing.

Today, I would tell you I hate my job. (I hate my job.) But I cannot quit my job, and I never intend to, but I still won't call it my career, because that would imply that it is something I had a hand in choosing.

It feels like hypocrisy, that's the thing, and after thirteen years it becomes increasingly impossible to ignore. But you still have to do it, you still have to trudge along down that path, because you're not walking alone anymore, and that's the scariest thing of all, the thing that keeps you up at night, the thing that makes you embrace your hypocrisy and your guilt and your self-hate and get on with it.

I have three children, and all of them are still asleep as the sun comes up and I'm washing placenta off my hands. I've been awake for close to twenty-four hours, on the job for eighteen, and my feet don't even ache anymore, that's how tired I am. I can go home in twenty minutes, if I make it out of the door before my name is screeched out over the hospital's PA. I can take a quick shower and steal a kiss from Jay before he starts the back-spraining work of preparing the heavy equipment for baling season. I can put on a pot of coffee and watch my children sleep for a few precious minutes before I wake them up and the shouted bickering kicks off another glorious Friday morning. I can't think beyond the next hour, and I don't have to, not right now, because right now, I have one more thing to take care of, one more thing to hate.

Mr. and Mrs. Elliot came into the emergency room at a quarter past midnight, him with his wife cradled in his arms, her overnight bag slapping heavily against his back. He was crying, she was laughing, and once we got a room set up for them, he joined her laughter, her joy, and proceeded to regale every nurse that strolled within six feet of the room with the story of his unnecessary yet charming heroics (she was only two centimeters dilated and her contractions were mild). They were having triplets, which surprised me until Mrs. Elliot explained that she'd miscarried when they'd tried the fertility drugs so they decided to gamble on nature. She didn't want any pain meds, but when the contractions worsened, she changed her mind.

The birth itself took four hours. The first one came with unsettling ease, two hard pushes and he was in my arms, but the second refused to follow her brother's example. When she did come, the umbilical cord was tangled around her neck and we had to work fast to cut it and clear her airway. By this time, Mrs. Elliot was exhausted and scared, but her husband held her hand and talked her through. That's when she started pushing out more blood than baby, and we discovered our third girl was breech and had to do an emergency caesarean section. It took its toll on the mother but her daughter came out just as small and loud and perfect as her siblings.

And that, all of that, suffering so bravely through that pain and that fear, won't spare them from what I have to do now.

She's in recovery, where she'll spend the morning just in case. Her husband is in their private hospital room, getting her oral-hygiene things from her overnight bag. Their babies are one floor below us in the nursery, crying at the sharp taste of oxygen and sting of the fluorescent lights. And I am standing at the sink, drying my hands, and trying to will my legs to move so I can meet the Liaison who's waiting for me in the hall.

He's worked on the maternity wing of this hospital almost as long as I have, ten years. He started here when we still referred to the wing as a "ward," until someone in the position to do so decided that "wing" had fewer negative connotations and changed the term. Personally, I thought ward was fitting, if not for my patients then certainly for me.

His name is Kevin Daniels and I only speak to him when I have to, which is more often than I like to dwell on. I've spoken to him twice since I started my shift, but he came in six hours after me. I spoke to his predecessor, Alice Richter, once before he got here. Did I say I did not like to dwell on the numbers? Well, it's still true.

In the hall, I don't greet him, I never do. We're supposed to be polite to the hospital Liaisons but I think a curt indifference suffices. He has stony blue eyes and long blond hair that he keeps neatly tied in a ponytail, no facial hair, though I suspect on the weekends he allows it to grow out. There are deep creases in his forehead but no lines in his double-breasted dark gray suit, and I would place him at about thirty-two, maybe thirty-four, nine years younger than me at least. He always smiles and nods when I come out but he respects my decision not to shake his hand or exchange pleasantries.

We walk down the hall together, he two steps behind me, arms clasped behind his back, polished shoes clinking against the freshly waxed linoleum. Every step is a struggle for me, every square tile I pass over is a mountain and I'm always afraid I'll fall coming down the other side. This part has always been hard but it's always been necessary, and it's only gotten worse since Monday, since that Liaison was in my home, invited in, yielded to, led directly to my children as directly as I lead this one now, and catered to almost as easily. Almost.

It's only because I've been doing this for thirteen years that I am able to keep doing it, to keep leading someone down the halls to the rooms of my patients, to turn the knobs and let them in, walk them to the sides of the bed, to the parents still in awe of what they've just created, introduce them, watch the parents' faces crack and break, and explain the process in an emotionless voice that scares me, wearing a vacant expression that haunts my dreams and carries me on the edges of a scream to waking.

We catch them laughing as we come in, but this stops abruptly when they turn to watch us walk through the door. In my experience, smiling doesn't help, hesitating only hurts.

"Mr. and Mrs. Elliot," I say, in that voice that isn't mine. "This is Kevin Daniels. It's time to make your decision."

With the experienced parents, this pill never sits well but it does go down smoother, without all that denial to block the way.

"Are you.... You're not serious?" the husband asks, his voice small and his eyes darting between Kevin Daniels and me. It's hard to look at his face but I make myself look. I always make myself look.

"I am serious," I say. "Mr. Daniels will approve your selection and we'll begin the process immediately. Once placement is set, you'll be allowed to know which program—"

My words are cut off by a deep, strangled noise spreading up and out of the wife's throat like a storm siren. She clings to her husband, and his face grows red.

"You don't have to do this," he says, his voice angry and demanding but it's still a plea. "You can't do this."

This is when I step back, literally, and let Kevin Daniels force the reality upon them. It's supposed to be easier when the news comes from their doctor, the person they've been with through the whole thing, eight months of uncertainty and doubt, the person they trusted to get them, and their babies, through this. But it never works like that. I start, and the Liaison finishes, and we spin around in this sick dance I wish I'd never been invited to.

"Mr. and Mrs. Elliot," he begins in a rational tone. I look at his ponytail and dig my fingernails into my palm. "This was all explained to you during your first appointment with Doctor Fontaine. We had your full compliance then and we expect your full compliance now. I understand how difficult this must be for you, but you must realize that we absolutely cannot make any exceptions regarding this matter. If it would help move this process along, you can waive your selection and we'll choose for you...."

"Evil," Mrs. Elliot mutters into her husband's shoulder, so low and muffled but I hear it. Then she turns her head and looks directly at Daniels. "This is evil," she whispers harshly, and her eyes flick over to mine. "You are evil." I can't help but flinch.

In the end, they have no choice, and they waive their selection, as most of them do. We leave them to comfort each other and go down to the nursery, the Liaison still two steps behind me. I suppose this is a tactical maneuver, designed to make me feel as though I am in control, as though I have any amount of power. Or maybe he just doesn't want to leave himself vulnerable with his back to me.

In the nursery, he looks over the triplets, finally settling on the boy.

"This one?" he asks, bending to pick him up. He was sleeping, but he wakes upon the Liaison's touch and begins to cry, loudly, achingly, prophetically.

I don't know if Daniels expected an answer from me but I don't give him one. I've spoken with him too much today.

The Elliots' chart is on the wall and I go to it.

"It'll probably be the Feed Program," he says. "But we'll contact you if this changes."

I nod absently. I checked the box before he even spoke.

+

AT HOME, THE CHAOS HAS already begun.

I haven't even cut the engine before Jordan comes tearing out the front door, followed seconds later by Jason, who's waving a doubled-up belt in his hand above his head like a crazed cattle driver. I undo my seatbelt as I watch Jordan vault over the porch railing and sprint around the far side of the house, those lithe and muscular legs making it look easy, making Jason curse and go around red-faced to the stairs which he hops down in a fury.

I pound my fist into the center of the steering wheel and the Civic's mild horn bleats loud enough to stop Jason in his tracks.

"What the hell are you doing?" I scream at him as I climb out of the car and slam the door behind me.

His mouth goes from startled oval to flapping lips as he searches for a believable excuse, finally settling on a resigned scowl as he howls, "Jesus, Mom, you let her get away with *everything*."

Less than two minutes home, haven't even kicked off my shoes yet, and I'm already Public Enemy Number One. The exhausting thing is that this is not a new record.

"Give me the belt, Jason," I demand, holding my hand out for it.

He looks at my hand in disgust and heaves the heavy sigh of the beleaguered teenager. He slaps the belt into my palm, not hard enough to leave a welt but hard enough to have been purposeful, and throws his hands in the air.

"You always take her side. Just 'cause she's a girl, I swear to *god!*"

"Jason, I just got home, I haven't taken anyone's side."

Zero to eye-roll in point-six seconds. "Whatever."

Jason has his father's build, which is a blessing considering the wispy men that hang limply from my family tree. Broad shoulders and barrel chest pushing out against the seams of his plain white t-shirt, standing a good three inches taller than his five-nine father, large enough to be intimidating but his face still retains its innocently rounded youth. If only he would shave more often I might be able to maintain some control over him, but his rough beard started to darken his chin two years ago and he became his father's charge. It seems all I can do for him now is provide a scapegoat.

He stomps back up the porch steps, mumbling a string of things I'm sure I'm better off not hearing.

"Just go inside and get dressed," I call after him. The front door slams in response.

It's my turn to sigh.

The sun is just beginning to peek over the prickly tops of the small spattering of pine trees that grow to the east of the house. Its early-morning glow paints the cloudless sky a hazy orange-pink. Dew drips from the long grass in the yard, and the air feels wet, heavy. I can hear the slight, tentative calls of our cattle in the fields, testing out the day. We have a rooster but he's shy. I finger Jason's belt in my hand and stand there, breathing in the morning.

I think about going after Jordan. She doesn't know that I know about her secret hiding place—the loft in the hay barn—and I'm sure that's where she's run to now, but I am also sure it would only upset her to be found. She wouldn't yell at me outright like Jason does, but she would look at me, her brow curved sharply to the bridge of her nose, the left corner of her mouth sloped downward, her light hazel eyes grown dark with disappointment. She is the only person I know who can pierce me with such guilt from one single look, guilt over trying to protect her. I can't stand that look.

One more deep breath, then I mount the stairs two at a time. I shake off my jacket in the foyer and hang it in the closet. Overhead, I hear the shower running, and think it must be Jeremy. Jay is a nighttime bather; it used to be one of our evening rituals, when I was home.

Jason is in the kitchen, cracking fresh eggs directly into the skillet and tossing the brown shells in the direction of the garbage can, falling about three inches short with each toss.

I set his belt and my purse on the kitchen table. "Jason."

I don't even have to finish (or, really, start) my sentence, that's how attuned he is to my tone of voice. It just must scream *nag* directly into his ear canal and he jumps to cut it off. With an even heavier sigh than the one he graced me with outside, he goes across the room to the garbage can and stoops to pick up his mess.

"Thank you," I say. I rub my eyes hard with one hand, trying to push out the exhaustion that has crept in at the thought of saying what I'm going to say next. It's a struggle not to sigh myself. "You want to tell me what just happened here?"

He's back at the skillet, sprinkling in some diced onions and shifting everything around with the black plastic spatula. He shrugs.

"You were clearly fighting about something," I try again.

"Don't worry about it, Mom," he says. "She's just a brat."

"Well, what did she do?"

Another shrug. He turns down the flame on the gas stove and comes over to the table to grab his plate. I touch his arm and he practically recoils.

"Jason, honey, you said you didn't want me choosing sides, and I'm trying not to. But it's hard not to be biased when the first thing you see upon pulling into the driveway is your son threatening your daughter with his leather belt."

"I wasn't going to hit her. I just wanted to scare her."

"Why?"

He scoops his omelet onto his plate with the spatula and takes the skillet over to the sink before he sits down. "I told you, she was being a brat."

"How?"

"Why does it matter, Mom? It's over. Can I eat now, please? In peace?" A forkful of egg is already in his mouth on the last syllable.

"All right, Jason, you're right. It doesn't matter. What matters is that you're eighteen, you're not a kid any more, okay, and she still is. So you can't solve your...disputes through threats of violence, intended or otherwise. Got it?"

"Mom—"

"I'm serious. You want us to treat you like an adult, start acting like one."

I can't believe those words just came out of my mouth. They remind me bitterly of all the times my own mother screamed them at me, before her hand came down. The difference is that my hand is at my side and my voice is even, and Jason will never appreciate this difference, and that makes me feel okay for saying the words in the first place.

Jason doesn't say anything, he just shrugs and continues his noisy chewing.

"Where's your father?"

"Still asleep. He wants me to wake him after breakfast."

"He doesn't want to eat?"

"I don't know, Mom, Jesus."

"All right, all right. I guess I've pestered you long enough." I want to reach a hand out and ruffle his hair, or bend a little and kiss the top of his head, and I nearly do, but there's that sighing again. I grab my purse and walk out of the room.

The shower is still on so I go to our bedroom. Jay is lying on his stomach, his large feet poking out from beneath the down comforter. His breathing is heavy but he's not snoring, so I know he isn't too deep into dreamland. I tiptoe to my vanity and sit in the chair to remove my shoes. The relief is like a bullet hitting me from behind, I don't expect it and it is incredible. I lean back in the wooden rocker and it creaks beneath my weight but not as loudly as my own bones snap and crack as I rotate my ankle in lazy circles. I slouch, I close my eyes. That's the stuff.

Shifting from the bed draws my lids open. Jay is sitting up, rubbing a hand across his bare chest, ruffling the dark hairs there, and breathing deep, looking at me over a big yawn. "'Orning," he says through it.

"I didn't mean to wake you," I say, smiling at his tousled hair, which he attempts to smooth down with dry hands.

"Ah, I shoulda been up an hour ago," he says.

"Jason certainly seems ready to go."

Jay stands and cracks his back, picks up a pair of jeans from the floor and pulls them on over his boxers. "Kid's got a lot of energy, and enthusiasm. He really likes running this place."

"Mmm." I close my eyes again and rub my temples. "Better he burn off all that energy helping you than chasing his sister all over the farm."

I hear Jay open a dresser drawer and a second later his voice is muffled by the t-shirt he's no doubt slipping over his head. "Siblings fight. It's what they do. They'll get over it."

"Jason's too old to still be doing this."

I feel him next to me before his warm hand cups my shoulder. His lips are centimeters away from my ear, his breath soft and inviting. "And you've worked too long and hard to be worryin' about this just now," he says, and kisses my forehead.

"Lower," I say, my voice as light as air.

I feel his smile, his laugh. "Like here?" His lips find my nose.

"Little lower."

"Here?" My chin.

"Tease," I say.

He kisses me proper, with so much tenderness I struggle not to melt right off that chair. When he pulls away, it's all I can do to keep from throwing my arms around his strong neck and digging my nails into his shoulders so he can never let go.

"Get some sleep, Junebug," he says, then he caresses my shoulder with his thumb and leaves the room.

No sooner has he stepped over the threshold than the front door slams and the screaming starts up again. I hear my husband calling for order and my son shouting curses he didn't learn from me, and then heavy footsteps clomping up the stairs to the attic.

In the hallway, Jay stands with his belt and socks still in his hand, shaking his head at the attic door.

"What did I miss?" I ask.

"June," he says, sounding exasperated, which is not a good sign, considering the early hour. "Get yourself back to bed, I'll take care of this."

"Well, what's all this shouting about now? Did she say something, do something?"

"It's… It's nothing, June. It started last night, she… Look, I'll take care of it, okay, I don't want you worryin' about it."

"'Cause keepin' it a mystery ain't worryin' at all," I say, my Southern syntax creeping out. He drops his socks and starts on looping the belt around his waist, still shaking his head, his mussed hair waving in the breeze caused by this movement.

The water for the shower finally shuts off. The silence is overwhelming.

"Jay…"

"She packed a bag." His voice is so low, yet I still hear those words as if he shouted them into my ear with a bullhorn, drilled them into my bones. He can't even look me in the eye when he says it; he's talking to the carpet but it's got nothing to say back to him.

When I finally find my voice, I squeak out, "When?"

"Last night. Jason caught her, tried to stop her, they got into it. I guess he's still pissed, but he'll calm down. Look, I made her put everything back, everything's all right."

The tears in my eyes steal the words from my throat. I just look at Jay and he can't even look at me; he never could keep eye contact and tell a lie at the same time.

I move toward the attic steps. Jay's gentle fingers on my elbow slow me but they will not stop me. I want to scream at him just to have someone to scream at but I am already halfway up the stairs and he does not follow. Maybe he does understand; everything is not all right—none of us are fool enough to believe it is—but we try, dammit, at least we fucking try.

Jordan's clothes are scattered all over the floor, as they always are. Her stuffed animals are in a neat bunch on the floor near a chair. The window is open slightly and the birds are singing to the sun. On the bed, Jordan is stuffing a bundle of unfolded underwear into the duffel bag we bought her when she joined the track team last year.

She knows I've reached the top of the stairs but she avoids turning her head to look at me. She reaches for a pile of jeans on the floor.

"What are you doing?" The words are wet and desperate, but she doesn't even pause. All of her jeans have holes in them; she won't wear the new ones I buy for her.

I stride across the room with a speed akin to flying and rip the pants out of her hands. "I asked you a question."

"You know what I'm doing" is all she says as she bends to pick up another article.

We never sent Jordan to preschool because the hospital opened a new daycare and it was free. But she wanted to go to school so badly; she didn't sleep a wink the night before her first day of kindergarten. We got her brand-new school shoes, sleek and black with straps and buckles just like the grown-ups wore, had her jumper pressed, matched the color of her lunchbox with the bows in her hair. She was so excited. When I pulled up in the parking lot she almost got away with leaping out of the car door before I'd come to a complete stop. She ran ahead of me into the building; we'd visited in May so she knew where the classroom was and she headed right for it. It was all I could do to pull her attention away from the other kids, all the new crayons and books, to pay attention to me long enough to say goodbye. That's when the fantasy broke, and the tears came, and the shrieking, and she clung to my arm and begged me to stay.

That fear is gone from her now, replaced with a coldness, a bold resolve that I do not recognize, and I do not like it. I can't see it in her eyes because she will not look at me, but I hear it in her voice. She has given up.

No.

"No." I take the clothes from her hand again, pick up the duffel bag and empty the clothes back onto the floor. "I won't let you do this."

"You don't have a choice," she says.

"Yes I do," I say, trying to put force behind it, conviction. "Yes I do. So do you. We all do."

"What—" and she finally looks at me, empty eyes and a wry smile, creases in her pale pink skin that she's too young to have, laugh lines and thought lines, stress, reality "—pack now or pack tomorrow? I choose now."

"You have no idea, Jordan," I start, but there are so many ways to finish that sentence:

You have no idea how much I've sacrificed for you, how hard I've fought. You have no idea the things I've seen and the things I've done, the things I know irrevocably and inevitably, and still I fight to hold on to you, to keep you safe, to shield you from these cruel truths. You have no idea how painful it is to drift through your days with a broken heart because your only daughter has given up, given in, given over, rejected your counsel, your hand, your love, and your hope. Most of all, Jordan, you have no idea what I will do, despite all this, to keep you with me, to keep all of my babies with me.

"You have no idea, Jordan... We don't know what's going to happen. Nothing has been decided. Put your things away."

"No." She stands up. She's almost taller than me, another heir of her father's strong build.

"Then leave them on the floor," I say, still hugging the duffel bag to my chest. "I'll take this."

She doesn't say anything else, and I take this as the best I'm going to get in the way of acquiescence. Tears are still dangerously close to the surface, and I turn to walk away so I can shed them alone. But her words stop me, her cold, unfeeling words.

"Goodbye, Mother."

The edge of my vision begins to blur and go black. I look at her and she meets my eye. Unblinking, she meets my eye.

"What did you say?" It's so hard to get the words out.

"I said goodbye." Her voice, so flat. So unbelievable. Then she shrugs. "Just practicing."

My hand shoots out. I feel the light duffel bag brush the tops of my feet as it falls to the floor but I do not feel her face against the skin of my palm. Her cheek is red but she doesn't touch it. I don't know if she cries out because all I can hear is the blood rushing through my veins, my heart furiously pumping. But there are tears in her eyes now. There are tears in her eyes.

Through clenched teeth, I instruct her, "Go. To. School." When only the water in her eyes stirs, I add sharply, "Now."

She runs for the stairs, swiping up a pair of faded jeans on her way. I listen to her fast feet scramble down the stairs and disappear in the carpeted hallway. I cup my hands over my mouth and scream.

# THREE
## JORDAN

THE BELL RINGS AND WE don't move. We never do. We never have to crawl through the halls with our partners in crime, snaking in and out of lockers, loading up for the next room, the next one and a half hours of staring at the back of dandruffed heads and failing to feign interest in the monotone drone that only occasionally finds its way to our ears. Ours is a larger room, two in fact, merged together through the careful demolition of one adjoining wall, and we only share it with a quarter of the ones who have to share those other rooms. We still sweat, we still stare, we still feign interest. We just do it, you know, apart.

This is the Learning Disability wing of the high school my parents make me go to because it is the "law" and we are abiding citizens despite what difference it makes. Not really a wing but a floor, the basement actually, renovated for us so we can go to the same school as the "normal" kids, the ones who don't need one-on-one attention, the ones who can slip through the cracks unnoticed because they're as mediocre as the kid next to them, and we can still feel "included," even though everyone sees you take the stairs down instead of up and the only space you ever share with them is the lunchroom—if they let you. I'm not bitter or anything, just realistic.

Here I am realistically sitting next to my obese neighbor who also happens to have a rare skin condition commonly known as Lack of Bathing-itis. If he lifts his arm to scratch at his armpit, which he does quite often, I have to look away and breathe shallow. There's a window I can pretend to look through, admiring the cracked sidewalk and tufts of brown grass, until it's safe to turn back. His name is Barney, unfortunately, and no one talks to him, at least they haven't in the entire year I've sat in this seat, wondering how much more weight his chair can take, counting the beads of sweat on his forehead when I'm particularly bored.

We share a table, we don't have desks. Another "inclusive" tactic. Two to a table, seven tables, fourteen kids. There are extra tables against the wall in the Activity Room (this is the Class Room); they bring them out if our numbers grow. Most people these days have the common decency to home school their deficient children, either that or place them in the ranks of the "normies" and it's not really surprising to me to see how easily they fit in, pulling down those good ol' C's and high D's. Avoid the stigma, live your life, not that it matters anyway.

For the record, I don't have a learning disability. I have a behavioral problem, and after several incidents of "acting out" and a neat little stamp on my permanent file declaring me the proud new owner of Oppositional Defiant Disorder, they didn't know where else to put me, so here I am. The quickest way to forget about me, I guess. Though, honestly, they could've just let me stay on the farm. What authority figures am I going to challenge there—the cows?

But here I am. So. I don't know what time it is; there's a clock above the white board but I don't care to look at it. We get out when we get out, counting the seconds only makes it worse. Mrs. Henrick handed out our mathematics worksheets a few minutes ago, before the bell rang. We're all at different levels but it doesn't matter in here; the book is divided into sections so we can work at our own pace. I worked ahead yesterday so today I can sit and listen to the hundreds of feet stampeding above me, an occasional eruptive chorus of giggle-girl laughter, and lean subtly closer to the window when Barney shifts his weight.

Mrs. Henrick is the main teacher for our class, but she has two aides who work one-on-one with anyone who's struggling. They're both young, younger than her by a generation, fresh out of college or maybe still in. Trying to make a difference, trying to convince themselves they care about us, our nation's youth, Our Future. The only ones who care about us are the Over, and we wish they didn't because then we would be free. But I'm tired of daydreaming and I never make wishes. Guess I'll work on some more algebra equations.

"Did they come for you yet?" It's Barney. I look at him sidelong. He's talking to the guys at the table behind us, Billy Rushman and Everett Scout. They glare up from their open workbooks and don't say anything.

I can't tell what Billy's problem is, but Everett is dyslexic and has a touch of ADHD. One of the aides is usually at his side for most of the day, except at math time. Numbers he gets. Everything else makes his face flush red and his fists slam into the nearest solid surface.

"They came for me on Sunday." Barney's going on, probably because they're still looking at him, he's encouraged. "Two more days and I'm safe, boy. It kind of makes me nervous."

"Oh yeah, tardo?" Billy finally responds, low and mean. Can't even come up with a better insulting nickname. "Are you scared? You should be, you have a *lot* to offer." He spreads his arms wide and wiggles around, like he's rolling blubber, just to make sure Barney gets it. Everett snickers.

Barney turns back to his workbook, red faced and sweating harder. His breath comes out hard from his mouth. Fuck it if he starts to cry.

"They came for me yesterday," Billy is telling Everett now. I can't tell if Barney is listening, but his shoulders shake. "What about you?"

"Nah, not yet." Everett is fifteen, he's been waiting two years for the Liaisons to come.

"He was such a homo," Billy says. "Double-breasted suit and some shit. Kept playing with his fruity cufflinks. I swear the whole interview I was just afraid he was gonna make a pass at me."

They both laugh at that. Then, "Hey, did they come for you?"

Something pokes me in the shoulder. I turn enough to see Billy and Everett looking at me, Billy's pencil extended across the gap between our tables. Great.

"Did they?" he asks again.

I just nod, one nod, quick and final, and turn back around. Barney's knuckles are whitening, bloodless, gripping his pencil. He's pressing too hard, his paper begins to tear.

"I bet they take her," Billy whispers to Everett, loud enough for me to hear. "Fine piece like her."

"Shut up, Billy," Everett says, but he's laughing.

"She'll go into Breeding, no doubt," he says. "At least I hope so. That's where I plan to end up. Hell, I'd volunteer right now if they'd let me!"

"Fucking sick dude," Everett laughs. They're getting louder, heads are turning, the aides are trying to ignore them. Mrs. Henrick looks like she might get up from behind her desk, but her dry-erase markers are oh so captivating.

"Hey." The poking resumes. "Hey, Jordan. Jordan. See you there, yeah? Try to stay fresh for me."

The laughter spills into my ears. Barney moves in his seat but I'm quicker. I push away from the table, knocking my chair into their table. Billy's fingers must have been on the edge because he yelps and flings himself back, and he's on his feet now and my hands are at the collar of his shirt. The aides are yelling and the kids are cheering and I yank and Billy's face hits the table and there's a cracking sound louder than the blood rush in my ears and I know I'm smiling and I want him to see I'm smiling so I pull on his hair and turn his bleeding face to me but his eyes are closed, closed and wet and fuck me if I don't smile wider.

Then hands are on my shoulders, of course they are, tugging, and fingers wrap around my wrist and pull me off him. They get me on the ground and I struggle, why make it easy? They're putting me in the Pretzel Lock, arms and legs pinned painfully against my back until I calm down. One of the aides is screaming in my ear, frantically trying to subdue me, ha. Her desperation floods into me and pushes all the anger out and I go slack. I can hear Mrs. Henrick somewhere above me, beyond me, placating Billy, asking another kid to take him to the nurse.

One of the aides releases her grip on my legs and makes her way around the room with Mrs. Henrick, trying to regain control. I let the other aide lift me to my feet and walk me to the door. Barney catches my eye and smiles. I hope he doesn't think this means we're friends now.

"What did you think you were doing in there?" The aide starts in on me, her voice still quivering. Maybe this is the first time she's had to break up a fight. If she were assisting in one of the normal classrooms she'd be a pro by now.

Her hands are tight around my wrists, which are pressed into the small of my back, like I'm in handcuffs. I bet she thinks she's doing something important, something Adult, leading me away, helping me. I bet she thinks she matters.

"What do you think that kind of violence solves, huh?" She won't give it up. We take the stairs up to the first floor, round the corner, hurrying down the hall. Heads peek out from the girl's bathroom. Ooh, drama, come have a look, tell your friends, sell tickets. "What did he do to you? To deserve a broken nose, or worse? There are no problems that can't be solved by talking it out. Absolutely not one. You could have come to me, or Miss Beverly or Mrs. Henrick, you know that, don't you?"

I don't say anything. We've reached our destination, the principal's office. Well, his waiting room, but I won't go see him. He only talks to the harmless kids, the class clowns, the peaceful disrupters. I'm here for Jonas Stephens, the counselor. One of. Our school has six, but I've only ever been to Stephens. He's even been to my house, god bless him.

The aide leaves me here, with one last deep and pouting I-hope-you-know-this-is-for-your-own-good sigh. Stephens's door opens slowly and dramatically a few minutes later, and a scrawny boy about my age is led out by the hand. His eyes are pink around the corners and he tries to hide this with his hair. He untangles his fingers from Stephens when he sees me, sniffs heartily and walks out of the room without saying goodbye to the good, sensitive, selfless Stephens.

Jonas Stephens has brown shaggy hair that looks like he spiked it too much in college, trying to fit in with a certain crowd that would never accept him because he was too stocky and too eager. He's still got the earring in his right ear, but that might be recent, to show he's "down" with us, the youth culture hasn't passed him by, no sir, not one bit. His suit is brown to match his hair, a lighter brown than his skin but darker than his eyes. His white dress shirt isn't tucked in probably because it won't work around his slightly protruding middle, or again, because it's the cool thing to do.

"Ah, Miss Fontaine, we meet again," he says, smiling. His teeth are yellow near the gums, a smoker. The yellowing on the first two fingernails of his left hand confirms this, but he never smells like smoke. An after-work hobby. More power to him.

He sits behind his big mahogany shield and I sit in a spindly, cushion-less folding chair, my knees nearly touching his desk, my elbows fighting for space between his potted fern and the adjacent chair. It's a tiny office but it doesn't take physical space to expand young minds, only hard work and determination. Thank you, inspirational wall posters, bulk manufactured for a profit that has nothing to do with my young mind.

Stephens begins by clearing his throat, as he always does. I fold my arms across my chest and slump casually lower in my chair, as I always do. Let the games begin.

"You got into another fight, I see," he starts, kind of weakly, if you ask me. "Billy Rushman. I got a call from the nurse's office; he had to be taken to the hospital. Seems you may have broken his nose."

I shrug. It's too much to yawn.

"This is serious, Jordan," he says, and it's obvious he really believes it is. "If he wants to press charges, you could be facing time in a juvenile detention center. Do you understand me?"

All the restraint in me can't stop my eyes from rolling. "Don't count on it," I say.

He starts to say something but shuts his mouth fast. He clasps his hands then unclasps them, and his eyes fall to his desk. He's starting to get it.

After a long moment, he says, "Jordan." He stops. Deep breath. "You've had your Liaison visit. When?"

"Monday," I say. My leg starts to shake. I shift in the chair and tuck it underneath me, awkwardly, but it stops moving.

"Jordan, you're aware that this does not mean you've been selected for the Summer Program. Twenty-six percent of Liaison visits amount to nothing."

"A stay," I say before I can stop myself. He raises his thick, carefully trimmed eyebrows at me, and the brown in his irises deepens. "You know, like a layover."

He shakes his head slowly and rubs his hand against the thin whiskers sprouting over his chin. "Even if you are selected—"

"Can you spare me the statistics," I say quickly. "Everyone knows them."

"This is important, Jordan." He leans forward, elbows on the desk, dislodging his pencil case to a precarious edge position but he pays it no attention. His eyes are unblinking. "You have to understand…I need you to understand…your behavior matters, now more than ever. You have to remain civil; you *have* to retain your humanity. Don't you understand that? That's something the Over can never take away from you, Jordan, from any of us. If we become animals, Jordan, if we let ourselves be pushed to that kind of cruelty, that kind of mindlessness, shamelessness… We become everything they want us to be. I won't let them do that to me, and I *refuse* to let them do that to you, to any of you."

The tears in his eyes stab at me but his words fall crumbling against my ears, broken before they reach me. But he really thinks this matters, he really does.

"I didn't break Billy's nose for them," I tell Stephens. "I did it because he's vile."

"Then let him bear the consequences of that," Stephens says, clearly ignoring the obvious conclusion that his broken nose *is* his consequence. "We can only judge ourselves, through our words and through our actions. We are responsible for the things we do and the people we hurt. We are *still* and *always* responsible. That is something we have a choice in, no matter how powerless we feel."

"Okay, I get it, I am the captain of my destiny." Blah blah blah.

"No." He shakes his head solemnly, and drops his voice. "That is out of your hands. But you *are* the captain of your choices now, of how you choose to react to your destiny. You're the captain of your soul, Jordan. No one owns that but you."

We sit in silence then. His wall clock ticks, I lose count. My soul, huh? I'm pretty sure that's part of the whole body package, and where it goes the soul must follow, round and round it goes, and where it stops everybody knows.

✛

BACK AT THE HOUSE, I decide not to give Stephens's note to my parents. Well, it's not really a decision in the sense that I consciously thought, *I shall not pass on this note*, just that it is in my pocket and that is where it will stay. He knows I won't give it to them, that's why he always calls anyway. It's just a waste of tree pulp if you ask me.

Jeremy can't drive yet but we take the same bus, which drops us off by the dirt road that twists and bends a mile through our wheat fields until it reaches the driveway. He doesn't talk to me on the bus; he sits in the front behind the driver and buries his face in a book, always. The loudest kids sit in back, hollering and shoving each other, boasting about how many cigarettes they'll smoke when they get home, how many roaches they snuck in between classes, how many girls they've privileged with a backseat romp. They laugh, they play. I sit by the side exit door and count the stops before our fields.

On the walk down the road Jeremy continues to read. I point out debris he might want to sidestep, large rocks or deep holes, by periodically calling "left" or "right," and he swerves, without looking up, in whichever direction I call. I realize the potential for childish havoc here, but Jeremy's a quiet kid, never did anything to anyone, and besides, I wouldn't want him to fall on his hands, those are his ticket, according to Mom.

At the house, Jason's in the front yard, dirtying his knees in the small herb garden to the right of the walkway. He looks up when he hears our footsteps in the gravel, lays down his trowel. If he still has it out for me he doesn't let on with more than a stony stare. Jeremy walks right up the porch steps and in through the door without a pause or a glance away from his oh so engrossing pages, but I stop. In the driveway, next to the rambling piece of crap Dad uses to haul dirt and wooden planks around the farm, is Mom's Honda. She's never home in the afternoon, unless it's Sunday, and then only to make us go to church, and then she's off to the hospital again. Babies don't stop for religious obligations. Not that I would either, if it were up to me.

But I do stop, here, right in the yard, right next to her car, and I just look at it. I know what it means, but I can't add it up, not with Jason right there, bent and sweating and purposeful, working working working. But Mom's home, and Jeremy just went inside, just like that.

I hear the screen door creak open, and look to see Dad step out. He's not wearing his work boots, not even his tennis shoes or loafers, just gray socks. His jeans are free of grass or mud stains, his shirt is bright and white and searing.

"Come inside," he says, looking at the grass. "Both of you."

He goes back in. Jason gets to his feet and picks up the trowel. Always put your tools away right when you finish with them, wash them and put them away, don't save it for later, that's the key to the running of a well-oiled farm, never put things off, especially the small things. So he takes his trowel to the porch and drops it in a bucket of warm water and goes in.

I bolt.

It's stupid and useless and childish but it's better than going in there and sitting and listening and waiting and holding hands and Kumbaya. I run around the house and vault the stone wall that separates the yard from the woods, so I can bypass the pig pen and chicken coop and take the long way through the grazing field at the other side of the trees, circling back and just running, the tall grass whipping against my legs, scratching, scarring, so I can think.

But I can't think, not until I stop, and I don't stop, not until I reach the barn and climb up to the loft and curl my knees to my chest and press my back to the wall and fiddle with a strand of straw sticking out from the square bales. If I look hard enough I can see the fleas scuttle through the loosely packed strands, making nests, making plans. I break the straw in two, pick up another piece and snap it, pick up another, and another.

Now I think, I think about her. She came and she told me straight, there was no getting out of it, and I believed her and I accepted it, I've always accepted it, what else can I do? But here I am, hiding, waiting, just the same as I've always waited, as everyone waits. She told me nothing can save me, she didn't say it like that but she meant it like that, nothing could save me, and she certainly wouldn't. The exact opposite, that's her job description, her choice. Who's responsible for her choices, Mr. Stephens? Who owns her fucking soul?

Someone's coming up the ladder to the loft. I breathe in through my nose and swallow baby powder and lemon hand soap. It's Mom.

"Jordan," she says. I look at her. She's wearing her Sunday best, of course she is, smart black slacks, casual emerald blouse, bangles round her wrists, not slender but not pudgy either. "Come inside, okay?"

I can't even tell her no because something is blocking my windpipe and I realize with disgust that it's tears.

"We're all together, honey," she says, taking a couple steps toward me, crouching when the roof begins to slant. "We're all going to be together right now. Please come with me." She holds out her hand. It's surprisingly steady.

"I don't want to," I say. I should've just kept my mouth shut because the tears come out too, the hot ugly tears, from my eyes, from my mouth, from my everything.

Then Mom is there, hugging me, or trying to, but I stand up, push my knuckles against my eyes, hard enough to see spots, red and yellow swirls, orange streaks. Her hands are on my shoulders. I break free.

I take the ladder down and she's a step above me. At the bottom, I fix my gaze with hers. My cheek throbs.

"Told you," I say, and go out the barn doors without waiting for her reaction.

✛

Maybe I'm just not one for family gatherings, group activities, circle jerks. I head up to my room without looking at anyone in the living room, ignoring him when Dad calls my name. I have work to do, right? Don't we all? Or are they only coming for one of us, or two of us? Well, I have inside information so I'm not going to sit around pretending I have a chance. No escape, no savior. Only a bag to pack and a goodbye to avoid.

When you're old enough to start going to school like the Big Kids, that's when they tell you. When you're old enough to hear things from the Big Kids, stories meant to shock and scare some precious little-girl tears out of you before naptime. Your parents usually want to make sure you come home sob-free, no extra monsters to add beneath the bed, so they sit you down before you go, all hopped-up on sugar cereals and dreams of the unknown, and they tell you, "Sweetie, if you hear the other kids talking about this, do not worry, they're only trying to frighten you." And then they tell you the truth, solid and straight, that in six to eight more years, when you've reached that far away age of the teenager, something might happen to you, something not good but not bad, something you shouldn't worry about but something you will have to face. And they give you the Summer Program rundown, abbreviated for your bright eyes and bushy tail: it's like a special camp, dear, where you'll do activities and be with other kids your age, and at the end you might not come home. But you might, always remember that, always cling to that, you *might*.

The kids at school fill in the rest for you, about Breeders and Feeders and Seeds. Growing up on a farm, no one had to explain Breed to me; I helped Dad deliver four calves before most boys experienced their first nocturnal emission. Breeding is simple mating, human-on-human, not human-on-Over, which I don't even think is possible. They breed you until you die, and then I guess you become food. Which should tell you what Feed is. No pretense, you're just slapped onto a silver platter and offered up, body and soul. Seed is murkier, I've never gotten a clear picture of this, but it pretty much amounts to a recruitment program. Not for Liaisons, though, those are volunteers. Anyway, you get this rundown, but you just don't really think about it, you don't think about it, because you have crayons that need your attention and Susie Haymaker who won't stop pulling your hair at recess and lines to hurry up and get into before all the chocolate milk is gone. And when you do start to think about it, when you're older, when reality grows thicker, persistent, no one wants to talk about it anymore, especially the ones who have been through the Summer Selection Program, the ones who made it through on that dangerously slim *might*.

Mom never went. She won't say it out loud but I can just tell, the way she shuts her mouth and looks away, she feels guilty. Dad went, but the only thing he ever says about it was that it "wasn't too horrible." Really, Dad? How horrible is too horrible? Give it to me in screams.

"Jordan?"

I'm piling my socks into the remaining space of the duffel bag I've already packed and unpacked twice this week when Jeremy's voice creeps up from the top step. He's standing there with hands clasped at his belt buckle, curiously devoid of his book. His bangs hang loosely over his left eye. He brushes the hair back but it falls again and he leaves it.

"I'm not ready," I say, the words croaking out. I hope there are no toads in the area that might hear it and confuse it with a mating call.

He shudders, actually *shudders*, a soft quaking that only moves through his shoulders, and then he swallows. "But she's here."

At first I'm confused and almost yell at him, but then I get it and go to my window. There, in the driveway, boxing in Mom's little silver Honda, is a plain white utility van, the kind you see TV repairmen driving, or people who want to remain inconspicuous in the movies. Touching my ear to the window pane, hot from the afternoon sun, I can hear that the van's engine is on. No rush or anything.

I turn back to Jeremy. He's still standing there, hands in his pockets now, rocking slightly on his heel, trying to decide what to do.

"Okay," I tell him. "I'll be down."

He hesitates then says, "Let's go back down together."

I nod. I finish shoving the socks into the bag and zip it up, and make a quick final sweep of the room. For a second I consider taking one of the stuffed animals but the dust would just upset my allergies, and then my eyes find the beaded bracelet I wore on her first visit, lying on the floor now, pushed up against the boxes that hold up my mattress. I grab it up and slip it on, hiding it under the sleeve of my long shirt. It's not for her anymore, but I like the way it feels against my skin, tight, secure. I brush past Jeremy without looking at him and take the stairs down faster than I intended to.

No one's in the living room anymore and I can hear voices coming from the front porch. I go out, Jeremy right behind me.

There she is, *Miss* Omalis, hair exactly the same, casual dress selected from the same Career Woman's specialty rack, except this time she's opted for black slacks instead of a skirt, something that can really breathe, really move. She's standing on the sidewalk in front of the porch, familiar clipboard in hand, reaching up the three wooden stairs to pass something off to my mom and dad, who just stand there themselves, arms at their sides, not taking it. I see that it is three pieces of pink paper, and I know immediately what that means before Mom's indignant voice breaks the stunned silence.

"All of them?" she says, low but angry, hand shooting for her throat. "*All* of them?"

Mom had six younger brothers and two sisters, a fertility-drug family before it became fashionably survivalist; four of her brothers went away for the summer, and one of her sisters, the oldest one. Only the sister came back. But I guess, when you only have three to choose from, your odds of being spared one are fairly dismal. Way to go organic, Mom.

Dad's hand comes out from his pocket and his fingers work the knot at the base of Mom's neck. I can only see the back of his head from my spot near the door but I'd bet anything he's screwed up his rustic, farm-hard face to be glaring at Omalis, absolutely boring into her all his outrage and denial, trying to appeal to her sense of common decency with a single well-placed scowl.

Omalis puts the papers back on her clipboard and sighs. She looks up at my parents, squinting against the lowering sun. "Mr. and Mrs. Fontaine, this is the decision that has been made. I know you are aware that this does not mean one or all of your children will not be returned to you at the completion of the Program. And of course, you will remain in contact with each of them, through me, and through scheduled visits and phone calls once they have been placed. If you have any questions or concerns you can always call our—"

Mom's laugh is so shrill and brittle it even startles me. Dad pinches her neck and looks at her. She wipes at her eyes and says through her dry laughter, "Concerns? Yeah, I think I may just have a few, now that you mention it."

But before she can say anything else something stops her, something inside her throat, but also Dad's shadow, falling over her like a shield as he steps in front of her and slowly, all hard-knuckles-business, descends the steps toward Omalis. She immediately unclips the papers again and holds them out to him. I expect her hand to be shaking but it isn't. Her eyes are steady, too.

"If we asked you to leave," my dad starts, and I have to take a sliding step toward him to hear the rest, his voice is so low and deep. "If we asked you, would you go?"

There is a breath of a pause; I imagine I can hear the wheat stalks exhaling into one another. I wonder if Miss Omalis gets this question all the time, this thin line between begging and threatening. I wonder what she'll say or do, but really, I think I already know.

"Mr. Fontaine," she says, rounded vowels as steady as her outstretched arm, "if I go, others will come. And you will lose everything, Mr. Fontaine." It's so quick, but here I think I see her candle-flame-blue eyes flicker over Jason, Jeremy, my mother, and then me, and back to Dad. "Everything."

Dad's arm shoots out and he snatches the papers away from her violently, crumbling them in his meaty fingers. He doesn't stop staring at her and she doesn't stop staring right back at him. Once, on Jeremy's tenth birthday, I got jealous because he got a bike and I'd been asking for one since I was six but all I kept getting were plastic kitchen toys and dolls and stuffed animals, and once a pair of plastic skates that I didn't even like but cried anyway when the wheels fell off. So I got jealous and I pushed Jeremy right off that bike and I took it and, not knowing how to ride it, I ran with it to the top of the hill at the backend of our yard, and pushed it down and watched it soar over the property line and fall and flip over a few times and finally land in a small creek, mangled and satisfying. Dad took me inside and sat me down and I tensed up for a spanking, but it never came. He just sat there and stared at me, so hard for so long, just stared and wouldn't let me look away. Finally, when I was ready to break down and apologize, he opened his frowning mouth and just said, "I'm very disappointed in you," and he walked away. I cried for days.

Now, he's giving Omalis the stare-down, but she's clearly not moved by it. I can tell Mom is about to lose it, the way her elbows shake. Shit, someone has to do something to move along the inevitable. I volunteer.

"Adios, mis parentos," I say in a poor imitation of Spanish and Drill Team cheer, hoisting my duffel bag onto my shoulder and trundling down the porch steps. When I pass Omalis she looks at me and I smile, the crinkles it causes at the corners of my eyes hopefully offsetting the fading redness. "Onward and upward. Vamanos!"

I hear my dad say my name in that stern way he does but I keep moving to the van, throw open the sliding side door and toss my bag inside, before turning back to the others. Mom is holding Jeremy by his arm now, probably permanently imbedding her fingerprints into his deflated biceps, her eyes on me and holding back tears. Jason steps around her, picking up his own gray gym bag from the porch as he goes. He stops at Dad's side and pats his shoulder, not like a son but like a man, like a buddy saying goodnight after a good poker game. Then he passes me without looking at me and climbs into the van after his bag.

Jeremy starts to go too, but Mom holds him back, and I have to look away when she starts kissing his forehead and he doesn't even try to struggle. Dad walks over to me, looms over me, I can smell his heavy cologne, like oregano and sweet sweat. He's staring at me but it's not a hard stare, it's not soft either, but it's new and I don't like it. He reaches out and squeezes my shoulder, pinching my neck with his thumb, almost too hard, but that's not why I can't breathe.

"You'll be okay." He stops and swallows a couple times, then licks his dry lips and says, "Take care of your brother." He means Jeremy, who's finally broken away from Mom and comes up beside us. Dad ruffles his hair and tries to smile and then walks back to the porch.

I hear Jeremy say, "We're really going," almost like a question but directed to no one and it sounds strange, like he said it but not from where he's standing, from farther away, from someplace else. He gets in the van.

I'm about to get in when Mom shouts my name, urgent and breaking on the last syllable. When she stands in front of me I can smell through the lemon hand soap her natural ammonia-and-latex smell, those long hospital hours seeping out of her pores, and I look at the neckline of her church clothes, wondering bitterly why she still dressed up, again, for this day.

"Jordan." She starts to say something else but stops in favor of leaning in for a hug, but it's too much. I back away only a step and finally look into her eyes that are so wet and so red and so much like mine must look right now, and I say, "Mom. I pierced my navel."

# F O U R
## O M A L I S

HEAVEN OMALIS DRIVES DOWN THE onramp with the windows rolled down. A chill drifts in from the west on the backs of gray clouds and the wind pushes against her loose hair, her cheek. As she accelerates her stomach dips and it makes her want to laugh; how odd that merging onto the highway can still make her anxious, how inappropriate. She eases the van into the center lane as the right quickly disappears, brings the speedometer's needle to rest between sixty-five and seventy, and flips on the cruise control. She cracks her ankle. After manually rolling up the old van's window, she flicks her eyes to the rearview mirror.

No one's spoken since they pulled away from the house, except for Jordan, to ask if she could turn on the radio. Some pop song Omalis is too old or removed from popular society to recognize spills out of the speakers, some child-turned-sex-object crooning in a key so close to whining Omalis is mildly concerned tears might begin to pour from the speakers along with the music, until the chorus hits and the tune takes an upbeat swing, and the child-turned-sex-object bounces with renewed empowerment. In the backseat, the boys sit tall and straight, looking out the windows on either side of them, not seeing the other cars stream by on the other side of the concrete median, the trees along the flat grassy fields. If they hear the music, which she doubts they do, they make no attempt to follow its beat with a nod or a gentle foot tap.

The girl, too, sits silently, but slumped, feet propped up on the dashboard, appearing casual, but if she were truly comfortable, Omalis thinks, she would've kicked off her shoes as well. Her hands are folded in her lap, fingers discreetly pinching a wrinkle in her shirt. Omalis looks at her only a moment, then turns her attention back to the road.

These drives are usually silent, when they're not filled with the sound of bravely suppressed sobs, so deafening in such a tiny space. Sometimes, when she's transporting more than one of them, the children talk to each other, ignoring her and their destination, trying to pretend they are only going on a day trip, a weekend getaway. Omalis hates it when they do this but she hates the crying even more, the silence the most, but she can think of no alternative she would care for anyway. She's grateful this is the only delivery she has to make today.

They drive on in silence for another forty minutes before Jordan speaks up again.

"Where are we going?"

The sound is strange at first and it takes Omalis a moment to react to it. She looks into the rearview to see Jason turn his head to look at his sister.

"I'm taking you to a private runway where you'll board a plane that will take you to your assigned camp." The words are stale and overused, but they come out almost bright, downright conversational, just like they always do, just like they're supposed to.

"Will there be other kids at the plane?" Jordan asks.

"*Jordeena*," Jason says from the backseat, "who cares?"

Omalis watches him roll his eyes and turn back to the window, his elbow bent against the armrest so he can hold his chin up with his palm. Beside him, Jeremy's knees squeeze tighter together and he drops his gaze from the window to the unopened book in his lap.

"Will there be?" Jordan asks again.

"I don't know," Omalis answers truthfully. "Sometimes there are, sometimes there aren't."

Silence follows, but Omalis can tell it will not last long. Sometimes the teenagers she transports start chatting with her, sometimes they ask her inane questions that calm them down—did she see the game last Friday? What does she think of all the construction on Route 52 lately? Sometimes they ask her other things, things that she wishes they wouldn't because they'll be answered in good time anyway, in proper course. And her history with this girl, Jordan Fontaine, tells her the questions will not be inane, and will most certainly not calm anyone down.

She decides to try to curb the barrage before it can begin, by turning the focus of the conversation, the questions, onto Jordan herself. "You told your mother about your piercing," Omalis says, looking at the road and smiling slightly. "I'm proud of you."

Jordan sits up straighter in her seat, stretching her legs. "Yeah, I confessed. Guess I don't need any priests to stop by the camp later."

"Jesus Christ!" Jason explodes from the backseat.

"Don't need him either," Jordan says quickly, "I'm cool."

"Will you stop it?" Jason shouts, leaning forward, straining against his seatbelt. Omalis rests her foot just above the break pedal. "Just shut the hell up. I don't want to hear your voice anymore, okay. Just shut up."

Beside him, Jeremy seems to shrink, the seat and the space around him swallowing him up. Jordan crosses her arms and opens her mouth and Omalis tenses. Jordan sucks in air and closes her mouth tight, her cheeks puffing out dramatically.

After a few seconds, Omalis can hear it but she is unsure if the others have caught it yet. Jeremy hides his head in his hand, the other clutching the tattered spine of his well-read paperback, but his small palm can't muffle the sound of his crying nearly enough for Omalis's ears. She sees in the rearview that he is trying to pull his knees up to his chest but he's too lanky for the seat and his feet keep slipping off. She wants to pull over and get out and take him aside and tell him to be brave, be brave for his younger sister and older brother, show them how to be a real man, but she knows she only wants him to be brave for her, so she won't have to listen anymore. His sobs grow louder, choked and fractured.

In her periphery she catches Jordan glancing back quickly over her shoulder, then folding her hands tightly together, pressing the knuckles of her left hand into her right, making the tendons in her muscular forearms and wrists stand out. Omalis knows Jeremy's crying is unsettling but she doesn't know what to say or do to quiet him. She drives on, switching over to the right lane, thinking she'll pull over if anyone starts shouting again.

She's never had to use force against the children she transports. More than a few times she has had to physically subdue a parent or guardian, but it is always swift and she only ever needs to take them down once and then they get it. Almost all of them beg her like Mr. Fontaine had, offering bribes or trades. But it isn't her call. Somewhere inside she knows they are aware of this, but she is there and she is a body, a person no taller than they, no larger, no less human. Their survival instinct kicks in and she becomes a target. She does not blame them for this; in fact, she regrets when they lunge at her or throw a punch or go for a weapon, because she knows it will only end with more pain for them, and—have mercy if this should ever happen—if they somehow overpowered her, she would never forgive herself.

Now, she looks in the rearview and sees Jason try to squash himself up against the side of the van, as far away from his quivering brother as he can make himself, pressing his forehead into the glass. Jordan drops her feet to the floor and begins to crack her knuckles. Omalis can see the tension building in her jaw and knows she is holding her breath. The pop music station cranks out another obnoxious chart topper. Omalis switches off the cruise control. She knows Jordan is bracing herself for something, and her mind races for a sentence, a word, a look even, that might diffuse the impending situation.

"Mind if I change the station?" Jordan asks, already reaching for the dial. Her voice startles Omalis, who blinks and swallows and shrugs her answer. She watches Jordan lean over and listens to the harsh static crackle between stations as Jordan spins the dial. Up ahead, a quiet suburb peeks into view, its sensitive inhabitants stalwartly protected against the intrusive traffic noise by a sound barrier twenty feet high, trees sprouting up around it, trying to blend the unsightly beige in with the natural greens and browns.

The static crackles in and out, punctured by a momentary burst of guitar chords or cymbal slaps or the indignant laments of some irate talk-show pundit, but the static comes back, the dial keeps on flipping. Omalis glances down at Jordan, whose fingers move almost frantically around the radio dial, her eyes closed.

"Jordan," Omalis begins, slowing down, prepared to pull over if the girl seizes up or faints, which is not uncommon. But her name is all Omalis can get out before Jordan moves, quick and sure, her hands grasping the wheel below Omalis's own and jerking it to the right. For one second Omalis is too stunned to counter the movement, but then she regains herself and tries to adjust the wheel. The van has already sped across the rough shoulder and the uneven ground crunches beneath them. Jeremy begins to scream and Jordan tightens her grip on the wheel. Omalis shouts and tears Jordan's hands away, simultaneously stepping hard on the brake, which is a bad move as the van is still turning and the tires slip and before she knows what is happening Jordan's window shatters inward and Omalis falls to her right. Her chest is caught painfully by her seatbelt, which knocks the wind out of her and brings a dizziness and a darkness to the corners of her eyes.

✢

WHEN SHE COMES TO, IT takes her a moment to realize she's even been out. She opens her eyes and the world is perpendicular, the horizon line cutting vertically through her line of sight. The static on the radio blares and beneath it she can hear the unsteady rumble of the van's engine. She smells cold air and petrol. When she tries to move, her chest burns. She fingers the seatbelt, pressed so far into her chest and side it might as well be embedded, and she inches her hand along until she finds its clasp. She is about to release it when she realizes the belt is the only thing keeping her from falling into Jordan, and then she looks and sees that Jordan is no longer there to fall into.

The passenger door is crumpled against the ground. Grass pokes through the broken window, the glass shards littered along the inside of the door and Jordan's vacated seat. Omalis shifts to look over her shoulder and sees that Jason is gone too, the sliding door on his side of the van partially open to the darkening sky. Then she hears it, the crying, which quickly melds into retching, and she cranes her neck over her other shoulder just in time to watch Jeremy vomit onto the cracked window next to his head.

"Jeremy," she says, but he doesn't look at her. His book has fallen from his lap onto the door and his seatbelt keeps him fastened awkwardly to his seat, even as he pulls against it with his hands. "Jeremy," she says again. "Don't move, I'll get you."

She says it to be comforting, to let him know she will help him, but it comes out sounding to her more like a threat. He just keeps on crying, mouth open and dripping, hands fidgeting.

As quickly as she can, Omalis unfastens her seatbelt, holding the armrest so she won't fall while she swings her legs down onto the passenger door, which has become the floor. She crouches through the space between the two front seats and kneels by Jeremy. She can smell his sick this close but she tries to ignore the sour sweetness of it as she touches his shoulder and says calm and soothing things to this weak and frightened young man.

"Jeremy, Jeremy, please, listen to me, listen. You're okay, you're all right. I'm going to get you out of here, okay? Come on, hold onto me, Jeremy, hold on to my shoulders."

When she finally gets him to wrap his arms around her he latches onto her with an unexpected ferocity that pulls her hard against him. He tucks his head beneath her chin and cries unabashedly into her shoulder, gripping the back of her shirt so tightly she'll be surprised if he doesn't rip it. She releases his belt and pulls him free. She hoists him like the small child he hasn't been for a long time out through the sliding door in what has become the roof, bends to retrieve his book, and then follows quickly after him.

Outside, she sees that they have traveled far enough away from the road that the cars speeding down the highway will not necessarily be able to see what has become of them, especially as the storm clouds roll in and the sky darkens for night. It is probably for the best that no one stops to help; they would only get in the way, complicate things with their own biases and concerns, none of which, Omalis is sure, would include the tracking down and reacquisition of two of her charges.

She wants to ask Jeremy how long she has been out, to determine how much time the two have had to run up or down the road, possibly hitching a ride, possibly finding themselves lost in the fields that stretch forever, the woods that sprout up here and there. But she knows it could not have been long, judging by the light, and Jeremy is in no condition to tell her anything.

Taking his hand and leading him a safe distance away from the still-running vehicle, Omalis sits Jeremy down in the grass and hands him his book. He takes it tentatively, perhaps unsure of what to do with it now, but nonetheless tucks it to his stomach.

"Jeremy." Omalis takes his chin, wet with tears and bile, into both her hands and makes him look at her. His eyes are bloodshot and mucus has built up in the corners at his nose. "Listen to me, honey. I'm going to go find your brother and sister. I need you to stay here. Are you listening to me? Stay here, Jeremy. I'll be right back. Please, stay here."

Jeremy nods his head only slightly. When she releases him she watches him long enough to see that he only rocks back and forth, his legs crossed in front of him, his stringy blond hair hanging in front of his face. She thinks she can hear him muttering to himself, but can only make out one word: "Why?" It isn't worth trying to answer.

Omalis takes off north at a fast clip, in the direction they'd been driving. There is a suburban neighborhood there, heralded by the looming sound barrier, which means people, which means salvation, at least for someone on the run. It is maybe two miles ahead, and Omalis wonders how fast Jason and Jordan can sprint. She remembers from Jordan's file that she is on the track team but she can't remember the times the girl has clocked at her meets; and Jason is strong but heavy, he might have the speed but not the stamina. Even if the two were able to make it to the wall they would have to find a way around it, which might take another mile or two of running, and then they would have to find a house with a sympathetic soul inside. This is more difficult to find than one might expect, Omalis knows. Still, she would prefer to catch them before they make it into the suburb; less of a game of hide-and-seek that way, and she is on a schedule, after all.

Sure enough, about nine minutes and a mile and a half later Omalis sees the lumbering shadowed figure of Jason, hunched over but still moving. She calls out his name and he stops, turning around to face her as she comes upon him, his face red and breath ragged.

"I tried to stop her.... I was trying to catch her."

After catching her own breath, Omalis asks, "Where did she go?"

He points to the suburb, shakes his head. "She's too fast."

"Go back to the van and wait with Jeremy," Omalis says. "Wait with him. Running can't help you, Jason. Jeremy needs you."

Jason continues shaking his head and obediently turns south. "I know. I know."

Omalis does not overtake Jordan at the sound barrier, as she hoped she would. The sun has completely disappeared behind a cloud, the stars not yet bright enough to lead her way. She stops at the wall and looks around; the wall continues north along the highway line and curves east for maybe a mile before it slopes down a hill and Omalis can't see it anymore. After a few seconds more of straining against the dim light, Omalis thinks she sees movement along the wall a few hundred yards to the east, and she launches back into her run.

When she finds Jordan, the girl is taking running jumps into the wall, apparently trying to vault herself high enough to reach its top, a good fifteen feet above her head. Omalis stops and just watches her, certain Jordan has not heard her approach over her own grunts that accompany her desperate lunges. Omalis can't make out all of the features of the girl's face, but she is certain she is crying, certain she is shaking, certain her heart is beating wildly, her mind racing. Where does she think she can go from here? What does she think she can do to change what has already been decided?

Omalis steps closer, saying the girl's name.

Jordan is startled and whirls around. She regards Omalis only briefly before spinning around and taking off along the wall again. Omalis shouts for her to stop but it's no use, she must give chase. It takes her significantly less than a minute to catch her and she regrets that she must pull her to the ground, kneel harshly upon her legs so she'll stop flailing, pin her arms to her sides to protect herself from being hit.

"Calm down, Jordan," she says, trying to keep her own voice soft, soothing, leading, but it is hard to do over the girl's uncontrolled pleas.

"Get off me! Let me go! Please, please! Help! Get off me, I want to go home, I just want to go home!"

Omalis decides the only sensible thing she can do in this situation is let the girl scream, let her wear herself out, exhaust her rage, and then Omalis can help her up and take her back to the van. She does not want to think about what she will have to do then. For now she is only grateful that she caught Jordan and her brother, and that, barring an hour-long hysterical tantrum now, she is still on schedule.

Jordan stops screaming any intelligible words and only moans and cries, her eyes shut tight against the world, or only against Omalis, she can't be sure. Omalis feels the girl's legs and arms grow steadily limper but she still struggles. Omalis relaxes a bit, a good-faith gesture of which the girl does not take advantage. She turns her head to the side as she cries and Omalis can see small cuts on her ear and on her cheek near her eye, probably from when the window imploded.

The sky darkens, overwhelmed by night, and then lightens as the clouds drift swiftly by and stars shine through. Jordan's breaths come in gulps and Omalis can feel her heart pulsing frantically in her wrists. She wants to be able to look away, to walk away, to leave this girl alone with her pain and her grief, let her figure it out in private without some stranger prying in on it, without the enemy lording it over her.

Eventually, Jordan speaks, an echo of her brother's earlier mutterings. "Why?"

"Jordan," Omalis starts, but she does not know what to say that won't potentially set her off again. The truth is, there are no words of comfort now, not here, not at this point.

"Why did you choose this?" Jordan stares up into Omalis's face, into her eyes.

Omalis looks away, at the ground beside her head.

"It doesn't matter," she says, trying not to sigh. "You wouldn't believe me anyway."

Omalis releases Jordan's arms and moves her own knees to the ground, so that she sits astride Jordan's legs.

Jordan props herself up onto her elbows. "Please just tell me."

Omalis allows her eyes to wander back to the girl's, which shine so bright and wet in the star's light, and something tugs at her chest, at her own dry eyes. She licks her lips and tries to keep her voice steady. "Because—"

"All right!"

A sharp beam of light punctuates the shout, a gruff greeting from an unseen man. Omalis raises her hand above her eyes to ward off the light and stands up. The man points the beam at the ground beside Jordan, exposing her left side and Omalis's legs in its castoff light. He remains in shadow, but he calls, "I'm an officer of the law, what's going on here?"

Omalis bends down and grabs Jordan lightly by the elbow, lifting her to her feet. "What's your name, Officer?"

He is close enough now that she can see his face, dull and mustachioed, and his blue and black khaki uniform, the thumb of his right hand crooked into his utility belt, the other hand gripping the flashlight.

"Hold on here, Miss," he says. "I'll ask the questions, right. I found a busted up auto couple miles back, and a couple'a scared kids wouldn't open their mouths to save their lives, wouldn't even get into my cruiser. You know anything about that, Miss?"

As he talks, the officer shines his light over Omalis's body and face. Omalis knows he can see the cuts on Jordan's face, the dirt and grass stains on her shirt and pants. She says, "Officer, I'll be happy to show you my credentials."

She steps forward and he moves his hand from his belt to the holster of his gun so fast he could've sprained his thumb. She reaches into the back pocket of her slacks slowly, so he'll see she is not trying to make any sudden moves, and hands him her ID. His flashlight scorches it and his eyes widen as he reads. He hands the ID back to her with a trembling hand and a catch in his voice.

"Right, Miss Omalis. Terribly sorry for the misunderstanding. I'm Officer Bradley. Can I offer you any assistance tonight?"

She can tell it is hard for him to say this last, but it is part of his job and, unfortunately, it is now part of hers to drag him into this. "I'll need your cruiser, Officer Bradley."

"Sure thing. I can drive you wherever you need to go."

"No." She clarifies, "I will take your vehicle and you'll stay here. You can radio for someone to pick you up. Understood?"

He nods his head, then hands her his flashlight and keys without her having to ask. "It's parked just up by the highway there."

Omalis thanks him and leads Jordan by the elbow through the tall grass, lighting their way with the pale light. When they reach the cruiser, Omalis holds open the passenger door for Jordan but she stops.

"You weren't lying, were you?" Jordan asks, small and sad, not looking at anything. "Nothing can stop this."

Again, Omalis finds herself wanting to say something comforting but the words fail her. She presses her hand lightly against the small of Jordan's back, damp from her sweat and the moist ground, and says the thing she always says. "I'm sorry."

Jordan looks at her. "I believe you," she says, and climbs into the cruiser.

✦

THAT NIGHT, THE CLUB IS emptier than usual, only a handful of regulars up front, drunkenly proffering their lowest bills, and a three-pack of obvious first timers hiding out in a shadowed corner booth, the whites of their eyes glittering even in the dim red light. Omalis sits at the bar in the back, not really wanting to sit or to stand, or to be here, waiting, the sweat from her untouched virgin Coke moistening her fingertips. She knows where she wants to be, and she knows this is the only way to get there. To get to her.

An older gentleman sits down two seats over from Omalis at the otherwise empty bar. He taps the rim of his Stetson with his index finger and nods at Omalis. His neatly trimmed brown mustache twitches when he winks. "Don't see many ladies in this place," he says, then produces a wheezing chuckle. "I mean, you know, aside from the fine entertainment."

Even though she doesn't look at him or respond he continues to talk to her, lighting up a fat cigar that smells like hot breath and stale sweat. She looks at him as he smokes, watching his yellowed teeth click together as he talks about this business trip that's kept him on the road for over a week, driving cross-country with only a battered old CB radio for company. That, and places like this.

"And now," he says, dropping his head so that his eyes peer out from beneath the Stetson's rim. "Maybe I got you, too."

Omalis downs her drink in one quick swallow, ice cubes kissing her lips before she drops the glass back onto the bar. The bartender, a middle-aged bodybuilder whose drinks all end up tasting the same if he has to mix more than two ingredients but whose neck is thicker than Omalis's waist, appears in front of Omalis, taking her empty glass.

"Get you anything else, Heaven?" he asks her.

"Get her another," says the cowboy before she can open her mouth. "It's on me."

"Well, now," says a voice from over Omalis's shoulder, a voice that makes her toes curl and all the hairs on her arms stand up. She catches the scent of her before she turns to look, a cinnamon and honey medley that captures the rest of her, causing her exposed skin to breakout in anticipatory gooseflesh. Pavlov's bell, she thinks, and if it weren't so unbecoming, she'd allow herself to salivate. Instead, she turns.

"I do believe I'm the only one allowed to buy my girl a drink in this bar," Marla finishes, directly beside Omalis now. One long thin arm reaches out and rests a soft hand on her shoulder, raising Omalis's body temperature and making her wish there was not this layer of fabric between her shoulder and Marla's fingers. Marla is wearing a barely-there crimson bikini and six-inch platform heels, her uniform. Some nights she wears a tiny plaid half-skirt and a black bikini top. She wants to put together another outfit but hasn't decided on anything yet, and Omalis refuses to help. Out of indifference or ambivalence, she's unsure.

The faux-diamond stud in Marla's bellybutton twinkles under the red lights of the club. Omalis stares at it, at the soft yet disciplined flesh surrounding it, wanting to run her hand along the curve that flows from Marla's abdomen down to her hips. But the Stetson man is still talking.

"My, my," he says, whistling through his teeth, the air causing his mustache to bristle. "But ain't you something, a real peach." His eyes slither up and down her body. "A real fine Georgia black peach."

"Mike," Marla calls to the bartender, "get this guy out of here."

Before Mike can move, the cowboy's cigar is down and his hands are in the air. He leans away from Marla and Omalis, his eyes wide and innocent, but also plotting. "Wait a minute now here," he says, "hang on. I know what you fine ladies have going on here, I see it. Oh yes. I have money, if that's what you're worried about, cold hard cash, a lot more than anyone else'd wave at you for a measly little dance."

He reaches into the back pocket of his Levi's and pulls out his wallet, fat with the bills he counts out onto the counter, slamming the fifty and hundred dollar bills with his palm. He looks back up, directing his arched brow to both of them, the corner of his mustache quivering. "What d'ya say?"

Any other girl in the club might blink, might pause and take a moment to review the offer. Any other girl might think about the other mouths she has to feed, the rent that needs to be paid, the lines to be snorted, the bus ticket that could be upgraded to a seat on the next Red Eye. Any other girl might say, "Just a second, let me talk this over with my partner." But Marla—Marla, the name burning just beneath Omalis's skin— Marla, without pausing for so much as a breath, says, "I'm sorry, cowboy, but no amount of paper could ever give me what I need. That's her job."

And she takes Omalis by the hand and leads her around the bar before the Stetson man can retort. They weave their way around the empty tables and chairs, to the side of the stage where the music is louder, some instrumental bumps and bops that are meant to be felt, not heard, through the backstage door that leads to the dressing room. All manner of skimpy clothing lies about, lacy bras and sequined panties, miniskirts and silver stilettos. Heaped in front of a row of vanity mirrors are mountains of makeup, glitter, and hairspray. Marla leads Omalis past all this to an uncluttered corner of the room, where a hard straight-backed chair awaits her. Marla sits her down and leans over and kisses her.

"What the fuck is a Georgia black peach?" Marla asks through a quick giggle, pulling back only an inch or two, enough for Omalis to still feel her breath on her lips.

She buries her fingers in Marla's dark hair, gently looping the small curls around her knuckles, and pulls her mouth back to hers without answering.

Again, Marla breaks away before Omalis is ready to let her go. "Stop," Omalis pouts. "I missed you."

"You always miss me," Marla says, teasing, and she sits side-saddle on Omalis's lap. Omalis runs her fingertips along Marla's naked thigh, an electric thrill passing between their flesh, shocking the minute hairs along Marla's leg, making them stand.

"Did everything go okay today?" Marla asks.

Omalis drops her head back, exhausted. "I'd rather not discuss it."

Marla emits a half-groan half-laugh that weaves a pleasant burn through Omalis's skin. "You never want to talk about it," Marla says.

And then Marla doesn't say anything for several long, straining seconds, as Omalis's lips and tongue find her neck and that space just below her right ear that always gets her into trouble.

But, of course, Marla is all business. She pushes Omalis gently away. Her hands ignite the sensitive skin across Omalis's chest where the seatbelt had grabbed her. "Tell me about the drop."

"Please," Omalis says, "I want you."

"And I know you," Marla says. Her eyes are deep and amber, and they make Omalis blush, especially when she fights hard not to. "Something happened. Whenever you're like this it means something went wrong. Tell me, babe."

"It's fine," Omalis says. "It all worked out. If it didn't, I wouldn't be here, would I?"

Marla stands up, looking down at Omalis with those deep eyes. Omalis looks back up and into them, and she wants them not to appear so tender; she wants them to grow hard, hard and sharp and judging, but they never do.

"Heaven," Marla says, and Omalis sits straighter at the sound of her name, the tone of voice behind it. When Marla begins to count, "One...two...three..." for a brief, curious moment, Omalis thinks about her mother, sweeping an olive-stemmed toothpick along the salted rim of her glass, leaning over Omalis in her childhood bed, her bitter odorous breath engulfing Omalis as she bends down for a kiss, whispering, as a sort of goodnight, "I may not believe in your namesake, child, but at least I can believe in you." When Marla reaches seven, Omalis hears the numbers ticked off with a sing-song lilt, like the nursery rhyme, and then she hears nothing at all.

✦

WHEN OMALIS WAKES UP THE sun is back out, tanning the backs of the birds who got the first worm and are now singing their good fortune. Marla's cotton sheets are damp beneath Omalis's skin and she feels hot, but nice. She opens her eyes to see a blurred outline of her girl drawing open the shades and pulling up the window, letting the cool morning breeze float in and greet her. Omalis's nipples grow hard. She frowns at Marla, turns onto her stomach and curls up and closes her eyes again.

"Heaven," Marla says, and her lips begin to kiss Omalis awake, starting at her shoulder and moving down the length of her back.

"Get back in," Omalis says, her voice muffled by speaking into the down pillow.

Marla obeys, wrapping herself around Omalis, synching their curves, settling heavy and content.

Their breath is all that fills the room for long minutes. And then Marla whispers, "I love you, baby."

Omalis pretends to be asleep.

# F I V E
## J U N E

WHEN THEY WERE YOUNGER, I never hit my children. I grew up with an iron fist always waiting for me on the right side of wrong and it was something I vowed at the age of twelve never to let myself do to my own future offspring. I can't lie and say it was easy, say there weren't days, small moments within days, when I wanted to do it. To raise my hand, just once, snap their father's belt, just once, and make them listen to me. Stop running through the house with muddy feet, stop pulling each other's hair, stop screaming, stop breaking the lamps, the flowerpots. Once, I discovered a clutch of chicks in Jeremy's room where he had made a nest for them on a pile of his good church clothes, and brought hay up for them to lie in. We had to have the whole house fumigated for fleas and other mites, and the stains never did wash out of his trousers and polo shirts. But I kept my hands in my pockets when I confronted Jeremy, all of ten at the time, scrawny as ever, and lonely, I knew. Even though I wanted to take him by his bony shoulders and shake some sense into him, I saw in his eyes that all he wanted was a friend, something to care for, something to talk to. So, instead, I put him in Time-Out.

That's where I feel I am now, in Time-Out, except it's more like Death Row Time-Out, for the hardcore offenders, the ones who can't be rehabilitated, population: me. In our house, we set a chair in the corner of the dining room, facing the wall, and sat the kids down and set a timer that they could hear sluggishly ticking away behind their backs, for fifteen minutes or twenty, depending on their crime. Often they would shout, throw a tantrum, especially Jordan, until she realized the time didn't count until her butt was in the seat. Then she took to sitting silently, slumped, like she had the weight of the world on her shoulders, thumping the heels of her feet against the chair's hard wooden legs until they bruised. That made me feel awful, like I'd caused her that pain, like I'd failed her anyway. But—stop this; it's all I do now, think about the ways I failed my children. There are so many.

Here, my Time-Out is self-imposed, in the semi-private bathroom of the nurse's locker room. No one's here, I made them leave, not with anything I said but with the look in my eyes, the uncontrolled tangle of my hair, the blood on my pale, bare hands. They rushed out, a few of them half-dressed, to catch up on the gossip, to see what I'd done. One or two have come back since to check in, to try to talk to me. I've locked the door to the shower stall and switched on the hot water to drown them out, drown myself out. Now, I'm just sitting here, still in the surgical scrubs I never changed out of, still with the blood caked under my fingernails and growing redder with the hot water that burns into my scalp and skin. I'm just sitting here, counting to sixty, fifteen times.

✛

IT's ONLY BEEN A WEEK. That's the reality, slow and agonizing, but it's also my husband's argument, obnoxious and pitying.

"It's only been a week, June. You need more time."

He's standing by the sink, letting the water run to fill it up so he can wash the dishes I've been ignoring since last Friday. He doesn't look at me when he talks, choosing instead to stare out the small window, partially fogged from the water's steam, at a pair of squirrels jostling for a perch on the plastic bird feeder his mother got us for Christmas last year. Done up in an already grease-stained white t-shirt and ripped blue jeans, he'd wanted to spend the day working on the tractor and its various attachments. Instead, he's snapping on a pair of yellow rubber gloves and having this conversation with me. Again.

"What am I supposed to do around here, Jay?" I ask him. He shakes his head and takes the ratty sponge, which I've been meaning to replace, to a glob of barbeque sauce that's beginning to sprout its own ecosystem on the bottom of our cast-iron skillet. He scrubs in such a way that answers me, *This, June. You're supposed to be doing this.*

I change my counter-argument to one I've used before, one that's still not been, for me, satisfyingly disputed. "*You've* gone back to work. Same as always. That's what you want from me, isn't it? To go about things, same as always?"

I'm wearing one of the bathrobes Jason cast off once he discovered he had muscles and learned that cotton doesn't show them off quite as nicely as a simple pair of boxer shorts and a white tank. It still smelled of him four days ago when I put it on; now it only smells of me and the showers I've managed not to take in just as long. At the sink, Jay sighs so long and forceful I swear I feel it over here, at the table, feel it ruffling the sleeves of the robe, wafting my own sour scent up to my nose. Well, I think, if he'd let me go back to work, maybe I'd shower.

I'm about to toss this nugget of compelling information into the debate when he says, "June, *of course* we can't just go on pretending everything's the same. When did I ever say I wanted that? I go on working because I have to; do you want the crops to turn? Or the cattle to run dry? I *have* to work. You, honey, you just don't *need* to; you don't need to go back to that place, not yet."

He's meticulously rubbing the sponge between prongs on all the forks he can rustle up from the soapy water as he says this. I watch him place them into the drainer without rinsing them and I don't say anything for maybe a minute. There's a mug of cold coffee, gone an unearthly beige from six packs of powdered cream, sitting beside my plate of uneaten scrambled eggs and buttered toast. I reach for it and sip it, tepid and sweet, thinking over what Jay's just said, and what he hasn't said, the thing he's most concerned about that he just won't say, because, to him, it probably goes against our marriage vows to even think it, that I'd be so stupid, so careless.

Mostly, though, I'm rethinking the thing that *I* hadn't said, hadn't got the chance to say and am glad for it. *If you'd let me go back to work.* Let me. It occurs to me, now, that I've been listening to Jay this past week not because his is the sagest of advice—"Take some time, stay off your feet, let this sink in, don't rush into anything, rest," as if I were only sick with the flu, *And drink plenty of fluids!*—but because he is the only one dispensing it. What might the ladies at the hospital have to say? My coworkers and friends who surely must have guessed by now the reason for my absence? Their opinion as to how much time off is necessary in this situation might just differ from that of my well-meaning but oversensitive husband. And who am I, a medical professional, not to take my own oft-given advice and seek a second opinion?

Slowly, I get to my feet, and carry the plate of uneaten food and mug of liquid creamer over to the sink. I scrape the food into the trash bin without a word and reach over Jay's arm to drop the plate in the water. My exposed wrist glances against his forearm, clammy with sweat and dishwater, and, for some reason, I blush. I set the mug of wasted coffee by the drainer, and walk away, more anxious now.

From behind me, Jay calls, "Where are you going?"

I don't stop walking. "To take a shower," I say.

✦

In the space between the stall door and the tiled floor, my husband's face appears. I can't tell how much of myself he is able to see from his crooked angle, but I can see the creases in his brow, the heavy bags under his eyes, the gray in his fine brown hair.

"Honey, open the door," he says, low, like he's only talking to me. As if a handful of nurses and doctors and orderlies and maybe even the janitor aren't standing behind him, eager to find out what happens next.

Margie probably called him; she was the first one to see me, after. Or Doctor Hanson, he was the one who tried to stop me. They are both friends, in the coworker sense, or at least were; who knows, now. I don't know anything, except that I'm not opening this door, not until this blood comes out.

"Honey," Jay says again, pleading. He's got his arm shoved under the stall door, replacing his face, bent and reaching for the handle that is just out of reach. If he wanted to, he could straighten out that arm and just touch my ankle with the tips of his fingers. And, at this moment, that's what I want him to do, that's all I want him to do, just reach out and touch my ankle, the very feather of a touch, nothing more. But he doesn't. His arm snakes back out through the space and there's his face again.

"Look, it's okay," he says, pleading again. "What—what is this gonna do, huh? Hiding in here? Just come out, okay Junebug, just come out. Let me…let me hold you, you'll see. It'll be okay, it's okay."

It is almost the same spiel he gave Jason when he was five and got the chicken pox, except instead of "let me hold you" it was "let me put the calamine lotion on you, you'll see, it'll be okay."

I ignore him and go back to my nails, thinking he is right. A little earlier, I'd pried up a piece of cracking tile near the drain and started picking at the drying blood underneath my thumbnail. I'm on my ring finger now, of my left hand, and the blood is running again but I'm pretty sure it's only mine. The hot water has cooled to warm by now, and I've started to shiver in my soaked clothes from the draft shooting in from underneath the stall door.

For a second, I allow myself to think, What am I doing? But this thought has come at least an hour too late and there's no point entertaining it now. And then, inexplicably but not entirely unexpectedly, I think about my babies. I wonder, for the millionth time, what they must be doing right now, what they must have been doing this past unbearably long week. This, of course, can't go on; I can't let it, especially when details try to push their way in: the brittle texture of the thin mattresses I imagine them lying on, the stifling heat of the rooms they must be crammed into, the overwhelming stench of the gruel they are forced to eat each morning. All in my imagination, thank goodness, and hopefully, certainly, *only* in my imagination. Because things can't be as bad as the frightful scenarios that play out behind my closed eyelids, things can't be that real. But, of course, I can never know how it is for them, can't even guess, as it has never happened to me.

But Jay went to the summer camps, more than two decades ago, early in their implementation, when no one quite knew exactly what to expect (or knew, but made themselves believe otherwise). And that is why, when he says everything will be okay, when he tells me in the darkness, as we lie chaste beside each other in our sterile pajamas, not to worry about our children, that they will make it through, that they aren't in any pain or harm right now, that we can see them soon and see for ourselves that they are fine so close your eyes and go to sleep and just stop worrying your pretty little head—that is why I don't believe him, and why I get so angry, at his lies, his denial. You can be married to someone for eighteen years, share a bed, their highs and lows, bear their children, bury their loved ones, and never fully know all of their secrets. But you can know that they have them, deep and rooted, hidden even from themselves. You can know their scars, the ones they won't talk about, the ones that may not be physical but that show all the same—in a look; in the way he tosses in his sleep; how close he holds you when you make love; how long it takes him to take the training wheels off your son's bike; in the stretching silences; the long hours he spends under the sun, working the fields. And you can know—deep down, rooted, hidden—just how far from okay everything truly is.

✢

WHEN I GET TO THE hospital, no one asks where I've been. Granted, I only pass a handful of nurses on my way to my office, one floor above the delivery rooms—the Hole, we call it, on a bad day—and they only know me peripherally, probably wouldn't recognize me without my surgical mask on, asking for suction. In my office there is one small window, one small square catching what little light peeks around the corner of the bank's corporate headquarters next door and tossing it across my desk, onto the letterhead, the appointment book, the framed family photos. It's not enough to illuminate the entire office, which is no bigger than a moderate walk-in closet, really, but it's cozy, comfortable, warm…like a womb.

When I walk in, I go immediately to the desk and flip the photographs onto their faces; I do the same to the ones on the walls, turning them to face the off-white drywall. Then I sit at my desk for a minute or two, trying to decide if I should close the window's curtains, as I've developed a sharp behind-the-eyes headache that might have something to do with the late-morning sunlight bathing my direct line of sight. I pinch the bridge of my nose and close my eyes. From the hallway I hear the soft, seasoned footsteps of nurses shuffling to and from one of the supply closets down the hall, their pleasant laughter, their quiet mumbled conversations. I think, It's just another day for them. I think, Jay was right; what am I doing here?

To keep myself from thinking, I open my appointment book and double-check my roster. Someone has blacked out my appointments for the week, assuming my leave of absence would extend into next. It was probably Doctor Hanson, head resident. So, no appointments, no scheduled deliveries. I twiddle my thumbs, I pick at my cuticles. A cloud moves across the sun, shadows move across my desk. I think of my children again, of saying goodbye to them, or, rather, doing everything I could not to say goodbye. I think of Jeremy, how hard it was to get my arms to leave him, to watch him climb into that van after his brother. Jason, so stoic, so much like his father, trying to lead by example, trying to be the rock for the others—and how I was too afraid, even, to touch him one last time, to let him know how much I care about him, too afraid he'd only sigh, or, scarier, tell me he cared, too.

And then, in the fading shadow crawling across my letter opener, I see Jordan's face, hard and vulnerable at the same time, looking at me with eyes that aren't quite experienced enough yet to completely hide her heart. I see her, again, at the van, and I see myself, reaching out to her, wanting, as with Jason, to make something of this moment, not to let her go without knowing, unequivocally, how much I care. But stopping short, failing again, and Jordan's mouth opening, and that venomous wit, that aching sarcasm, her final words to me, "I pierced my navel." And how much, once they had driven off, once the dust had settled behind them, I laughed, so full and loud, and Jay walked away from me, slamming the front door, and I knew I should have stopped and followed him in, but I laughed and laughed and didn't stop until the sun went down.

Light replaces the shadow. An airplane roars overhead. I cover my mouth, afraid I'll begin to laugh again. When the phone rings I jump and let out an involuntary yelp.

"Doctor Fontaine," I answer.

"Oh!" comes a surprised voice through the handset. "I didn't know you were back. I was only going to leave you a voicemail."

"Who is this?" The voice is female and deep, rusty, like it hasn't been used for anything other than to request another pack of cigarettes at the liquor store.

"I'm sorry," she says, "this is Penny Baker, I'm the new RN. How are you this morning? Oh, I suppose it's getting on to afternoon now."

The pain behind my eyes throbs anew. "Can I help you with something?"

"Oh, I was only calling to leave a voicemail. I heard you were on temporary leave. Well anyway, I was just going to leave you a message that your client, Miss Reynolds? She delivered early so you can cross her delivery date out of your books."

Quickly, I flip through my calendar. Reynolds isn't due until late July. "Jenny," I say, "She's five weeks early. What happened? Were there complications? Why didn't anyone call me?"

"It's Penny," she says, then there's a pause. I can hear muffled static and faint voices, like she's placed her hand over the phone and is consulting with someone else, trying to figure out how much to tell me. But I'm not new to this business, as she surely must know; I can guess what has happened, and I know what will happen next. The throbbing in my head moves down to my chest.

Finally, Nurse Penny gets back on the line. "There were complications, yes." Another short pause, an intake of breath. "She's recovering well, though."

"Penny," I say, struggling with the volume of my voice. "What. Happened."

"I'm sorry, Doctor Fontaine," she says in a rush. "Doctor Hanson alerted me to your own personal situation, and he feels that Miss Reynolds's situation might be slightly—" Then there's a rustling, more muffled voices. I'm standing now, pacing as far as the phone's cord will let me, ready to drop the handset and all this bullshit and go down to the nurses station and cause a scene until someone tells me what happened to my patient's babies.

Then Doctor Hanson's voice is in my ear. "Fontaine," he says. Then, softer, "June. I thought you'd be taking more time off. You are allowed, you know. You're not the only one who can handle umbilical cords and afterbirth around here."

His forced laugh makes me furious. "Tell me about my patient," I demand. "How many made it? How many, Dan?"

His pause isn't long, but it's revealing. "One," he says, and I feel as though the pain in my chest has throbbed its way out, broken my ribs as it went, dragging my heart along the shards behind it. "Two were stillborn. One's in NICU, but it doesn't look good."

Now it's my turn to pause, to struggle for breath, for something solid to hold onto. Hanson waits patiently; I can hear him swallowing, and I imagine him preparing what he'll say next, what words of comfort he'll try on this time, which soothing platitudes to conjure up for this occasion.

Before he can speak again, I ask, "Has the Liaison gone in yet?"

"June—"

"I want to be the one, Dan. I want to be the one to tell her. She's my patient. It should come from me."

I'm sure he only hesitates for the benefit of the nurses listening in on his side of the conversation, because I know him and I know he'd make the same request. "All right, Doctor. She's in 412."

✦

THERE'S A NOISE, PENETRATING, SHRILL. I look and see at least four different pairs of shoes underneath the door, moving around, dancing. But they're not in step with the music, jaggedly pulsing through the air, vibrating the tiles, making the little pools of water by my knees ripple and slosh. Then, a large metal screw clangs to the floor and rolls toward the drain. The door creaks on its one remaining hinge. Oh.

✦

KEVIN DANIELS WAITS OUTSIDE OF Miss Reynolds's room. Hands behind his back, dressed in a casual-Friday navy shirt, unbuttoned at the collar, unwrinkled Dockers hemmed perfectly at the ankles of his Doc Martens. He catches my eye and raises his eyebrows at me.

"Doctor," he says, nodding. "They asked me to wait for you."

"Stay here," I say, walking by him. My hand is on the door handle when he says, "Pardon?"

"You're staying here," I tell him, meeting his eyes. "I'm handling this alone."

"I'm afraid that's against protocol," he says.

My fingers clench around the door handle as my headache surges. "Fine. But you do not speak, do you understand me? Not one word. Not even a hello."

He nods again, with a gracious smirk, letting me know his cooperation is a courtesy, a favor. I turn from him and push open the door.

Magdalene Reynolds is thirty-four, a self-employed architect whose small mostly-family firm specializes in designing and constructing miniature golf courses and other small-scale family amusements. She's widowed, with no children from her marriage, as her late husband had had a vasectomy. She herself had undergone tubal ligation after he died, for reasons she never shared with me, but two years ago she realized it wasn't another man in her life she needed to complete her, it was her own children, and so she had the surgery reversed. When she first came to me, it was to consult on in vitro fertilization and to get a prescription for the fertility drug. Her pregnancy seemed stable throughout our consultations, and she glowed with it, with the health of her unborn children, with the promise of their future in her life.

She's still radiant now, lying with her head turned so all I see when I enter the room is her profile, her flushed right cheek, still glistening a little, her thin pale lips curved in a gentle smile. I knock politely on the open door. A wisp of dark hair falls over her forehead as she turns to me, and her smile widens.

"Doctor Fontaine," she beams. "They told me you were out sick. I'm so glad you're here."

She holds her hand out to me, inviting me further into the room, but she drops it as if it has become too heavy for her to hold up. "Oh," she whispers to no one, and I see where her eyes have gone, beyond me, to Daniels.

At first I find I am unable to speak. A thousand words play through my brain but I am unable to latch on to a single one of them. I stand and lick my lips and try to catch her eyes again but they seem glued to Daniels. Who, at this moment, begins to clear his throat.

"Magdalene," I say, her name leaping out of me, landing on distracted ears; I don't even know if she's hearing me, or if she's already listening ahead to what she knows is coming. Where do I even start? How can I say this?

"Maggie." I step forward, close enough to take her hand but it seems inappropriate. "I'm…I'm sorry. Your child—"

"My daughter," she cuts in, finally looking at me. Our eyes lock and the uninhibited pain in hers is the only thing that keeps me from looking away.

"Your daughter." I swallow. "We…she…The process has to begin immediately. I'm so sorry."

Tears come, and her face seems to fold in on itself, her body seems to shrink into the bed, and she turns her head to stare at the blood-pressure gauge on the wall.

I consider touching her, giving her shaking shoulder a comforting squeeze, but then I think, were I her, the last person I would want touching me was the person who just told me I'd lost everything.

From behind me, Daniels clears his throat again. When I look at him, I imagine I must be glaring because all I can see is darkness outlining his blurred red body, a beating black thing in the center of it. He takes no notice. My eyes focus enough to see him mouth the words, "Shall we?"

✛

I THINK, NOW, NOW THAT I can think, I think I decided to do it on the way down to the nursery. I let him walk ahead of me this time, so I could watch him, the ease of his step, almost jaunty, his ponytail swaying as if caught in an updraft in a lazy meadow somewhere, his hands clasped behind his back, just so. He should be whistling, I remember thinking, or humming.

When we reach the nursery, he goes in ahead of me, straight to Reynolds's daughter. I can smell them, all of them, these new lives, fresh as talcum powder, as barely ripened fruit. And Daniels leans over the daughter, picks her up and tickles her with an index finger to her chin.

"Fairly strapping," he says. "Remarkably healthy after coming out of all that." He means her traumatic birth, in which two of her siblings died, the third waiting his or her turn upstairs in the Neonatal Intensive Care Unit. "I'll say Seed for now. I'll let you know if anything changes."

He's bouncing her up and down in his arms now, which her little face scrunches up to enjoy, thinking he is playing, but I know he is only weighing her, sizing up her future in his eyes. As I look at him, something happens, something changes, and I only see her, the woman who did the same to my children, if through different methods; sized them up, and took them down.

"Doctor," he says to me, looking at me as if I'd gone somewhere. "Aren't you going to mark this down?"

That's when I notice he's laid the baby back in her cradle, and that's when I act on my previous decision, trying to pretend I only just thought of it now—or, rather, that I didn't think of doing it at all, but only *did it.*

"Can you grab me the clipboard?" I point behind him.

When his back is to me, I run at him. I scream, some sort of desperate cry, some sort of warning, and then I have his ponytail in one hand and his throat in the other. I pull hard. His neck jerks back and I hear him yell and feel something ripping, ripping right off into my hand. He grabs the wrist of my right hand but the more he tugs on it, the more it tugs on his ponytail. I bite his ear, trying for a chunk but ending up with only a nip. I dig nails into his throat, so deep, trying to gouge, to stab, and scrape them along, hoping for a vein.

Then I'm flying over him and hitting the floor, blacking out for only a second, coming to on my back, looking up at him, hearing footsteps running, and another man's voice calling my name, asking what I've done, what do I think I am doing. And Daniels's head, leaning over me, looming over, one hand on his neck, the blood standing out in tiny magnificent droplets.

"You shouldn't have done that," he says. I wish he'd said it like a threat, I wish it made me angrier, ready for round two. But he says it sad, pitying, and it frightens me. It frightens me into getting up, into pushing Doctor Hanson aside, into running through the hall until I find the locker room, the shower stall, the silence of the rushing water, the company of my own shallow cuts, the comfort of my blood washing away the memory of his.

✦

"June? Junebug. Drink this, okay? Just a little sip, please? You'll feel better."

The cup is warm in my hands, hotter against my lips and tongue. I swallow it, knowing before I do it that he's put a sedative in it, something to make me drowsy, something to make me sleep while he, my stalwart husband, figures out a way to take my incoming bullet.

I'm back in my office. After they used a drill to take off the shower door's hinges, Jay picked me up and carried me here; I was too busy crying to protest. Someone had given him towels to give to me. They line my chair now, to keep me from soiling the leather. One is wrapped, turban-like, around my hair. The hot chocolate comes from the machine in the waiting room; the sedative probably came from Doctor Hanson.

Jay kneels in front of me, one arm draped across my knees, the other absentmindedly scratching at a spot on his thigh. He's still dressed the way he was this morning, his jeans and shirt bearing the grass and sweat stains of his recent labors. I take another long drink of the hot chocolate. I notice my headache is gone.

"What are you thinking?" I ask him, my voice already sounding thick, strange.

He shakes his head. "I don't know what I'm thinking."

He rakes his hand down his face and I see the sweat still beading along his hairline, down the side of his cheek.

"I'm sorry," I say, because I can't think of anything else.

"Don't," he says, squeezing my knee in his big, calloused hand. "I didn't want this to happen. I…it's my fault. I should have…I should have looked after you closer, made sure… You never should have been here."

An old anger flashes through me, but is quelled by whatever drug swims fast through my blood stream. "You're right."

"I don't want to be right," he says, the anger coming to him too, turning his ears red, and straightening his back. "Goddammit, June, I don't want to be right. This…I can't take this. I *couldn't* take this. If…" He looks at me, his face becoming a blur, but I can still read him, like I've always been able to, no matter what face he tries to put on for my benefit. "If I lose you…I won't be able to keep on. I just won't."

I set the cup down on my desk and take his hand in both of mine. I can't think of anything to say, and I'm quickly losing the energy for that anyway, so I just hold his hand, and he holds mine back. We just look at each other, every bit of each other, until my eyes start to close.

A shrill ring makes me jump, makes Jay pull his hand away from mine. He answers the phone, and looks at me, and asks the caller, "Why?" After a few seconds he frowns and hands me the receiver.

"I can't," I start to say, but he stops me, saying, "It's Omalis."

I don't even have the energy to hate the sound of her name, or the obnoxiously elegant lilt of her voice, her pretentiously crisp consonants, her languid vowels.

"Mrs. Fontaine," she starts. "I've heard some rather disturbing news. Are you all right?"

It's really the last thing I'd expected her to ask, let alone start off with. I choose not to say anything, preferring instead to sway unsteadily and blink rapidly against the exhaustion that's consuming me.

"Listen to me," she says. "Your behavior today is unacceptable. There are strong consequences for lashing out at a Liaison. You know this."

"I know," I say, so tired, so ready. "Just let me say goodbye."

"Mrs. Fontaine—"

"No," I say, "No, wait, I don't want them to know. Don't tell them. I'll…I'll write them a letter… Jay will…Jay will give it to them… Only, give me enough time to…."

"June," I hear my husband's voice, but I've closed my eyes and he sounds far away. "What is she saying? What is she telling you?"

"Mrs. Fontaine," she says again. "That won't be necessary. I've spoken with Mr. Daniels. He's agreed to report this incident as an accident. There'll be no need for goodbyes."

I open my eyes halfway at her words, at the meaning that begins to sink into my ever-hazy mind. I look at Jay and want to tell him what she's said, but can only manage a smile.

"What is it? June? Give me the phone."

But Omalis is speaking again. "You have to remember that this sort of leniency is not to be expected again. You have to remember that, Mrs. Fontaine. Now more than ever you have to be careful. If not for yourself, then for your children."

At the mention of my children the anger flares up and, with it, the words I've wanted to say since hearing her voice again. "Miss Omalis," I say, slowly, so as not to slur. "When I was hurting him, I was thinking only about you."

I let the receiver fall from my hand, hear it clatter to the floor and listen to Jay scramble to pick it up and ask Omalis to repeat what she'd said to me. And then my eyes grow heavy, my head grows heavy, the world grows heavy, and then, thankfully, it all goes away.

Mostly, it's like group therapy. I figure I have a leg up on how to deal over most of these other girls, who still sit in the circle on their cold metal folding chairs, backs straight and legs crossed, ears at attention and eyes front and center. They still don't realize their number's been up so long it's seared into the claws of the Over, which are dug so deep into our backs we won't see 'em until they're ripped out of us, only to be replaced by another set, or something worse. At least, that's how I hear the things do it, with their claws, more like talons, like a vulture's. I've heard more stories about them here in one week than during countless playground hours. I believe every horror story, no matter how contradictory, because the alternative is denial, and that's just fucking sad. Anyway, they don't make me sit in on the group sessions anymore, and I guess that's why Omalis is back here now.

It's day seven, I know because I've been scratching the days into a floorboard under my bed, right beside the days marked down by every other girl who's lain awake on this cot before me. We wake up early because there's a bell tower somewhere nearby that I've never seen that sounds more like a gong and it bangs and bangs and bangs until every last one of us is up and standing around the flagpole in the recreation yard, hands on hearts, belting out "God Bless America." Well, in all fairness, it's not a requirement, it's just something I do, get the blood pumping for that star-spangled banner that streams ever so gallantly. There're no flags on the flagpole, but when I try real hard, by golly, I can see it, and feel it, feel it right there in my heart. I made one of the girls cry the first time I did it, and she joined in. She says it right along with me each morning, only she probably really does feel it, and she probably talks about that in group, thinking anyone who matters now will relay this information to her executioners and they'll throw her a pity party instead of a wake. I don't know her name; we're all numbers here. She's Five. I'm Jordan.

I think that was the scariest day, the first one, when our plane landed and my stomach dropped because I thought one of the Over would be there to escort us through our final days, but that was just nerves. Our hosts, of course, were just like us, only older and with dry eyes and faker smiles. When Omalis dropped us at the hangar where a tin-can of a jet awaited us on the tarmac, the flight attendant took our bags and stowed them somewhere I think was probably a garbage can because we did not get them back when we landed. And yes, there was a fucking flight attendant, and she was a brunette who wore too much lipstick and cucumber-melon body spray and tapped me on the shoulder to ask me if I preferred Coke or Pepsi and served us a micro-waved mini-pizza. Jason ogled her cleavage every time she leaned over to refill Jeremy's spring water, and I think he probably told Jeremy to pretend to be more thirsty than he was because she refilled it at least six times. There wasn't a bathroom on the plane.

I watched the sun rise over the clouds and set again and then we were landing. I tried to count the hours but I fell asleep a couple of times. Not that it mattered if I could somehow calculate our location; we were Nowhere, Earth, and if anyone made it out long enough to relay our locale, it wouldn't really matter. Who was going to come rescue us, or any future crop of kids from this place? Our parents, our government? They're the ones who put us here in the first place.

When we got off the plane, my brothers went one way and I another. There was a field of other planes, small jets like ours, all de-boarding at once, and all the girls followed the women in pink polo shirts carrying peach-scented clipboards and all the boys followed the men in blue polos carrying sports-decaled clipboards. I didn't say goodbye to my brothers and they didn't say goodbye to me. I kept my head low and snapped my bracelet against my wrist until it went numb. Then they took that away from me, too.

We got on yellow school buses, and someone's leather-skinned grandmother checked our names off on her clipboard and handed us buttons with adhesive backs to stick to our shirts: our numbers. On my bus, there were ten girls and six "counselors," for lack of a better term. They wanted us to call them "mentors," as they'd be our guides through this six-week process, our hand-holders, our open shoulders. The engines rolled over and our counselors passed back brown boxes with our numbers on them, and told us to change right there on the bus. Inside the box were two pairs of gray sweats and sweatshirts, two pairs of white socks and underthings, and one pair of white sneakers. They told us to put everything we were wearing into a canvas bag that they passed around after we changed; we'd get it back at the end of the program. The girl next to me started crying, quietly, but she also started to untie her shoes.

I opened my window and tried to shove the box through it but it was too big. I had to take the items out one by one. The leathery grandma grabbed my elbow after one sweatshirt and both socks went out. She was surprisingly strong, but I could see it in the wrinkles on her burgundy face that she didn't have much stamina.

"What do you think you're doing?" Her voice was constructed of cooking sherry and uppers, and her breath smelled like someone's grave. She shook my arm until I dropped the box.

"Gray isn't my color," I said. Someone behind me laughed. Another, younger, counselor came over.

"You need to change with the other girls," this new one said. She wore glasses and she pushed them up on her nose and sniffed in air. I expected an "or else" but only got another shake from Grandma.

"Come on, Eleven," Grandma said. "There's no need to make this difficult."

"My name is Jordan," I said, tearing up at the woman's pincher-like fingers digging into my bone.

"No," she said, "no names here. You're Eleven. We're all numbers here. You're no different than anyone else, you got that?" That was when my eyes found the button taped to the breast of her polo shirt, right next to the tiny alligator, declaring her number Fifty-Six. Then things got a little more blurry and her hand left my elbow and traveled to my knee, where it just lay there softly, gently.

"Come on, kid," she said, low, like reading me a bedtime story. "Just put on the clothes, okay?"

But these were my favorite jeans, the ones I had to fight for in the middle of a Target last August because Mom said they were too tight and I said they make me look taller and I won because I can get a lot louder than her and don't care who's watching; and this was my third favorite shirt because I cut the sleeves off two Halloweens ago when it was too big for me but now it fits just right and I wanted to go as a body builder and I needed to show off my arms, freshly decorated with press-on tattoos of butterflies on mushrooms and a woman with devil horns, but then later in November it got colder and I wanted the sleeves back which I saved because I knew this would happen and

Mom sewed them back on with only one *tsk* and a small admonition to take better care of my things, which I thought was pretty big of her; and this was the bracelet I made in art class when I didn't really want to be doing it but I took my medication that morning and didn't have the energy to argue my way into getting to sit in the corner and pretend to read while really I napped so I made the stupid thing while the really LD kids made macaroni art and I wore it when this all started, for the woman who told me she couldn't, or wouldn't, save me, and I wore it today because I could hide it under my sleeves and snap it against the big blue vein in my wrist and feel okay; and now they wanted me to give them these things, these things that made me more than a number no matter what kind of bullshit they pinned to me, and I didn't want them to have it, I wouldn't let them take it.

I glared up at them both with wet eyes, gripping my bracelet, willing my shirt and pants to stick to me. "Make me," I said.

And they did.

That was seven days ago, according to my mark on the floorboard which I make with my fingernail, which is the sharpest thing we're allowed to keep around here, and even those they make us cut and file every couple of days. I don't know how else I would keep track. We get up when the bell sounds which is probably right around first light, and we're ushered back to our cabins when the sun goes down, though no one really sticks around after that to make sure we go to sleep right away. I guess they don't have to, because of the cameras, which are everywhere, barely hidden behind their dark black spheres in the corners of our rooms, in the dining hall, the boat house; there's even one on the flagpole. The only place I haven't found one is in the bathroom of our cabin. Maybe they think they're letting us keep some of our dignity this way. Some of us are fooled by this, think it means there's hope for some reason. Some of us think the cameras are just better hidden there, to catch us trying to hatch escape plans or developing codes to include in our letters to our parents. But I know there aren't any cameras there, or they would've taken Taylor away by now.

There are ten of us in the cabin, just like on the bus except it's a different group of girls. We keep our boxes under our cots and we all have the same thin blanket and flat pillow. We all look the same, tired and scared but trying to fake it through, except our hair is different, and I'm still waiting for someone to come in with a pair of clippers and move us all on to Stage Two. My cot is right next to the bathroom, because I got to pick last, because I'm the youngest in our cabin. These things still matter, I guess; I guess the older girls feel safer if they treat this like some high school sleep-away camp.

Taylor's cot is next to mine, that's why I heard her get up that first night. I watched her shadow move into the bathroom, and saw her reflection in the mirror when she flipped on the light, before she closed the door and I got up. She has dark hair, she lets it hang down to the middle of her back and doesn't do anything with it, at least not here, which my mom would say is such a waste. What kind of impression are we making if we can't even take care of ourselves, hmmm? Her face is small, and pale, and the shadows under her cobalt-blue eyes grow deeper every day, and her cheekbones grow sharper, and she looks at me more and more like she wants to tell me her secrets but really she hasn't spoken to me at all since that night.

I went to the door and listened, I don't know why. Because I couldn't sleep, because it was either listen at the door to the sound of her showering or peeing or whatever, or lie there on my hard cot and listen to eight girls try not to cry themselves into unconsciousness. That night she was a number, number Fifteen. I put my ear to the door and I heard her sobbing, and then I heard something else, like something ripping, and then I heard her cry out, and then I opened the door.

She stood in the shower, her pants on the floor, her hand beneath her, pulling something out from between her legs. She didn't stop when I came in. She cried out again and pulled and I let the door close behind me. The thing she pulled out was in a bag, there was blood on it, but not much. She threw it on the floor, at my bare feet.

"You can use it too," she said, her voice wet, not looking at me. "If you need to."

She turned on the shower and started washing her legs. I stood there for a minute, trying, and failing, to think. I picked up the bag. It was a Zip-Loc, and inside was a cardboard carton, no bigger than a matchbox, with white block letters declaring a company logo, DO IT BEST. I opened the box. A single razor blade, the kind guys shave with, fell into my palm.

Fifteen turned the shower off and dried her legs with one of the off-white towels in the pantry, hung it over the shower rod. I watched her pull her pants back on. She held out her hand. "I'll take that back now, Eleven," she said.

But I couldn't give it back to her, not right away, because my name was Jordan and I wanted her to know that, and I wanted to remember it, and I didn't want anyone to be able to take it away from me, like they were, so goddamn easily, able to take away my clothes, my brothers, and everything else.

"My name is Jordan," I said. I put the blade to the underside of my arm and it didn't hurt as much as I thought it should. I looked at her while I did this, started to cry and tried to suck it back in, looking at her watching me, watching my arm, the cross-top of the J appearing in bright red on my skin. Then she grabbed my wrist, not the one holding the blade but the other.

"Wait," she said, "don't do it there. Pick some place no one will see."

I had to stop and examine my body, actually had to look myself over, trying to remember the parts of myself that stayed covered most often.

"Here." Fifteen rolled up the bottom of my shirt to my navel, and traced a finger beneath the hole where my piercing used to be. "Right here. Don't go too deep."

I pressed the blade to the spot she'd touched but I didn't feel it, only the lingering warmth her skin left on mine. Then I couldn't feel my own fingers, couldn't grip the blade right, scared, fuck it, too goddamn scared.

Without a word, Fifteen took the blade from me. With her right hand she pushed and pulled the blade through my skin, lightly, delicately, so it stung, but only like a scrape, like a bee sting. Her left hand gripped my right hand, mostly around the thumb, steadying herself, steadying me. I closed my eyes and listened to the blood drip onto the tiled floor.

When she was done, my face was wet and hot from trying not to breathe. But I have them now, the letters, my name, the only thing I get to take with me here. The letters are jagged and they don't connect well; it looks like a third grader wrote it, just learning his cursive alphabet. But it's there, my name, forever.

Fifteen washed the blade in the sink and gave me a towel to hold to my stomach, pressing it there herself until I stopped shaking and replaced her hands with mine. She straightened up, taller than me, looked into my eyes, and just said, "Hello." It was the last thing she said to me before she put the blade to her own stomach, lower than where she'd done mine, along the indentation of the waistband of her sweatpants, and that's how I learned her name is Taylor. That's how I know there are no cameras in that bathroom because the razor blade is still hidden under a loose tile in there, where she checks it every night to make sure, where it will stay until she needs it, or until the next girl does, if Taylor's lucky.

That's what got me into trouble with the group thing, those six letters that mean so much to me now, all I am reduced to a scar I have to hide but at least it's something, more than these other girls have. Well, really what got me kicked out of group—which, if they think that is a punishment they are as deluded as the genius who came up with high school suspensions—was their refusal to let me keep my meds. Mood stabilizers, so I don't act out, or, you know, feel too much of anything. But everything we had on us when we arrived was taken and traded for those numbered brown boxes and I tried to explain but it doesn't matter. They took 'em, I lose. I bet they pass 'em around at night, in their camp counselor suite, to take the edge off the coming day. If there's any left by now, which I bet there aren't. Anyway.

We didn't start with these group meetings until Day Three. Before that we didn't do much of anything, it seemed. They took us one by one from our cabins to a tent near the mess hall that had a big red cross on it, and inside they said this woman was a doctor and this man was a nurse, and to sit on this wooden table they covered with a paper sheet and let these two people look in our ears and up our noses with their tools and open wide and say ah. They even checked for lice. We took some written sort of psych evaluation later, the ones with those oh so relevant true/false statements that reveal you sometimes want to punch people who smoke, or you consider it poetic justice to take Post-Its from the office's storage cabinet. Mostly, we were just left alone, to wander around but only in the yard or to each other's cabins or to the mess hall at meal times. No one interacted much, except the desperately positive girls, the ones who preferred to braid each other's hair and list their favorite pop stars over sitting on their bare bunks contemplating the usefulness of drawing up some sort of will; the ones who could take one look at me eating oatmeal by myself in the morning and picking at the scab they couldn't see and know not to invite me to their slumber parties. But Day Three began a stricter routine.

If you sleep in a cabin together, you don't go to group together, though it is about the same number of girls, give or take. Groups meet after lunch, and every day, and they start like this:

"Okay kids, it's Share Time. Everyone think of one thing they miss about home, and one thing they are happy to be away from. And let's not forget to use our Emotions Vocabulary! Who wants to start?"

The woman leading these merry sessions is number Eighty-eight; she's waif thin and has the stringy hair of a street-walker, and it's almost all gray but the lines in her face put her at about thirty-five, maybe closer to forty. Her voice rises at the end of her sentences, turning all of her statements into questions. She narrows her makeup-less eyes and purses her chapped lips at whomever is speaking, tapping her pen, which is practically glued to her fingers, against her knee and leaning forward like she's oh so interested in the puppy you won't get to see grow up and the nightmare of grass-stained jeans you'll never have to worry about scrubbing out. I started calling her Gertrude immediately, because she looked like a lady I used to see in the feed store at home, who bought sixteen pounds of chicken feed every week when everyone knew she lived in her son's basement in a two-family Tudor, and the closest thing they kept to chickens was a zebra finch that died when I was about ten. They do have a shed in the backyard, but it's pretty small. Maybe she ate the feed herself? Anyway, she died because she was old, and her son moved. I call the group therapy leader Gertrude, and she hates it.

I guess when I say hate I mean she was pretty indifferent about it. More so I think she got peeved when I wouldn't participate in Share Time. When the room got quiet and everyone looked at me, waiting, a link in the circle of chairs but feeling like I was in the middle, called out, stupidly, to talk about some inanity that was so far beneath any of us now, I couldn't open my mouth, because I might have laughed, or I might have cried. Or I might have told them about my mother and how she chews her food as if she's masticating a living creature and I can't eat in the same room with her or I'll want to stab forks in my ears; and how, when she told me there was no such thing as Santa Claus when I was seven and getting wise but still wanted to believe and she told me, I called her a liar and I threw my teddy bear into the fireplace because it was something "he" had given me and if he wasn't real then neither were any of his gifts. But that's when I knew it was therapy, and I had enough of that at home, and maybe I should have said that was something I was glad to be away from, but, see, here it was again. So I crossed my arms. I closed my eyes. The talking picked up again without me, more sharing. Getting to know each other, sans proper nouns.

The session when I got in trouble, yesterday, when they kicked me out, that was the day everyone shared what animal was their favorite and which ones made them kind of uneasy, like bats or spiders, which isn't an animal but no one split any hairs about it when Four brought it up. And after this, Gertie opened up her clipboard and pulled out a laminated copy of a photograph, and said, "Now I need each of you to look at this picture and try not to react to it outwardly, but do react inwardly, and pause on that reaction, and think about it, and when everyone has finished looking at the picture, we'll discuss our inward reactions."

The picture passed through five girls' hands before it got all but pitched into mine. The first girl gasped—very little self control, must not have been held enough as a baby—and tried to fling the photo at the next girl, but our fearless leader admonished, "Don't be so hasty to pass the picture on, Twenty-six. Look at it, at all of it, slowly. Don't fight your reaction, but hold onto it, keep it inside. Go on."

And so it went, and so I was curious, watching everyone pull faces they quickly tried to cover up, and watching Gertie, too, sweet Gertie, watching these reactions like she was watching some secret porno she "accidentally" picked up at the video store and her boyfriend would be home any minute and boy would her face be red, but how exciting, getting caught looking. And then I had the picture, and my inward reaction took a flying leap from my gut out through my throat in the form of a sound I hadn't heard since Omalis came to our house that first time.

I laughed.

The picture was of a boy, too hairless to be a man, lying naked on his back on a stainless steel table. His face was covered with a sheet pocked with cherry bloodstains, his skin peeled back from his chest. There was an embalming tube half inside him, with the gloved-white hand of his coroner holding back a fold of skin, directing the tube. I understood why some of the girls would gasp, or crinkle up their noses at the blood, or at his ash-grey hue of death, the clinical incisions, so close up. But those weren't the only things I saw when I looked at the picture, they barely even registered, really. What caught me, what tickled something inside me that decided to burst out so absurdly, was his tattoo; inked into his left forearm, a simple darkened outline of a woman, the kind you see on truck mud flaps, something he didn't pay too much for, or did himself, with initials underneath it, M.P. And I thought, in that instant of seeing it, I thought about another girl, or a woman, or a boy, or a man, being handed this same picture, in this same circumstance, and seeing first the shocking muscle tissue inside his chest cavity— and taking a moment to pause and react—and then flicking her eyes down about a centimeter, and there it is, that mud-flap lady with those initials, calling to her, glaring, screaming, "Hey, hey you, don't I look familiar? Didn't you wonder where'd I'd gone? Didn't you wonder why I stopped coming to class, or delivering your paper, or fucking you in the backseat of my Dad's Cutlass? Well, you found me."

And so I laughed, at the absurdity and the cruelty of possibility. Gertrude didn't think it was funny, neither did the next girl I passed the photo to, or Twenty-six, whom I thought of as a Brenda, who started to cry. I took in a deep breath to stop laughing, to maybe start trying to explain, but Gertrude stood up.

"Clearly, Eleven," she began, her high notes brought down an octave but still church-choir worthy. "Clearly you have difficulty following instructions. Your behavior is most disruptive, and it is not a positive influence on this class or these girls."

"Class?" I couldn't help myself. "What exactly are you teaching us?"

Good ol' Gertie chose to ignore me. "What do you think I should do about your behavior, hmm? Clearly it is unacceptable, at this juncture."

"Clearly," I said, still not over the eye-rolling I enjoyed so much back home. "I guess the only thing you can do is send me home. Let me burden my mother, she's used to it."

I almost got a snicker out of one of the girls to my left, I swore I heard it. But then Gertrude said this: "Or we could accelerate the program, Eleven. How would that be? Get you out of here expediently, as you've expressed quite unquestionably to be preferable to joining in our activities. Yes, perhaps I should phone your Liaison, have her inform your parents that your tract will be decided at the end of the week? Hmm, Eleven, how does that sound?"

"Sounds kind of like murder," I said. Twenty-six-Brenda gasped again, and the snicker came again, and Gertrude turned ember red.

She raised her pen like a sword, or like a shield, close to the chest. "Now, Eleven—"

"My name is Jordan."

"Enough of that."

But I wasn't talking to her anymore, I was talking to the black sphere in the corner of the cabin, to whomever was watching, to whomever might watch later.

"My name is Jordan Fontaine, I'm fourteen, I live in Silver Lake, Utah. I have two brothers and a mother and a father and I go to Silver Lake High School and I don't play sports anymore because my therapist says it's hard for me to get along with others on account of my—"

That was when my head hit the plank wood floor. It felt like I was back in my old classes again, just like I'd been only last week, which had become old now, I guess, and something to miss, being tackled and twisted like this into the pretzel hold, which I guess they teach everybody how to do if you're going into some sort of social service work, which I guess you could call what these women do a social service but that seems kind of ridiculous. I struggled, of course, and some of the other girls screamed, and they all got up to back away, and one or more of them probably ran to get some help. Gertrude wasn't strong but she made up for that with enthusiasm. During the struggle I guess my sweatshirt rode up and her hand brushed my naked stomach and it made her stop, and it made her look, and then she was the one who gasped.

So now I'm waiting in a special room, one I hadn't seen until they led me here this morning, which is actually really big, like a great big lodge where you might hold a wedding reception, if you could bring yourself to get married in some place that used to be a camp, or if you'd gotten married before it became one. Inside it's all hallways, though, and so many doors, and behind one of those doors is me, waiting at a table with two chairs, cushioned, which is nice, and a hardwood floor that someone laid a rug over. The table sits on this rug, whose dark green frayed edges I pick at with the toe of my assigned sneaker. The corners of the room are empty, only lonely right angles, bare pine walls, not even a knot-hole to hide in. No cameras.

That's how important she is, I guess. How loyal. I don't really want to meet with her, but there isn't any alternative. I just have to wait here, and I'm shaking a little because I didn't eat much this morning, low blood sugar or whatever. Why did they call her? I don't want to see her. She's late, though, maybe she won't show, just tell them to let me alone, because she knows my history and everything, she has my file, right, so, it's not my fault, what I did, and nothing needs to be accelerated, even though it doesn't matter, but I still can't keep my stomach from dropping a thousand miles when I think about it, so, yeah, yeah, that's what I'll tell her, I'll say, when she gets here, I'll say—

"Good morning, Jordan." Her lips make my name sound like poetry breathed to life through her rounded vowels. I want her to say it again. I want it to be the only thing she says.

She doesn't sit down right away. She's wearing a short skirt that will ride up and expose her knees when she sits, no stockings. The door brushes the skirt as she glides it closed behind her, ruffling the smooth slate-gray pleats. Her blouse is white, long-sleeved, and she'd look like just another school teacher if it weren't for the soft shadow of cleavage that peeks out below the third undone button. She doesn't wear a necklace so it's hard not to look lower, but she does wear earrings, the same small faux-diamond—or real, maybe, I don't know her salary—studs, and her face, again, bears only a light patina of blush-eyeshadow-lipgloss. Today, she smells like cinnamon and something sweet.

Her shoes make no noise as she walks to the table and sets her briefcase on top of it. She pulls out her chair. She smiles at me, closed-mouth, and sits, knees together, elbows on the table, hands clasped as if in prayer.

"Truthfully," she starts, drawing my eyes to her mouth. I can see saliva in the corners, cracks in her gloss, the slick pinkness of her tongue. "Truthfully, I hadn't expected to see you so soon."

If she expects me to say something, apologize maybe, I don't. I'm not close enough to smell her breath, but I bet it is spearmint, or I want it to be spearmint, or just pink, the smell of pink, like the girls all together would smell after showering when I used to take a gym class.

"How has your week been?" Omalis unclasps her fingers so she can touch her face, her chin. Her sleeve falls down, revealing her wrist. I hold my breath.

"Jordan?"

I look at her eyes. They seem deeper, the color and the pupil, so black. I listen, and I hear her heart beat. I want to move closer, remembering, now, with her across from me, how it was, earlier, long ago, when she was on top of me, when I was running and she was on top of me, holding me down, saving me, saving me from myself. So long ago. I can still feel how warm she was.

"It's a struggle for everyone," she says. "In the beginning."

"Isn't this the end?" My voice is thick. I swallow but still feel wet, though my lips are dry and cracked, like hers, but I know you're not supposed to lick them, it only dries them out faster, something about the salt in your spit.

She doesn't say anything for a few seconds, just looks at me, and I feel the heat again. I'm trying to remember the things she said to me, all of the things, but I realize she never really said much of anything besides what she was instructed to say, the script she memorized through sheer repetition. And what did I say, when I wasn't crying or screaming to go home, which I never really wanted, I don't really want that, home. I hear her voice again, and I feel her fingers grasping my palms, though she hasn't moved. A phantom pressure, it makes me blush.

"I'm not going to tell you everything will be all right," Omalis says, stopping my heart, my lungs. "There are things you'll have to do here if you want to stay here, like everybody else. If you will not do them, if you cannot, Jordan—you will be taken directly to the Feed Program."

My eyes burn as hot as the rest of me. I have to look away from her because I don't want her to see me cry. It's all I ever do around her, when she's smiled with me, at me, for me, even laughed. All I do is cry. I close my eyes and smell her. I lick my lips.

"At least you don't lie to me. I like that you don't lie to me."

"Maybe you'll return the favor, hm?" Even with my eyes closed, I can feel her smile, the small one, the smirk. "Will you look at me?"

I do. I start on her eyes but it's too hot, so I refocus on her nose, which is average, only the lines that droop down to cusp her mouth are too enticing not to follow, and then I'm back to the lip gloss, a different flavor this time, I think, something with more citrus, to complement the spearmint. If I leaned a little closer I could shatter my illusion. I cross my arms and lean back, refocus on her eyebrows, light and trimmed, which makes it look like I'm looking at her eyes, which might be a kind of a lie, I guess, but here we are.

"What did you use to cut yourself?" She asks, which is kind of nice, kind of nice she didn't start with "why," that tired question so revered by therapists and school administrators.

Of course, I have to lie, but it's not really my lie, it's not for me. It's for Taylor, who's probably in her own group right now, looking at more pictures or sharing more hopes and dreams and disappointments, just trying to get by, get through, like all the rest, like I should have done, like I should be doing, like my brothers are doing, like so many more will do long after we're all done.

"They didn't make us cut our nails until the second day." I hold up my hand, fingers spread, nails eclipsed by rough skin. "They were a lot longer, then."

"May I see what you've written?"

"No," I say, a knee-jerk no, like when Mom yells up the stairs for me because I know whatever she is going to ask me I won't want to do. I fold my arms over my stomach.

Omalis arches an eyebrow, a sharp stab up, like the lines on a heart monitor, and drops it back down again. I feel myself blushing again, I can't stop.

"All right," she says. "I suppose we'll just have to start filing down the fingernails upon initial arrival."

She says it like, "and that's that," but I can tell there's more to come because she hasn't moved to get up yet, and they wouldn't have called her down here to give up so easily. She shifts slightly.

"It's my turn," I say before she can speak. "I get to ask you a question now." But my statement comes out as more of a question—"Is that okay?"—and if she were paying closer attention she would catch that and have her turn back.

She nods, a smile in her voice, condescending if it weren't so innocent, "I suppose that's only fair."

All eyes on me. Everything dries up again. Well, almost everything.

"Tell me about South Africa," I say.

"That isn't a question. It may be your game, but you still must play by its rules."

How I want to smile, but I don't. I take a deep breath and try again.

"Did you get caught in the war?"

"Yes, if you can call it that. I think of it more as a decimation." She never takes her eyes off me, but she tucks her hair behind her ear, the nervous gesture equivalent of shoving your hands in your pockets. "My turn, then. What's your favorite color?"

"What?" Now I'm tucking my own hair behind my ear.

"Your favorite color?" she repeats.

"Um…I don't know… I don't think I have one."

"Oh, everyone has a favorite color." Her cheeks brighten with the sharp points of her smile. "For instance, mine is pink, though I would never wear it in public, but I love it on other people. That's a freebie," she says, and her right eye closes in a quick wink.

I shove my hands in my pockets.

"I don't really like pink," I say.

"Few people generally do." She thinks a moment; I watch it in her eyes, how they quiver, flick down to the table, then just as quickly back up to me. "Your bracelet," she says, stopping my heart, "it was made of very bright colors, yellows and oranges, a spot of green in there. Any of those your favorite, perhaps?"

Again, I fumble. I feel my underarms begin to sweat. I want to leave, or at least change the subject. "Yes, all of those. My turn. How did you get out of there? I've never read anything about the survivors or anything."

"My father was a fisherman," she says. "My mother smuggled me to the marina and we set sail."

"I think you're lying," I say.

"Why would I lie? You can count that as my question if you'd like."

"They wouldn't have let anything that noticeable leave the continent," I say. "That place was like ironclad lock down."

She looks bemused again, with her half smile, tilting her head to the side, like suddenly I'm a child again. "What books *have* you been reading about South Africa?"

I shrug. "History books. In school." I don't want her to think I've been doing any extra reading-up on her birthplace.

"I see," she says. "Well, it is your choice not to believe me. After all, I've never had my account of things published in a textbook. But then, you've never heard stories from a survivor, you said. Who's writing these books, then, I wonder?"

"I don't…" I'm getting distracted. "Anyway, it's still my turn. When did you decide to become a Liaison?"

"A long time ago," she says, but she can only be thirty-five or so at the oldest, so this answer is too vague to count. But she jumps back in before I can say anything else. "Did you make the bracelet, the one you wore before?"

"Why do you care?" I snap, forsaking my stupid game, avoiding her eyes now, giving up. I wonder if I can just get up and leave, or do I have to wait for her to dismiss me.

"Why do you care about my upbringing?"

I can't answer her. "Look, I'm sorry I got into trouble or whatever. You know they took away my meds, so. It's not like it's all my fault. I just…I didn't mean to get into trouble."

Dammit, I'm sulking, which is close enough to crying to really piss me off. If she doesn't leave in the next thirty seconds, I will.

"I'll see what I can do about that," she says. I am looking at the carpet, but I hear her chair slide back and her clothes rustle as she rises. Her shadow peeks onto my knees. "In the meantime, if you have anything you'd like me to pass on to your parents, a letter perhaps, you can give it to one of your mentors and she'll pass it on to me. All right?"

I can't even nod, I don't even have that left. She doesn't say anything else and then she is gone. When I look back up, there's something on the table. My bracelet. I feel like I can't move, but I grab it before counselor Ninety-Seven comes to take me back to my cabin.

On the way back, we pass by the small lake, a handful of two-man canoes lined up across its bending shore. There's a boathouse near the short plank-wood dock but they don't keep anything in there except for a few barn swallows, on account of how old it is, and how the weather has worn out its boards. The roof is already caved-in in spots, the walls and floor rotting. They don't tear it down because some of the kids like to go there to smoke, and they turn a blind eye—a sympathetic one, maybe—to that one and only refuge.

As we pass, I see a shadow through the barn-like opening. The brief flicker of the end of a cigarette lights up Taylor's face. I stop and tell the counselor I'm not ready to head back yet. She reminds me that dinner is in thirty minutes, and I nod and walk away, not looking back to see how closely she may watch me, how long she waits to make sure she knows where I am going.

At the boathouse, Taylor stands half in and half out of the archway. It's begun to drizzle, and her arm gets wet from the elbow down, the droplets clinging to the light hairs there, but she doesn't move it. She moves the cigarette to and from her lips with her left hand, the one in the safe dry shadows of the boathouse. I stand inside the boathouse, sneakers creaking against the wet and rotted floorboards, arms crossed and looking at her arm. She hasn't said anything to me since our first night here, with the razor, our secret. I don't know what to say to her, or if she'll say anything to me, but I know I don't want to go back to our cabin just yet, because I'll be alone while everyone else is in group, and I'll have to start thinking about today, and about tomorrow.

That's when it occurs to me, she isn't in group either. Well, it might be flimsy, but it's an opening at least.

"Did your group end early?" I ask, casual, avoiding accusation, like the soft way adults speak to me when I'm coming off an "episode."

She sucks in smoke from her cigarette and holds it behind her words. "Ducked out. You?"

"Something like that." I don't know why I'm being coy, after the razor, after the things I saw, the things she let me see. But if she's pretending it never happened, I will too; she's older, I'll follow her lead.

"Do you want one?" I shift my eyes from her dampening arm and see she's proffering her pack of off-brands to me with her other hand. *You can use it too.*

I look at the ceiling, at the corner, the black sphere hanging ominously. Some of the counselors will give you cigarettes but only one match. And then they'll watch you, in person or through those black, deceptively dormant eyes. I shake my head.

"Yeah, smoking will kill you." She tucks the soft-pack back into the waistband of her sweats.

"If you're lucky," I say, kind of wishing I'd taken one now, just to show her I mean it.

She laughs a little with her throat but her lips stay pinched. She's old enough and she has hair dark enough to need to wax around her upper lip, but that's a luxury we're not allowed to smuggle in with us here. I wonder what her armpits must look like, and turn away, pretending to find something interesting in the mud clumping up in the corner on the other side of the boathouse.

"Right," she says, kind of light, like maybe I was making a joke, or maybe she is making one. There's a lull then. I watch a barn swallow swoop in through the back entrance of the boathouse, the one facing the lake, and land on a crossbeam overhead. Three small, pink bird faces peek out from their nest of sodden twigs and grass. The mother dips her head to them and spills a worm from her mouth into theirs.

"You had your Liaison meeting," Taylor says, not a question. I keep looking at the swallows, waiting for the inevitable follow-up. "We're not supposed to have them for a few more days. You got yours early. Guess they found out, huh?"

"They found out about me," I tell her, looking over my shoulder at her. She's finished her cigarette, put it out on the floor with the rest of the legion of discarded butts. Arms crossed, she's full in the boathouse now, the rain falling lightly just beyond her back. "But it's okay. I told her I did it with my own fingernails." I shrug.

Taylor nods, almost smiles. "Thanks," she says. I nod back. She swipes a hand across her right forearm, brushing the cold from it. "Your Liaison is a woman? I have a man. He's fat, seems like the kind of guy who plays Santa for his umpteen kids. His suits always smell like a woman, older, with that perfume like grandmas have, you know? Like potpourri that's been closed up in a closet for a few years."

I smile. "Mine doesn't smell like that." Then I blush.

"Your grandma or your Liaison?"

I laugh, a real laugh, quick but there. She laughs too, a mirror sound. She steps a little closer to me. I turn fully to face her.

"What's she like?" Taylor asks. "Your Liaison?"

"I don't know. Probably like all of them." When Taylor frowns, I add, "She's South African."

A light goes on in Taylor's eyes, her eyebrows rise at the significance but she swallows any excitement that might be building in her voice. "Wow," she understates.

"Yeah. Fucked up, huh?"

"Why?"

I really need to explain it? "She went through the war. She…*survived*. And now she works for them. Kind of a fucked-up decision, if you ask me."

"Maybe nobody asked her," Taylor says, dropping her arms in front of her, picking at the side of her thumb with her other thumbnail. "Maybe it wasn't her decision."

"Whatever."

Taylor comes closer and gives the stomach of my t-shirt a light tug. "It's almost time for dinner," she says, cocking her head to the boathouse archway. "Come on, all the good gruel will be gone."

I smile. She smiles. It's almost normal. It's almost just another day at summer camp.

WHEN SHE SHOPS AT THE market on Banquet Street, she never brings a list. She goes straight for the candy bars, filling her basket with M&Ms, Snickers, 100 Grands. Next, she grabs a bag of chips, salt and vinegar, and a couple packages of microwave popcorn. Three apples, six oranges, a cheese ball, a box of green tea. The greeting cards she saves for last, selecting whatever is closest from the Any Occasion rack. She pays with cash.

It's late evening, the sun is finally settling in for the night, dropping down behind the low buildings on Banquet Street, no clouds to hasten its progress. It hasn't rained since April, the farmers are getting nervous, taking special care this summer to maintain their irrigation systems, which for a number of the smaller operations means stocking up on children's sprinklers. The market is having a sale on umbrellas. Omalis buys one on impulse on her way out.

In her car, she lets the engine of her Miata warm up while she divides her purchases into five separate groups. There are brown boxes she picked up from the post office earlier in the day on her backseat, and she fills them all, seals them, and digs around briefly in her purse for the labels she printed out yesterday. She delivers them personally, even though the Over don't require it, but the labels help her keep track of which one goes to whom. As if she would ever forget.

Her first stop is the Fontaines'. She would save them for last but she has a feeling—rather, her experience allows her to *know*—that their visit will prove the most difficult and she wants to have the energy to give them the attention she knows they will need.

It's been nearly a week since Mrs. Fontaine's incident at the hospital, and Omalis knows she has not been back to work. This will leave her restless. This will leave her vengeful.

Omalis pulls into the gravel drive. Mr. Fontaine's truck is gone, but his wife's Honda Civic is parked off to the side, near the lawn. Omalis cuts the engine, picks up one of the packages, and gets out slowly, taking her time walking to the door, giving Mrs. Fontaine time to prepare herself. Although she did call ahead, no one answered, and no one responded to the message she left on the answering machine. It would not surprise her if the Fontaines went out for the evening to avoid this visit. In that case, Omalis would turn around and continue the rest of her visits, and call back to reschedule this one. It would not be against regulations to leave the package at the door and be done with it, but Omalis never does that.

She raps on the door with her free hand. This evening, she's wearing a pair of straight black slacks that mask the curve of her hips, a light V-neck sweater the color of twilight, and her black sneakers. Her hair is down, straightened this morning, falling just below her shoulders, bangs brushed back from her eyes. Casual Friday, a couple days early.

After a moment, she knocks again, louder without becoming insistent. She feels the house shift and hears movement inside, footsteps on the stairs. Another moment and the door opens.

Mrs. Fontaine is wrapped in her downy bathrobe, hair pinned up in a towel. Her skin is dry.

"Have I come at a bad time?" Omalis asks, affecting a smile, a jovial lilt.

"Yes," Mrs. Fontaine says. There's redness around her eyes, puffiness to her cheeks. Familiar features, to Omalis.

"My apologies," she says. "I suppose you didn't get my message. I'd be happy to come by another time."

Mrs. Fontaine considers for a moment, her face hard, her eyes uninviting. Omalis is patient. Finally, a sigh. "Just come in now."

The living room hasn't changed much since she was here three weeks ago, except there's dust on the end tables and it smells like tomato soup instead of cookies. Mrs. Fontaine sits on the couch, in the middle. Omalis sits on the same chair she occupied three weeks ago. She puts the package on the coffee table.

"Your children put this together for you," she says, nodding to it. "Jeremy thought it silly that the children should be the only ones to receive care packages, said it didn't seem quite fair."

Mrs. Fontaine looks at the package for a long moment. Omalis waits for her. Somewhere in the kitchen, a clock ticks, a quick, tinny sound, probably a battery timer.

"When my brothers were away," Mrs. Fontaine says, "my parents received letters, drawings, little crafts. With my sister, it was a care package, chocolates and a card."

Omalis waits for her to say more but she doesn't. Omalis snaps open her shoulder bag and pulls out a business card.

"I wanted to give you this, Mrs. Fontaine." She holds out the card. "It's a number for parents. Parents with children in the program. I've taken the liberty of adding my own personal number to the back."

Mrs. Fontaine takes the card and puts it in the pocket of her bathrobe without looking at it. "Is that everything?" She's still looking at the package.

"No." Omalis stands up and moves closer to Mrs. Fontaine, who doesn't move at all. She sits down next to her, speaking to her profile. "I want you to know, Mrs. Fontaine, that I'm not only here to act as liaison between you and your children. I'm here for you as well. For anything you might need."

Mrs. Fontaine clasps a hand to her mouth and begins to shake. When she turns her head to face Omalis, her eyes are wet but sounds of laughter escape behind her palm. She drops her hand, spit building up in the corners of her crooked mouth.

"I want to kill you," she says through her teeth.

Omalis doesn't flinch. She waits.

"Do you have children, *Miss* Omalis?"

"No," she says tightly, waiting.

"Do you have anyone?" The spittle at the edges of Mrs. Fontaine's mouth has trickled out, falling onto her chin. She doesn't wipe at it. "Anything you care about more than yourself?"

"No," Omalis answers.

A gruff laugh bursts free of the woman's throat; some spittle flies onto the shoulder of Omalis's sweater. "Why am I not surprised?"

Silence, then. A flat buzzing from the kitchen.

"My laundry," Mrs. Fontaine says absently.

Omalis stands, giving Mrs. Fontaine room to go around her to the kitchen, but she stays sitting. Omalis stands for a second or two longer, finally unsure. She decides to sit back down, wait for Mrs. Fontaine to speak again, to ask her to leave, or to threaten her, or to cry.

"How are they?"

"They're well," Omalis tells her. "They are all very well."

"Would you tell me anything else?" But she answers her own question. "No. My husband…even he won't tell me anything else."

"Where is your husband?"

"He had to sell one of our bulls on auction, since my salary's been suspended." Mrs. Fontaine stops herself, glares over at Omalis as if she just manipulated a confession out of her. "You don't need to speak to him."

"Right," Omalis says. "But if he should need to speak to me—"

"He has nothing to say to you," she says.

Omalis nods. "Then it appears we're all set. If you have any letters or small gifts you'd like me to pass along to your children—"

A burst of laughter again, this one softer, sadder. "What can I give them now?" She speaks to her hands, clasped at her waist. Omalis wants to leave, then, leave this woman to her private conversation with herself. "They're lost to me."

"No." Omalis clasps her own hands together to keep from reaching out. "A letter, something simple, something to let them know you're with them in spirit, means all the difference. Something real, something of yours they can touch, to remind them."

Mrs. Fontaine looks at Omalis, her face still hard. Her hands unclasp. "Do you mind waiting?"

✢

TWO HOURS LATER, HER PACKAGES all unloaded but feeling weighted still, Omalis reclines in her single window seat on the small private jet, alone save for the pilot up front and the flight attendant who knows to keep himself busy pretending to grill the Salisbury steaks until Omalis gestures for her in-flight meal. They're over the ocean now, flying west, and it will be another seven or eight hours before they touch down. In another hour she'll have her dinner, and when she's finished she'll try to nap but sleep will refuse her. Instead, to pass the remaining hours, she'll thumb through her itinerary again, make sure all her papers are in order, maybe fuss over her makeup a little in the jet's coffin-sized lavatory. But for now, she has a headache, and another kind of ache, one less common but all the more piercing for its infrequency.

She aches for the thing she promised Mrs. Fontaine she could deliver to her children: something real, something she can touch, to remind her, remind her of something good.

But since she does not have this—cannot have it, will not have it—she calls Marla Matheson.

"Hey, sugar," Marla's honeysuckle voice croons through the transatlantic static on the plane's phone. "How did today go?"

Omalis suppresses her sigh. "Fine, it always goes just fine. I don't want to talk about my day. Tell me about yours."

"Uneventful," Marla says, "which is always nice. Though I'm bone tired; remind me I'm not as young and limber as I used to be, can't go covering girls' shifts back-to-back."

"I'm sure you've lost nothing for the years," Omalis says, allowing Marla's southern semantics, even thousands of miles away, to slip into her own speech.

"Well, that's what I'm saying, sweetie. Gained a few pounds, a few bags, and a mess load of unseemly veins."

"And a couple fistfuls of cash?"

Marla laughs, a balm as cooling as a breeze in the desert. "Won't be worrying about rent for a while, no."

"So it was a good day."

"It was a good day."

The silver-tongued static crackles in Omalis's ear. She's silent, straining to hear Marla breathing beneath it.

"You there?"

"I'm here," Omalis says.

"I want to take you out when you get back," Marla tells her. "Someplace extravagant, someplace beyond our means."

Omalis smiles. "Whatever you want, darling."

"You really must've had an exhausting day. You usually put up at least a pretense of a fight whenever I want to do something for you."

"I just wanted to hear your voice, Marla. Doesn't much matter what the words are."

Another pause. The plane gives a slight jump and then another. The ice in her plastic cup of water tinks together.

"Well," Marla says, drawing it out. "I can't decide if that's a sweet sentiment or if you're just being an asshole."

"Pick one," Omalis says, a little dryer than she means to.

"Fuck, Heaven," Marla hisses, and her next words whisper along with the static, almost as if she were talking to herself, or to someone else on her end. "I don't have time for this."

"I'm sorry," Omalis says. "I'm just tired. You know I'm tired."

"I know you're tired, baby," Marla says, her voice dropping low, sad, repentant. Omalis is about to call her out on her sudden change in tone, when she is frozen by her own name, and the ticking off of numbers that always leads to memories, memories she never recalls willingly.

This time she's on her back, looking through the cracks in the floorboards, staring up into a darkened room. She can feel her mother's hand in hers, sweating so much it's hard to keep their palms together for the slipping. Her mother is breathing shallow, silently, and Heaven mimics her, but she's scared; scared more of her mother than of the smell that streams down into their musty hiding place, the smell that precedes death, or worse, for some. And then the floorboard that hides her, protects her, rips away with a violent tearing sound like flesh ripped from bone. She's screaming, still looking into blackness but this blackness is *alive*, this blackness is moving for her, and then it is on her, *in* her, and she's screaming and she's kicking and above the noise, above the stench, above the pain, her mother's voice, her mother's final plea, her fatal promise: "Wait."

Omalis wakes up as the wheels touch down and the jet taxis on the runway, coming to a jerky halt. She rubs her eyes, stretches and yawns. Her stomach growls. She really must have been tired, to sleep through dinner.

✢

Jordan Fontaine looks worn down. There are shadows under her eyes, her cheeks are drawn and pallid and her hair is mussed, uneven at the roots, indicating she may be pulling at it, willingly or in her sleep. If she sleeps very much, as Omalis suspects she does not.

The girl slouches into her place across the table from Omalis, and looks blankly at her. "Come to spring me?"

Omalis can't help a pinprick of a smile. The girl is down but not out.

"Not quite," Omalis says. "Checking in, merely."

"Merrily?"

"*Merely*," Omalis says. "It means simply, or only."

"I know what it means," Jordan says, shaking her head. "Trouble understanding you, with your accent and everything."

"Right." Omalis nods, straightening the papers she has in front of her. "That old preoccupation."

"Getting tired of it? I thought we were building a rapport."

There's that aching again, someplace lower than the grumble of the hunger pains, someplace deeper. Jordan's voice triggers it this time, that hollow, hopeless desperation disguised beneath a cracking patina of sarcasm. She was not like this a week ago; she had more life in her, more fight. Omalis knows it is because the program has accelerated, inevitably, redoubtably. But, still, that ache.

Omalis steers directly into it. "How are you dealing with the changes to the program?"

There's a pause in which the girl's eyes seem to go somewhere else though their focus never leaves Omalis's face, and then they are back. "I guess I'm dealing how they want me to."

"And how would that be?"

"I don't want to play this game," Jordan says.

"Which game would you rather play?"

Jordan flinches slightly, no doubt not quite anticipating such a response. Instead of answering, she asks, "How many weeks are left? Three?"

"Four," Omalis says.

Jordan sighs and straightens her back a little, then lets it slump back down.

"You seem disappointed."

"I just don't like waiting."

"You can do more than wait, Jordan," Omalis says. "You can try."

"Really?" Jordan's eyes refocus, making Omalis realize she hasn't been looking into her eyes at all, but in-between them, not seeing them, until now. "Because I have a theory, more like a bet, I guess. It goes that my death certificate was signed the moment you showed up at my house, mine and my brothers', and any other's kids' you or yours visited three weeks ago. Now it's just a matter of how it goes down, how long it lingers. Seems to me the shorter the better. So, I guess I am disappointed."

For a long moment Omalis says nothing. She watches the girl's eyes shift down to the table, then her cheeks flush with color, and her hands comb through her hair, trying to hide her sudden redness but not in too obvious a manner.

"Our last visit, Jordan," Omalis begins, "you were less inviting of your fate."

"Well," Jordan says, "a lot's happened since then."

"What sorts of things?"

"I'm sure you can get the list from one of the Gestapo."

Omalis almost laughs, tries not to register her shock at the reference, but is too curious to let it lie. "Where did you learn that term?"

"A lot of people know it," Jordan says, eyes as evasive as her words.

"A lot of *elderly* people know it," Omalis corrects.

"*You* know it," Jordan counters.

"At any rate, its history is no longer part of the public curriculum. You must have made a friend who is Outside Educated."

"What history?" Jordan asks, and Omalis can tell she does not know. She's only using it as a word, a synonym, perhaps, for warden, guard, soldier. "What's the big deal? Is it offensive or something?"

"Not to me," Omalis says, deciding to get back to the task at hand. "Have they begun the physical exams yet?"

Jordan's hesitation is all the answer Omalis needs. "Yeah."

"Which ones?"

When Jordan doesn't reply, Omalis gets the most embarrassing out of the way first. "The gynecological exam?"

Jordan almost recoils, dropping her hands down to cover her lap. "No! Are they… are they going to do that?"

"It's quick," Omalis says, "and quite painless." She is struck by how small Jordan has become in her chair, how so like a little girl, a toddler afraid of the world simply because she has not yet known it. That is why she shivers, why she makes cavalier comments about death, why she hides behind other things to distract her, the things that make her blush, make her feel older.

And that's when Omalis wants to leave, and when she knows she can't leave. She has one more thing to do.

"Before I go," she says, aware of the change in her voice, the dropped octave and thick, stilted words. "There is one test I must administer to you myself."

"What is it?" Jordan asks, curious but not afraid.

Omalis walks around to her side of the table, kneels down so she is eye level with Jordan. Jordan is looking in that space between her eyes again, and she's holding her breath, the redness beginning to creep up from her neckline.

"It's quick," Omalis says slowly. "And quite painless."

She draws the uncapped syringe from her loose jacket pocket and stabs it into Jordan's shoulder in one movement. She's certain the girl doesn't even see this motion, just feels the piercing needle and the rush of something hot through her, and sees the needle for the second before Omalis draws it back out and puts it back into her pocket, and tries to connect all of these things in her steadily heating mind. The question is on her lips but it doesn't get to escape before the seizure starts. Omalis catches her before her convulsions throw her against the table, and lays her on the floor on her side. She goes to the intercom next to the door.

"I need a medic in room three," she says into it, calm, strange. Rehearsed.

# EIGHT
## JORDAN

I WAKE UP TO THE distinct smell of Bactine. This triggers some sort of sensory memory because I see my mom even though my eyes aren't open yet. She's bent over me in my bed, rubbing a cotton swab covered in the stinging medicine along a jagged scrape on my elbow. I guess I expect to see her when I actually do open my eyes because my heartbeat grows rapid as my lids flutter open, and then all but dies when she is not truly there.

It's dark, wherever I am, and I can barely see two feet in front of my face. There's a faint glow to my left, and when I turn my head I can see a console like the face of a complicated radio, all dials and knobs and blinking lights. It's hard to tell, but I don't think it is hooked up to anything; it's sitting on a metal cart or table a few feet from my bed. Other than my own breathing, all I hear is its low hum, and the wind outside.

I look around and think I am in a tent. The ceiling is low, kind of curved in and meeting in a V-shape at its top-most point maybe four feet above my face. It's some dark color I can't quite make out. When the wind picks up, the ceiling and walls bend in slightly. There's a draft wafting up from below me. Yep, tent.

The bed I'm in is little more than a cot with guardrails. Thin mattress, thinner pillow, not even a blanket. I'm wearing the same old sweats. There's no scrape on my elbow, but there's still that Bactine smell. I lift my hands and smell them, lift my arm and sniff. That's when I realize it's not coming from me, but from all around me, from the bed itself. It's a shadow smell that's soaked into the mattress and the pillow, and it's obvious where I am: a medical tent.

But how did I get here?

I feel okay, except a light throbbing in my right shoulder, but when I put my hand there it feels smooth, no bumps or scratches. My head feels a little groggy and my stomach a little achy, but I think that is because I have not eaten in a while. Although, I'm not entirely sure what time it is. The color and thick nylon fabric of the tent are too dense to allow any light inside, even if the sun were shining. There's only the pale blue light of the machine next to me. I look at it again. A heart monitor thingy, like from a hospital? But there's no line spiking up and down, and no numerical display. Besides, it isn't hooked up to anything, least of all me.

I think I want to get out of here. No, I definitely *know* I want to get out of here, *especially* because I don't know *why* I'm here. Maybe it was the food, like food poisoning or something. I remember the last meal I ate was breakfast this morning—if it *was* this morning—and the eggs were really runny and the gravy tasted kind of sour and old. But I didn't eat a lot of it; in fact, Taylor ate most of it for me. If I'm ill, Taylor should be too, but she must be in another tent as this one is definitely single-occupancy.

Of course, I don't think it was food poisoning. I don't think Taylor is here. I wish she were. The drafty air is getting colder, and trying to think over the meaning of this new situation isn't making anything any warmer. It'd be nice to have her with me, holding my hand, making her own postulations about the predicament, laughing at some stupid joke I made in an effort to make us both feel better.

The scariest thing about being here is that nothing is *keeping* me here. I'm not strapped down or plugged into anything. My eyes have adjusted to the dark just enough to see that across the "room" is the front of the tent, complete with zippered flap. It zips up from the outside but that shouldn't be difficult to manage. Yet, I can't move. I may be allowed to go, but should I go? If this is some sort of test, some sort of measurement of something of mine that might determine whether or not I have a future, what the hell am I supposed to do to pass it?

I sit up, starting to shake, trying to stop. I look to the corners of the tent, near the top, checking for cameras. There are none. My eyes find the machine again. Maybe it *is* some sort of monitoring device, after all.

I hear a metallic *vizzzzzz* sound and whip my head toward the front of the tent. The zipper is down and flaps are cast aside and a shadow enters the tent. If I thought my heart was beating fast at the expectation of seeing my mother when I first opened my eyes, I was an idiot. I could power a small village with what's happening inside my chest right now.

The shadow is swallowed by the darkness in the tent, and I am frozen. I follow the faint outline of its form with my eyes as it circles around the left side of me. I feel a scream welling up, and visions of things hiding under my bed, creating worlds in my closet when I'm not there. But instead of going for me, the shadow goes for the machine. The blue light is smothered by its hand, and, after a series of clicks, the walls of the tent catch fire.

As I blink the room comes into focus, and I see that the tent's walls and roof are lined with strands of tiny, bright yellow bulbs, like Christmas lights. The machine is indeed connected to something, the plug for the lights, down near the wheel of the cart it sits on.

The sudden light brings relief, but the air I might have let out in a nice deserved sigh is quickly sucked back in at the sight of the "shadow."

I've never seen her before, but then, this camp is probably a lot larger than I think. She wears the same gray sweatpants and shirt that all the other counselors wear, except something is off. It only takes me a second to find it: the right breast of her shirt where her numbers should be is blank, just cool slate-gray cotton. Her skin looks creamy in the yellow light, and it glistens at her neckline. She isn't smiling at me, like most of the others would have, trying to keep me calm, placid. Instead, she's almost frowning, her dark eyes narrowed severely, narrowed at me.

"Hello, Jordan," she says, taking a step toward my cot. Hearing my name on this stranger's lips is like a balm; it loosens me, makes me feel I can do anything. But then I remember where I am, I remember myself, and all the things I've forgotten, or never knew.

I sit up straighter. "What's going on?"

"You'll be all right. My name is Marla Matheson." Then she does something that almost has me rolling: she reaches out her hand to shake mine. Like we're at a fancy dinner party, or a parent-teacher conference.

But I can't laugh, not in here. Not anymore. And I can't take her hand, because I don't know why she's offered it, not really. I look at her hand as she realizes I won't be roped into some meaningless pleasantry and draws it slowly back to her side. I get a flash of the inside of her wrist; something is written there in dark ink, a tattoo. Maybe a scar.

"I came here to speak with you about something vitally important," she says. She uses these fifty-cent words but her accent is painting pictures for me of a past spent trying to talk her way out of the back of a good ol' boy's pickup 'cause she still needs to get home in time to finish her chores around the farmhouse. The kind my mom sometimes lets slip out when she's angry, kind of tough, kind of rocky. "I know you respond best when you're not talked down to, Jordan, so I'll try my hardest to be straight with you."

There's a plunging feeling in my gut. "Oh god," I hear myself say.

She blinks. "What is it?" Eyes darting over me, leaning forward, looking concerned. She plays her part so well, this Marla.

"This is it, right?" Saying this could make things worse, but…but…could it, really? I'm not so sure anymore. "You're here to take me, right? To…to…prepare me? The program … it's over for me…isn't it?"

She leans back and breathes a sigh, as if relieved. Presses a hand to her heart, the one with the faded black ink. "Oh, Jordan, no." She shakes her head and almost laughs. I almost drop a load.

"I'm here on an entirely different agenda." Serious again. "I want you to know—no, I need you to know—how serious this is. How real. How much I am trusting you by coming here, hoping that you might trust me in return."

She pauses here, for effect or for a reaction. My insides plummet again. Outside, the crickets start up, crying out their midnight song for mates.

"I'm a member of the Resistance, Jordan. I'm here on a mission for them. I'm here to fight back. And I need your help."

It takes me a minute to take in all the sounds she's just made and turn them into words, then to sentences, then to anything that makes any kind of sense. I go cold all over, start to shiver. There's no blanket, no goddamn blanket. What kind of medical tent doesn't stock any blankets?

"Are you all right?"

It could be a test, is my first thought. It could be for real, is my second. A or B, gotta pick one. Which one is your money on, Jordan? The biggest risk has the biggest pay out.

"What do you want from me?" I ask.

"A lot," she says. "Can I trust you?"

"Can I trust you? What if I scream for someone? Will you run? Or stay and… shake hands?"

"I'm afraid I'd have to kill them," she says, no joke, just like that. "Then I'd run, yes."

"Jesus."

"We have to try to get along without him now, don't you think?"

I press my knuckles into my eyes, still see the brightness of the tent between my fingers. A headache's coming on, pushing its way from the back of my skull to the front.

"What have you got to lose?" she asks me.

Huh.

I tell her, "You can trust me."

"I can't make you do anything, you understand that, Jordan?" Those severe eyes softening a little, or maybe it's just the light. "All I can do is lay out what I need from you, show you all my cards, and you decide what you are able to do with them, for us. Understand?"

"So, lay 'em down then."

"I know you've heard of other resistance movements; I know you think fighting back only gets you killed quicker. You're right to think that. Our faction is no different... Well, it's marginally different. Do you know what genetics are?"

I shake my head. "Like biology?"

"Yes, like biology. Specifically, the science of heredity, of the make-up of an organism. The study of genetics was outlawed immediately following the war, that's why you'll only hear your grandparents talking about it, if they dare to. Well, and people like me."

She smiles, waits for me to return it. I'm still trying to deal with this whole being-vitally-important issue that we seem to be taking a lifetime to get to. She clears her throat and goes on.

"You see, for as long as we as a species have been oppressed, we've fought back. We've turned to technology, to science, to help us. We think that because our enemy is bigger and stronger, that we must make ourselves bigger and stronger to defeat them. This means weapons, this means war. Even when this method fails, we remind ourselves it was because our weapons were not big enough, and we embark on making them more powerful. Our enemy meets us every time. They aren't winning because they're bigger and stronger, Jordan. They're winning because they are smarter, and they are smarter because we've let them dumb us down."

"I thought they were winning because they're immortal," I say, trying not to sound too blasé, but, I mean, come on. I think I make a pretty good point.

Her dark eyes seem to shimmer with new life. If I were close enough to touch the skin on her arm, it would quiver with excitement. "They only want us to believe they are. That's where genetics comes in."

She paws at the front of her sweatshirt and lifts it up, revealing a slim fanny pack strapped around her stomach. She pulls it free, still talking. "My father was a genetics professor at Yale. Even before the order to burn all texts dealing in any way with genetics came down, he started hiding his collection. Over the years, parts of it were discovered and destroyed, but a few volumes survived."

From the fanny pack she produces what looks like a small video-game player, flips it open, and sets it on the rail of the bed.

"Of course, to learn anything worthwhile about an organism, to discover what makes it tick, what gives it life and makes it able to pass that life onto others, it isn't enough to read a few books. Especially when the species you really want to learn about has not been captured in any text."

She presses a button and the screen blinks on.

"That's why we have a live specimen."

The screen is about five inches in diameter, the resolution dim and shaky, but there is no mistaking what I am seeing. It's one of them, bound to a bed or table by a cage of wires that seem to encase its entire body. The camera moves over this image, gliding along above the coarse dark hair, which is all I can see of it until the camera reaches its face. "Face" is not the right word. It only has eyes, eyes in the middle of its pimpled head, yellow filmy eyes that have no pupil. These rest an inch or two above its beak—which is a funny word, too funny for the damage that sharp, serrated thing can really do. It's a sword, it's a spear. It's nothing compared to the thing's talons, which the video screen, mercifully, does not show.

"Turn it off," I say, barely audible.

Marla presses the button again and the screen goes black.

"You're insane," I tell her.

"We've learned so much from only this one creature," she says. "Don't be afraid of it, Jordan. We've learned its strengths and its weaknesses. Believe me, it has many weaknesses."

"You think they don't know you have one of them?" I want to scream it but my words are still coming out like swallowed whispers. "They'll hunt you down. They'll rip you apart. They'll—"

"I promise you they do not know." She reaches her hand out to me but I pull back.

"I don't want to," I say. "No, no. I don't want to do this."

"Okay," she says. "I can't make you. Will you listen to what I have to say, though? Only that, only listen."

I point at the video device. "Put that away."

She obliges.

"We know the Over have no idea that we have captured one of their own because their primary form of communication is telepathy. Those wires you saw in the video?

They are connected to machines keeping the thing alive in body only, not in mind. Think of it as the creature is in a coma, brain dead. It can't talk to anyone."

This isn't soothing but I nod my understanding so she'll finish her speech. Before she can say another word, there's movement outside the tent, close by. Voices. I stiffen, but Marla doesn't even seem to notice.

"I'm not going to ask you to decide anything tonight," she goes on, "but I do want to make you perfectly aware of two things. First, there is absolutely no guilt or blame if you decide against joining us. What I'm asking of you is huge, it's beyond huge. It's a burden I wish I didn't have to ask you to carry, and it's okay to hand it right back over to me. Do you understand?"

I nod frantically, eyeing the flap of the tent as the voices draw nearer.

"Good. Secondly, deciding to help us will not save your life. What we need you to do requires you to be selected for a certain program. We will not rescue you once your task is carried out. You will not come back. Do you understand that?"

"Yes, I get it," I say in a rush. "Suicide mission, check. Someone's coming, don't you hear them?"

But the voices begin to fade almost immediately after I say this. Marla is smiling again.

"Thanks for keeping an ear out," she says. "But you're right, I shouldn't overstay my welcome here."

She stands up, refastening the fanny pack around her stomach. As she works the strap around the pack, her wrist twists so I can see the underside where the flesh is lighter and the ink of her tattoo darker. I make out the word SHALL.

"What does it say?" I ask, pointing.

She pauses in her work and turns her wrist over, pushing the sleeve of her shirt back for a better look. "This too shall pass," she says.

"What does that mean?"

"A few things." She finishes adjusting the pack and tucks her shirt in over it. "I'll tell you later, if we meet again."

She goes to the light machine and makes to turn it off, then stops and turns back to me. "I almost forgot." She lifts her shirt back up, unzips a pocket of the pack, and produces a small green plastic bottle.

"For your ODD," she says, "if you feel you need them."

I take the bottle and stuff it in the waistband of my sweats. "Thanks." I want to say more, but I don't. I want to ask more questions, but I just sit there and watch her turn off the lights. I follow her shadow to the front of the tent, listen as she unzips the flap.

"Jordan," comes Marla's voice in the dark. It is at once soothing and terrifying. "Do think over what I've told you tonight. I'll make contact with you again next week."

She goes, leaving me with the soft hum of the light machine, the delicate pounding of my heart, and a bottle full of pills that could easily make my decision for me.

The only time Heaven Omalis allows herself to feel guilty is when she is in bed with Marla Matheson. When she is curled behind her, one hand cupped around Marla's soft breast, the other rubbing fast-slow-fast against her, sliding her own wetness against the back of Marla's thigh, Omalis will close her eyes and whisper in her mind, *Murderer.* Marla likes to look into Omalis's eyes when her fingers are inside Omalis, so when this happens Omalis will bite the sides of her own tongue and try to come as quickly as possible. Once, she bit her tongue so hard that she cried out and blood splattered her chin. Marla tried to pull out of her, but Omalis held her hand in place until she climaxed. After, Omalis's sleep was deep and dreamless.

Last night is the only night in three years that Omalis has not slept in the same bed with Marla. Some nights they only sleep together, side by side, not even touching. These nights are torture for Omalis. It is not that she wants Marla, it is not that she sleeps better after they fuck. It is the silence, the silence in which Omalis turns herself off, in which she is not haunted, not reflective, not concerned. In the silence, she might as well be dead.

Omalis did not share Marla's bed last night not because she was afraid it would be another night of numbing silence or that her tongue could not take another scar, but because she passed out in her car in the apartment's parking lot. One of the mandates of her job prohibits the ingestion of drugs or alcohol, and Omalis usually adheres to this rule. But last night, something was off.

She was off-duty, just returning from her trip to one of the camps. The airport had a bar and when she started to walk by it, she stopped. In the corner near the top-shelf liquor was a television. A pharmaceutical ad was on, rolling by images of happy people on happy drugs, people playing with their children, people playing with their pills. Omalis watched the commercial and then went up to the bartender.

"What do you recommend?" She asked him.

"How about a gin and tonic?" He had a lazy, distracted way of speaking, as though perhaps he had something better to do but he'd forgotten it, so might as well do this. He wore a plain blue t-shirt and simple jeans, a military-style hair cut that framed a face too young to have served at any significant time, and a wedding band. His brown eyes took in her chic form, and he added, "Most popular drink with the ladies."

Omalis arched a brow. "And if I were a gentleman?"

"Bourbon, neat."

"Give me a bottle of tequila. Something expensive."

When she showed him her ID, he blinked and insisted she keep her money. Some of them do this, because they think it will buy them leniency, down the line.

When he turned his back—a dark sweat stain already spreading down the spine—to fetch the tequila, she asked, "Do you have children?"

"Yes, ma'am." He said to the shelf. "Seven daughters."

"No sons?"

He shrugged, turned around to set the bottle on the counter without meeting her eye. "Maybe someday." But Omalis could tell, could read it in his face, that that day had come and gone. Whatever sons he had, they belonged to the Over now.

Omalis gripped the neck of the warm tequila bottle. "How old are they, your daughters?"

"The triplets are eight, the quads are eleven."

Coming up on the time, then. Two more years and his family will really have to start to worry about her. As politely as possible, she asked to see the bartender's ID. He handed it to her slowly, his movements mimicking his speech pattern. She slid it back to him across the bar, and when he put his hand on it, she touched his fingers.

"John Davenport," she said, looking at his forehead because his eyes refused to leave the bar. "Relax. I won't be taking your children from you." He did not relax. She leaned in close and whispered to his sweating face, "You're not in my jurisdiction."

Her intention was not to drink the bottle herself. It was a gift for Marla, to whom she knew she had recently been a dick. On the plane back to Utah, Omalis briefly thought about calling her back, apologizing for being short earlier, cooing and placating and making Marla feel better. Ultimately, though, she decided she was too tired for all of that. With the bottle of tequila, however, she wouldn't have to say anything, or very little. She would present it to Marla right before she headed out the door for her shift at the Shake It Lounge, kiss her cheek, breathe hotly into her ear, and mumble something about having a nice night. In six hours, when her shift ended, Marla would come home, dancing slightly on her heels, too tipsy to remember that they might have been having a fight, too thirsty or too tired or too giggly to care.

Omalis drove from the airport to Marla's without thinking about the bottle, which lay unimportantly on its side in the passenger seat. She thought about the billboards that she passed, the car with the broken taillight in front of her, the current talk-radio program on UTAM. She looked both ways at an intersection before crossing; she tapped her indicator light a full five seconds before her turn. She swished the saliva around in her mouth, realizing she was hungry, remembering she had some mints in the glove compartment. Upon searching, she came up empty. She checked the pockets of her slacks, thinking she might have transferred them there yesterday before she left the car at the airport's long-term parking terminal. No, her jacket. She would have put them in her jacket.

At a stoplight, she reached into the backseat and pulled her blazer into her lap. Something fell out of the pocket onto the floor. When she grabbed it blindly, she felt its cylindrical shape and thought it must be the mints. It was a syringe, the small needle neatly capped.

Omalis was curious but not alarmed. She set the syringe on the passenger seat next to the tequila, finally found the mints and popped one in her mouth. She pulled into the apartment complex and parked in one of the guest spaces. Cut the engine, pocketed the keys. Picked up the syringe. Hm.

She didn't remember having this when she left for the airport. She didn't remember being out of sight of her blazer long enough for someone to have slipped the empty syringe into the pocket. She saw that the syringe was pressed down, and pulled back on the plunger. Maybe it had been filled with something at one time, maybe it was brand new. Maybe someone injected her with something while she napped on the plane.

Omalis flicked the needle cap off with the tip of her thumbnail and stabbed the needle through the cloth of her pants, into her thigh. It was such a small needle that she did not even feel it. If she pressed down on the syringe, air would flow into her blood stream and suffocate her. But the Over had done a fine job of eradicating her and any other Liaison's suicidal tendencies. She took the needle out.

Grabbing the tequila bottle, she stuffed it between her legs and twisted off the cap. She took the needle out of the syringe, tossing it carelessly onto the passenger seat. Plunging the head of the syringe through the neck of the bottle, Omalis pulled back and loaded the instrument with tequila. She thought of the pharmaceutical ad, happy people, happy pills. She squirted 500 mg of tequila straight down her throat so that she did not even taste it.

She drank one more from the bottle, then tipped it back again. The sun had been down for a while when she threw up the first time, rolling down the window only half way before it shot out of her. She considered going up to the apartment then, but it was three flights and the elevator was only for handicapped residents who have a key. Though, they would probably make an exception for her. She took another drink.

She does not remember passing out. She remembers a giant fish using maracas to bang on a steel kettledrum, and then her eyes peel open and the sun materializes before her. At her left ear, Marla bangs on the driver-side window.

Cold air rushes in when Omalis pushes the door wide with her foot. She can smell Marla's sweat, sweet with her strawberry perfume, slightly muted by cigarette smoke.

It takes a moment for Marla to speak, her eyes roving over the pathetic woman before her, the pathetic scene, what a mess. God, how Omalis wants to kiss her, but she can still taste bile in the back of her throat.

Marla says, "Let's get you inside."

This is how it is with Marla. Sympathetic smiles, conveniently blind eyes, often stitched up mouth. Few questions, when she can see how Omalis is hurting. She is good at that, Marla is so good at that. At seeing through Omalis, at knowing what to say, what not to say. The right places to touch, to heal.

In her kitchen, Marla boils water in a silver-plated teapot. Omalis watches her take down a bag of coffee from the cupboard. Marla has a French press; she likes to work for her addictions. Waiting for the water to boil, she fills a cup from the tap and brings it to Omalis in the adjacent living room. She hands it to Omalis without saying anything; Omalis sips at it, still tasting bile. Marla starts to untie Omalis's shoes.

Omalis met Marla three years ago at the Shake It club. She wasn't even supposed to be there, Omalis. It had been a hard week, everyone in the jurisdiction was going. Her colleagues, her friends. She never called them friends, but she thought of them that way, because that was supposed to help. Before eleven o'clock, Shake It was just a bar with hot waitresses. After that, the dollar bills came out and the clothes came off. It was so thoroughly American.

They did not drink or smoke and perhaps that was why they frequented places like Shake It. Places like that could make them feel normal. Normal enough, until they caught someone looking at them, until they let themselves feel the tension in the air, the stolid distance the other patrons kept, that let them know they'd been found out.

People tolerated the Liaisons—deferred to them, even—because of the laws. But Omalis knew—they all knew—they were hated. Hated more than the Over. Because the Liaisons were human; they could be killed. But they could also be replaced. They were always in danger, despite the laws that kept them theoretically protected. This danger, though, this was why they went out. For Omalis, at least, it was intoxicating, better than any alcohol she had ever tasted. The people's fear, her own mortality. Finest cocktail ever mixed.

On that first night at Shake It, no one knew what they did because they dressed down and they left their IDs at home. They sat in a booth to start with, with the guys breaking off in twos or threes to sit up at the stage. Occasionally, one of the women went with them, laughing. Omalis watched the girls dance, strip off their one layer, make their living. She watched all of them, until Marla came on. When Marla came on, she felt ashamed. She turned away. But Marla, she found out later, was still looking at her.

"Most gorgeous woman I've ever seen," Marla said through gasps, later, in the passenger seat of Omalis's Mazda. She straddled Omalis, kissing her neck, letting Omalis play with her panties beneath her skirt.

"Why?" Omalis asked.

Marla stopped kissing, ran a hand down Omalis's cheek, through her hair.

"I don't know," she said. "Maybe it's your eyes. Maybe it's your tits." She lifted Omalis's shirt off over her head and cupped her breasts. "Definitely the tits."

That was how she was when they started. Funny, carefree, a laugh a minute. She did not even know who Omalis was and she never asked. Omalis never would have told her the truth but she was recognized. A mother at the supermarket—Silver Lake, what a fucking small town—a mother who used to have five kids, shopping with her remaining son. Omalis remembered sitting with the woman in her dark living room, holding her limp hand, delivering the news that the Over, for all their monstrous bravado, were too chicken-shit to deliver themselves, never mind the excuse that they don't have mouths. At the market, the woman had to be restrained by store security, but she was still shouting as they led her away. Omalis took Marla aside then and had to tell her, explain the woman's mad, justifiable ravings. She wished she could have been drunk to tell her, or a gun held to her head.

"We all have to make a living," Marla said. She kissed Omalis. "I love you, baby. You're sacrificing. I know you're sacrificing."

It was enough for Marla to know that Omalis did not want this life, hated it, could not escape it. But Marla did not know, or refused to acknowledge, that she herself was part of Omalis's abhorred life, not an exception to it but a rule, a cog that kept Omalis's wheels turning, for better or for worse.

Back in the apartment, her shoes on the floor, water slowly soothing the burn in the back of her throat, Omalis slouches on the couch—the one they bought together at a flea market two years ago when Marla moved in here ("But it's a flea market, Heaven. Kind of doesn't bode well for the condition of the couch. *Flea.*" "But I like it.")—and tries to avoid Marla's eyes.

"I'm assuming you don't want to talk about it," Marla says. Omalis sighs. Marla echoes her, and clicks on the television in the corner, just so someone is talking.

Sometimes Omalis imagines Marla becoming angry. Not exasperated or irritated, as she often is with Omalis, but all-out, red-faced, straining-neck-veins *angry*. She imagines Marla yelling, shrieking unintelligible insults, picking up things in her vicinity at random—the lamp, the tea kettle, an idle chopping knife—and hurling them at Omalis. She sees Marla drawing blood, she sees Marla crying, sees her breaking down and taking Omalis with her. Omalis thinks if this ever were to happen she could love Marla, not blindly, the way Marla seems to love her, but knowingly.

In the kitchen Marla pours the water into the press and selects two mugs from the cupboard. Omalis sets her glass of water down and rubs at her eyes with her fingers, not quite able to reach the ache that's building up behind them. On the television, a male monotone recounts the scores of yesterday's football matches.

"Can we change the channel?" Omalis asks.

Marla comes into the room and hands Omalis one of the hot mugs. She takes the seat across from the couch, a mid-size recliner in which she usually reads because the light is better nearer the window.

"Are you going to be okay?" she asks.

"I'm always okay."

"I mean…I mean with them. The drinking…."

Omalis has to make a report to the Over later that day, as she does every day. They would know about the drinking, of course, but Omalis was not worried about any repercussions. Her performance for them so far has been pristine. She may be punished but not severely, which is just as well.

"Don't worry about me."

"How am I not supposed to worry about you, Heaven? You're acting…spastic. And now you're drinking yourself into a stupor in the parking lot? Yes, this is entirely normal behavior."

"The tequila was for you."

"How thoughtful. Heaven, you have to talk to me. Something's wrong."

Something is wrong. But Omalis doesn't want Marla to analyze it. She doesn't even want Marla to be a part of it. How many times has she lain awake, Marla's sweat still drying on her own skin, and thought about a way to leave her? How much easier would it be to go this alone, to ride out the shame by herself? But Omalis, for all her fantasies of pushing Marla aside, doesn't want easy. She doesn't deserve easy.

Omalis pats the cushion beside her. "Sit next to me."

"No."

"Come on."

"No. Tell me something. Did you have a bad meeting at the camp?"

"I want to hold your hand."

"Was there an incident with one of the parents?"

"I want to smell you."

"Did you get a new assignment?"

"You're gorgeous."

"Heaven."

"Marla."

"You're avoiding me."

"I'm calling to you."

Marla sets her cup down on the coffee table. She leans forward, running a hand through her loose hair. "Heaven," she says, not looking at her. "You're slipping."

Omalis wants to respond to this but the monotone voice issuing from the television breaks with barely contained panic and Omalis's attention splinters.

On the screen, a male anchor, forty-ish, hair already silvering around the ears, presses a finger to his earpiece and stares at the camera, eyes gleaming. The little video box in the corner of the screen plays a video of a Fourth of July parade, sans sound. Finally, somebody stops tape, and the video freezes on the jovial green face of a made-up Statue of Liberty, throwing candy on the street for the children.

"…Sightings are being confirmed…in…Kyoto, Japan," the anchorman continues, eyes scanning the camera face, as if reading from the TelePrompTer. His fingers grow pale and his ear red from pressing so hard on the earpiece. "….Oh…Oh my… It appears that the Over are launching an attack…"

"What?" The question slides out of Omalis like a last hope. She goes and stands directly in front of the television. From behind her, Marla uses the remote to turn up the volume.

To someone off-screen, the anchorman now asks, "Do we have audio? Can we get audio on this? Loyal viewers of UT-41, this is…this is breaking news. The Over have been conclusively spotted in the area of Kyoto. They are amassing as a…a swarm. Do we have video? Do we have anything?"

"Change the channel," Omalis says, almost dreamily, "CNN."

"Heaven, maybe we shouldn't…"

"Do it."

Marla flips to the appropriate channel. Immediately an image of downtown Kyoto appears on the screen, a man-on-the-streets camera shakily zooming by buildings and pedestrians, all running. The camera tries to angle up but keeps being jostled by people running by. On the bottom of the image, a news ribbon scrolling quickly by, dramatic all caps text screaming: THE OVER ATTACK DOWNTOWN KYOTO, COMMUNICATION WITH LIAISONS LIMITED.

"We've lost audio," says the anchor, this time a woman, trim and refined, stern professionalism masking emotion in eyes and voice. The image of Kyoto is now in the top right corner of the screen. The anchorwoman directly addresses the camera. "We'll try to get that back for you, in the meantime… Wait… Okay, we have visual, visual confirmation of the swarm."

Back on the screen, an immense darkness, writhing, squirming. The anchorwoman's voiceover: "Can we pull it back?" The camera zooms out to reveal the tops of skyscrapers, neon lights flashing the only brightness against a sky gone oil black. Like violent storm clouds, the Over spiral in the sky, cavorting, swarming. As dangerously graceful as ravens, their jagged knife-shaped beaks piercing the sky around them, their giant wing-spans stretched to the limit, circling, circling, vultures biding time. God, how Omalis wishes they could screech.

"Okay, what we are looking at here is a swarm of roughly four hundred Over," the anchorwoman's steady voiceover cuts back in. "They are flying low over Kyoto, the people are in a panic, seeking shelter indoors. There have been a number of accidents, car accidents, injuries reported as a result of a rush to vacate the streets. We're getting reports now that the Over have not, in fact, attacked anyone, they are…they are simply gathering, gathering in flight above downtown Kyoto. No official word from any Liaisons at this time as to—"

In a blink, the spiral becomes a column, a sharp-nosed dive of Over ten strong down to the streets. The cameraman isn't quick enough to track them; when the lens finds them, they are already ripping into two dozen pedestrians, whose own cameras are flung from their necks, their faces twisted in screams, blood spilling like rain to the streets

"The Over appear to be attacking, they *are* attacking, in waves of ten, of ten at a time—"

Then the camera drops to the ground, the image flashing into gray static for a brief second when it hits pavement. Feet race by, darkness descends, screams go unheard. The camera is crushed.

Back to the anchorwoman. She swallows hard. "We've lost…we've lost visual."

The text on the news ribbon changes: BREAKING NEWS: 400 OVER LEAD MASSACRE IN DOWNTOWN KYOTO, HUNDREDS INJURED, NUMBER OF DEAD UNCONFIRMED; NO LIAISON CONTACT.

"Why are they doing this?" Omalis doesn't realize she's spoken out loud until she feels Marla's reassuring hand at the back of her neck, fingers pinching her taut skin, trying to keep her steady, keep her here.

"It's okay, baby," Marla says.

"It's happening again."

"No…."

On screen, the anchorwoman straightens up. "A Liaison has made contact. We're setting up live feed now. We're speaking with…with Henry Matsumoto. Liaison Matsumoto has an official statement from the Over. We're going to him now."

Matsumoto sits in a straight-backed chair, a plain blue backdrop behind him. Shot from the shoulders up, he is dressed in a bright beige suit and brown tie, hair greased back, glasses horn-rimmed and perched on the end of his pointed nose. His eyes look directly into the camera, into the eyes of the world watching him; he does not read from a TelePrompTer. The words come straight from the Over, from Matsumoto's own head.

"Citizens," he begins, his monotone disconcerting if it weren't so expected. The English translation of his words runs across the bottom of the screen. "Be assured the events you have just witnessed are not the beginning of another war. In fact, if you will simply learn from your mistakes, they can act as an *end* to this tiresome hostility between yourselves and the Over.

"Last night, two Liaisons were attacked by a mob of students and mentors at Camp Seven-Sixty-Eight in Kyoto. Yuki Katzen and Randall Clark were making their weekly visit when an organized group, armed with weapons supplied to them from their mentors, overpowered and murdered the unarmed Liaisons. This type of unprovoked violence against the Over will not go ignored.

"These students and mentors, young men and women like most of you watching today, have been detained and will shortly join the Feed Program. But their punishment is your lesson: The Over have the power; you—all of you—have the choice. One misguided decision and all of you suffer.

"Citizens, is this what you want? Is this the world of blood and fear in which you wish to live? Have you forgotten your responsibilities in this contract? The Over have not forgotten theirs. Every day, there can be massacre. Every day, there can be blood and war and death. Every day, all of these things can be yours. Or, you can have peace. When you strike against the Over, you only kill yourselves.

"The incident in Kyoto today is a lesson. Please, Citizens, learn it."

Matsumoto's face dissolves back into the anchorwoman, whose blank eyes blink once—her humanity betraying her—as she readdresses the camera. "Thank you, Liaison Matsumoto. We now have additional reports coming in from Kyoto. The Over have dispersed; medical personnel are now onsite. A complete list of injured and dead cannot be provided at this time, but the damage is extreme. We'll have more cameras on the scene and be able to give you additional information within the hour."

The ticker tape scrolls by: MURDER OF TWO LIAISONS LEADS TO MASSACRE IN KYOTO. OVER'S PLEA: "UPHOLD OUR CONTRACT, UPHOLD PEACE."

The screen goes black. Marla has switched off the news because Omalis is on the floor, on her knees, and her eyes are closed and she is swearing softly, swearing, saying *shit shit fuck shit.*

Marla kneels down beside her, hand returning to the back of Omalis's neck.

"You see," she says. "An isolated incident. Scare tactics. All dictators throughout history have done this." She's trying so hard to be reassuring, but Omalis hears the tears Marla hides. Marla cares about those people—all those people the Over wasted in zero seconds flat, them and their families too who've lost them, and those students and mentors who will go to their graves blaming themselves for all the blood and loss.

Omalis knows how much Marla cares; her own blood runs hot with envy.

"I have to go." Omalis tries to rise but Marla keeps her kneeling.

"No, don't go anywhere. Stay here. Talk to me."

"I have to report in. There's going to be…pandemonium."

"Let someone else deal with it."

"It's my job to deal with it."

"Fuck them," Marla nearly shouts. Her voice is filled with venom, so close to rage that Omalis pays attention. "What if I need you? What if it's pandemonium in *here?*" She slaps a hand over her heart and her voice softens. "Can't you deal with that first?"

Omalis leans into Marla, lets Marla hold her, awkwardly, there on the carpet, both kneeling, shoulders angled sharply. Then she pushes her brusquely away.

"No."

She gets up.

"Heaven, wait."

Omalis waits. Not because of anything Marla has said, but because of the way she has said it. Her tone reverberates through her, through Omalis's bones, pleading but demanding as well. Irresistible. Like her mother's, so long ago. *Wait, Heaven. Do this thing for us. Do this one thing. You can save us. I know you're frightened, baby.*

Omalis's headache blooms with the memory, and she shakes it away before it can burst. She reaches out to Marla, now standing, and pulls her hard. She smashes their faces together, kissing hard enough to bruise, digging fingers deep into Marla's hair, feeling Marla's tears wet their mouths and still not letting go. Her mother in her head lying, *It won't hurt, baby, I promise it won't even hurt.* She kisses harder, biting.

Marla plants her hands heavily against Omalis's chest and pushes, whipping her head back to tear their mouths apart. "Stop!"

Omalis wipes her mouth and spits red-tinged saliva onto the carpet. Her blood or Marla's, it still tastes sweet. She says, "Now I'll be late."

Absurdly, Marla begins counting. The numbers sing in Omalis's head, searing themselves over scar tissue beside her mother's face: *One, two, three, four, five, six, seven, all good children go to Heaven, when they die their sin's forgiven, one, two, three, four, five, six, seven.*

Heaven loses sight of Marla. She is back under those floorboards, sight—and all other senses—consumed only with fear, with apprehension. Marla leaves her there for a moment while she walks to the sink to rinse her mouth and scream into a dishtowel before beginning their session.

In the living room, Heaven stands exactly where Marla left her, tottering there, drool gleaming on her chin, eyes half-closed. Marla steers her to the couch and tries to make her comfortable. She makes a few false starts when she first opens her mouth to speak, afraid some emotion might sneak out. She swallows hard, sits on the coffee table, resting elbows on knees, snaps her finger in front of Omalis's face and begins.

"Heaven, do you know where you are?"

Heaven's head sweeps the room, but her eyes, though open, exist in another time and see nothing. Her voice, tired and thick, says, "With you."

Marla resists an impulse to hold Heaven's hand. "How do you feel?"

"Afraid."

"Of what?"

"Guilt."

At the beginning of every session, Marla asks how Heaven feels. Her answer is invariably different. Heaven is afraid of many things: Shame, Pain, Marla, Love, Complacency, Forgiveness. "Guilt" has made the list on several occasions. Not once, not ever, has Heaven responded with "the Over."

"Don't be afraid. You're not afraid, you're...you're proud, and calm. Proud to be useful, calm because you know it will all work out. Do you feel proud and calm?"

Heaven remains a blank, unreadable slate, but she says, "Yes, proud and calm."

"I need to see Jordan again."

"Yes. She's ready."

"You think so?"

"Yes. She's strong. Smart. Ready to die, not ready to be killed."

"All right." Marla got this sense herself, in her brief meeting with Jordan. Though the girl was undoubtedly frightened, she was brave, curious but cautious. "How can I see her again, privately?"

"The medical tents are private."

"It's too risky to try the same thing twice. Is there anything else? Some other place easily accessed?" Although Marla has infiltrated a few camps over the years, each operates slightly differently within their layout and their security measures. She needs to be certain of privacy.

"Yes. Detention Row. Small, box-like barred cabins. Isolated. Irregularly patrolled. No one likes to do it." Heaven startles Marla by emitting a child-like sigh. "It's boring."

Marla smiles, pinches her knees to keep from reaching out. "Okay. Okay. How can you get Jordan there?"

"She likes to fight."

"Yes…"

"Fighters go to Detention Row."

"Would it be possible… Could you get her to fight you?"

"I'm feeling afraid again."

"Nothing extreme, no fear. Just…" She brings her fingers to her own swollen mouth. "A bruise. One shot at you."

"Why would she hit me? She likes me."

"You'll have to provoke her. What can you use against her?"

"She likes me."

"Yes, but—"

"The way you like me."

This gives Marla pause. Finally, she asks, "What?"

"She's shy about it, but she's obvious. Blushing, overly interested in my personal life, excited to see me. She doesn't want to like me."

"All right. Okay. We can use this. You can use this. I have to think. Does she like anyone else?"

"Yes. Taylor Reed. Sixteen. One of seven sisters to be selected for the camps. History of depression, history of passive resistance. Slated for Breed."

"She and Jordan are friends?"

"Yes. Always together."

"How does Taylor feel about Jordan?"

"Don't know. Jordan is shy."

"So…if you were to let Jordan know that you're aware of her crush on Taylor, would it embarrass her?"

"Yes."

"And that would make her angry?"

"Jordan translates almost every emotion into anger."

"Angry enough?"

"I can make her angry enough."

Marla's mind says, *Of course you can*, but she forces her mouth to say, "Good. Here is what you will do."

✦

OMALIS SITS UP IN HER car. Her neck creaks a bit and she feels the waning (perhaps waxing) throbs of a headache behind her eyes. She looks at the passenger seat and finds it empty; no tequila bottle, no jacket, no mysterious syringe. Remembering the syringe recalls images of the day's massacre, causes Omalis to imagine the two Liaisons whose murder ignited the Over's hostility, whose murder was plotted and planned and carried out with no regard for consequence. If someone is plotting against Omalis, she only hopes they'll get it done already, and try to make it look like an accident.

A horn blares behind her. In the rearview mirror she watches a silver SUV continue backing out in front of a compact sedan, ignoring its mechanical cries for attention. The sedan pulls indignantly into the vacated space. Omalis looks forward. She's at the office.

She barely remembers driving here. She presses at her eyes with her thumb and forefinger and gets out of the car. Her mind screams numbers at her: two one five, two one five, two one five. She struggles, but she can't unpack it.

The building is innocuous. It is surrounded by dozens of other innocuous buildings, a couple of fast-food places, and three coffee shops. There's no sign or indication of what type of business might go on inside, but only the people who should be there ever go in. Something about the energy of the place, something about the whispers from inside. If someone did wander in, the doorman would kindly validate their parking and send them away, smiling.

Today, the doorman is Jameson Peters, a late-fifties man who only owns three pairs of pants—the tan and black slacks he interchanges for work, and the basketball shorts he wears at any other time. Every six months or so he has to buy new slacks up a pants size, but the basketball shorts have an elastic waistband; he hasn't replaced those in two years. He also wears suspenders and one of seven short-sleeved collared shirts. He goes through shirts faster than he goes through pants; the sweat stains eventually find a point even the Tide can't wash away.

Usually, Jameson Peters is all smiles, not only for the occasional wanderer, but for the Liaisons, who are in and out of the building at all hours, their moods unpredictable but mostly subdued. Jameson Peters likes to try to make them laugh, even if it's only a pity laugh to get him off their backs. It may not be in his job description, but Peters likes to go that extra mile; his position finds him within hundreds of yards of the Over and he's upped his anxiety meds twice in six years; he can only imagine how the Liaisons must feel. So he cracks a smile, he cracks a joke, and on his way home, he cracks open a plastic can of strawberry icing and eats it straight from the container, his tongue as a spoon.

This is the back story Omalis has invented for Jameson Peters. She does not even know if his first name is Jameson; his name tag only reads Peters. She has only ever said hello to him, and goodnight.

Today, Peters's growing jowls pull at the sides of his face. His eyes barely find Omalis.

"Afternoon, Peters," Omalis nods at him as she passes.

"I don't know anymore," he says, addressing his black loafers. "I just don't know anymore."

Omalis wants to tell him it will be okay, wants to pat his meaty shoulder with her slender hand and break out the platitudes and affirmations, but she lies enough in one day as it is. She strides past him as he closes the door behind her.

The building ostensibly has ten stories but the elevator only goes from the ground floor to the top. The lobby today teems with Omalis's coworkers, some she's seen before, others she only vaguely recognizes, and still more whose paths she's never crossed. There is a waiting area on the top floor, outside of the briefing room, but it must be full to capacity. Whenever there is a crisis—and in all her years, there has not been one like this—the Liaison offices are always backlogged.

"We're by appointment only today," Dillon Snyder strides over from the water cooler to tell her. He's young and lanky, his suits invariably an inch too short, as if his mother still picks them out and sends them, and he is too generous to tell her he's grown. "Mine's not until four, but I thought I'd pop in and see what kind of information I could get. Seems I wasn't the only one with that idea. You heard anything?"

Omalis regards his close-cropped blond hair, the remains of teenage acne he attempts to hide behind a light layer of beige makeup, the pinhole in his left nostril that hasn't closed up since he removed the ring. She resists the urge to roll her eyes at his eagerness, and simply walks away.

On the wall hangs a clock the size of a basketball backboard. The time is two-oh-five. The numbers in Omalis's head ebb into a soft simmer. Not two-one-five, but two-fifteen. The time of her appointment.

Omalis belongs to the largest generation of Liaisons—those recruited during the war—but there was an entire generation before her, small and less conspicuous, and although sanctioned by the world's governments, far less protected from the world's people. They were recruited when people actually thought of it as "recruitment," as a choice; when siding with the Over seemed avoidable, even with Australia gone from the earth. Sure, the continent was still there, but its nuclear mass was abandoned to the

Over, who, far from having been eradicated by the bombs, instead thrived there, long enough to multiply, long enough to "recruit," long enough to plot and plan and launch what would become the War. Although there have been other wars, past and present, between nations, between states, between cities, between cultures, this is the only war anyone talks about when they talk about war. That first generation of Liaisons is long gone; dead or retired in seclusion. Omalis and her cohorts, then, are the oldest line, but there are new, younger arrivals all the time. Most of the older generation behave cordially to the newest arrivals, many take a flock or two under their wings, show them the ropes, lick their wounds. That kind of thing is not to Omalis's tastes. She prefers to keep to herself. Before Marla, she had a small group of coworkers who, if not friends, were at best acquaintances, but since Marla, Omalis has backed away from, as she sees it, unnecessary cavorting.

Today, however, it is near impossible to avoid talking to someone, because everyone is talking. Even the ones Omalis used to admire for their stoicism and envy for their cloud of evident self-hatred, even they are huddled in corners and running from group to group, soaking up the chatter and spilling it for someone else.

Omalis goes as briskly as she can to the elevators and presses the glowing up arrow.

"Have you been called up?" Angela Capelli asks from her shoulder in a conspiratorial whisper that almost makes Omalis laugh. When Omalis chooses to ignore her, Capelli can't contain herself. "We're by appointment only today," she goes on. "Everyone is, because of the overflow. I mean, it makes sense; there's going to be a lot of fallout from this. A lot of fallout. Have you heard anything? I heard the Over are going to stage a public execution of the attackers. Can you imagine! I'm sure nothing as lewd as a hanging, oh dear no, but something, you know, to show what they can do."

"They've shown what they can do," Omalis says.

"Oh yes, well, I'm only telling you what I've heard." The elevator arrives and the doors swish open with a loud *ding*. "Oh, here you are then. Did you have an appointment, though, or…?"

Omalis enters the elevator and presses the button to close the doors. The silence in the small steel box is almost as inviting as a bullet, as the slow scrape of a knife across her throat.

On the top floor, Omalis finds the waiting area is empty. The large oak double doors of the briefing room are closed. When the Over are ready for you, the doors open. Omalis stands before them and waits, ticking off the seconds by tapping a finger against her wrist.

Her palms begin to sweat. Heat rises from beneath her arms. She wishes for her blazer, to hide the smell. Not that scent matters so much to the Over. The line on her chest where the seatbelt burned her all those days ago begins to throb. Her mouth and throat go dry. The blood in her ears pulses rapidly. She has a few seconds to irrationally regret drinking that tequila, and then the doors open.

Rebecca Hartmeyer walks out. She appears a little dazed but otherwise quite herself. She even smiles at Omalis. She is older by ten years, the wrinkles around her mouth and eyes curving attractively. "We'll get through this," she says, offering Omalis's elbow a quick comradely squeeze. She walks away before Omalis has a chance to ignore her.

In the room, the windows are blacked out. Before the door closes behind her, from the little light bleeding through from the waiting area, Omalis sees the Over, only one of them, who may be but is probably not the same one she sees every time she comes here. There is nothing in the room except for it, and now her. It towers there against the blacked-out windows at the other end of the room, its monstrous nine-foot frame caught in the yellow light from the waiting area, a light that appeared normal out there but is all too sickly in here, gleaming against the slick dark feathers of the thing's wings, which, for the moment, are folded in to hide its talons. At the instant of complete dark, when the click of the door's latch catching reverberates hollowly through the room, the thing's eyes flash bright orange, like the flick of a candle, and flame out.

Omalis doesn't hear it breathing, though of course it breathes, through the holes at the top of its beak, beneath its eyes. It breathes and it moves, but she doesn't hear that either. She is listening to the pounding of her own heart, the rushing of her blood, to which it, of course, also listens. At the moment of contact, Omalis always screams, always, and thanks whatever cruel god created the Over for rendering them without ears.

She screamed as a child, too, the first time. Her birth, kind of like a birth, she thinks, like a rebirth, the first step to becoming a young woman, the young woman they made her into. The young woman her mother forced her to become.

*Wait*, Omalis hears with her little-girl ears, *Wait, wait. Please wait.*

Her mother was pulled out of hiding first, yanked up from beneath the floorboards with no warning, only her screams trailing behind her, exploding into Heaven's own face, where she tried—triedtriedtried—to burrow deeper into the hard earth beneath their kitchen floor. And her own screams bulleting out of her, *ratatatat*, as the sharp talons grabbed her too, ripping through her shirt, stopping just short of her flesh.

And there is her mother, crying, screaming, *Wait*; and there is Omalis, little Heaven Omalis—Heaven Silamo then, before she crossed the ocean and buried her family name as deep as the reversal of a few letters would allow—her mother's last hope, all her faith rolled up into a then-eleven-year-old girl, all of her salvation.

*Wait. Isn't there something, isn't there anything, anything I can give you?*

Little-girl Omalis thought money, little-girl Omalis thought baseball cards, pocket radios, bite-size candy bars, because these were things the boys at school would bully her for, and if she handed these things over, the boys stopped, and if she fought back, the boys kicked harder. And these things were bullies if there ever were bullies, Kings of Bullies, Overlords of Bullies, and if we give them what they want, little-girl Omalis thought, they will leave us alone, even as the houses in her neighborhood burned, even as the sirens wailed and the guns fired and the bombs dropped and the people screamed, Omalis thought it and believed it and prayed it, *Give the bullies what they want and they will leave us alone.*

It never occurred to little-girl Omalis that the Bully Overlords might want *her*. It never occurred to her that her mother would even offer.

That first time, that first connection, Omalis felt the pain not from the thing's teeth, but from her mother's voice, her vacant eyes, her final sobbing words. *Take her, take her. I'm old and worn out. Take her, take her.*

"Take me," the words falling from her mouth as they have a thousand times and will a thousand times more. The Over's claw splays against the base of her neck near her spine, the teeth in its palm opening and piercing her skin, digging something deep into her nerve endings and catching. Her scream dissolves into a whisper and then into a memory. Her senses spiral into a blur as the Over rakes through her mind and takes from her her report. It takes from her mind into the collective mind of the Over all of her memories since her last report: her drunk and vomiting, her angry and fucking, her visiting homes and ripping families apart one pink slip at a time. The things it does not take, the things it can't go deep enough to scrape up, even Omalis is unaware.

When it's finally finished, the suction dies and the mouth slakes off with a slick peeling sound, leaving the back of Omalis's neck red and wet but not bleeding. The bleeding only lasts for the first few times, and Omalis is nothing if not a veteran. The doors open behind her and Omalis turns to exit them on wobbly legs, not wanting to see the thing again. On her way out she gets the message, not in words but in some complex jumble of nerve firings that after all these years she can easily decipher as their voice. *Do not do it again*, referring to the drinking, and, *Keep peace*, referring to the work she must now do to smooth things over with her frightened clients.

As Omalis stumbles out, Blake Jefferson catches her arm and stares at her, agape. "Are…are you okay?"

She looks at him, puzzled that he has to ask. "No," she says. Finally, the truth.

# TEN
## JUNE

IT FEELS LIKE EVERYTHING'S CHANGING, but nothing is. Here I am at the grocery store, trying to remember we only need one box of meatloaf mix now it's just the two of us, and buying two anyway because I guess I'm just that stubborn. Here I am at the check-out counter, resentfully leafing through tabloid and fashion magazines, sneering at the young and the beautiful and the talented who get to keep their youth, beauty and talents until their natural deaths, thinking, My kid could've been you; my kid is a thousand times more young, beautiful and talented. Here I am outside of a Rent-a-Center, plastic bag of meatloaf mix and *USA Today* dangling from one hand, fitting the key in the door of my Civic when all the televisions in the store-front window blare out the news behind me: *The Over swarm above Kyoto....*

Everything is changing. It's Sunday, the streets crowded with shoppers and churchgoers out to brunch, school children playing in sprinklers in the park, riding their bikes in the street, leash-less dogs padding this way and that. We all stop in front of that store-front, paralyzed by the images, the thoughts. Some rush inside the store to hear better, others pick up their children and race home. I watch until the story starts to repeat itself, the blurred images looped around the same disconnected scrawl of ticker tape, and then I get inside the car and I scream.

My phone is already ringing. It's Jay, of course.

"Baby, don't do anything," he says.

"Do anything? Do what, Jay, what would I do?" He's been this way for weeks now, since that thing at the hospital I refuse to think about. It's worse than walking on eggshells—he's trying to hover completely over them. When did I become so frail and yet so dangerous? He's afraid I am going to lash out again, even though I've been taking those antidepressants our doctor prescribed—he knows because he watches me swallow them down each morning, checks under my tongue and everything. He's afraid I will shatter what little stability he believes we still have.

"Just come home, we'll talk about it."

He's thinking, Never should've let her out of the house. Never should have left her side. He should be thinking, Never should have let her take our children away. Never should have even let her get close.

Because we talked about it, talked about it when I first conceived, years before the One Child Rule was enacted, when we didn't have to worry about that decision but there were plenty hard times ahead. We'd been reading about conditioning, how to raise not a child but a statistical probability. Athletes are thirty-two percent less likely to be chosen for camps; children with an extraordinary aptitude for academics are forty-six percent less likely, those exhibiting prodigious musical talents twenty-three percent, or especially proficient in other arts and sciences, fourteen percent. Jay is from farmer stock, a family of laborers, necessary but too prevalent to be special; both of my parents are doctors. With Jason, we pushed him to science but he had no appetite for it—he wanted to play, chase girls, be a kid. Jay was happy, he had his son, his strong boy, to help him, maybe even succeed him. I think he forgot about the camps. But Jeremy reminded him.

Poor Jeremy. He was a crier from the start, normal, weak. My baby. I remember tracing his small infant fingers with my own, measuring his hand against the mold we pressed of his brother's two years earlier. Long fingers, I told Jay, remarkable hands; he'll be remarkable. We tried him on so many instruments, hoping for guitar, praying for cello (the classical string instruments had the highest success rate in keeping kids out of camps). Of course, piano, that's a string instrument too. Jeremy loved it, so much fun; we thought we had it locked, we thought, at least, we had this one saved. But Jeremy, bless him, he didn't like competition, he couldn't take it, got physically sick. That first recital, not even officially up against anyone, seven years old and heaving up his dinner backstage, all the way to the bile then to the blood. Had to take him to the hospital, feed him ice chips. It was a long time before he played again, and then he never played for anyone else. I caught Jay watching him one night, listening to him play something he wrote himself, so sad and longing and gorgeous—and Jay, standing there in shadow in the doorway, just shaking his head, shaking, shaking.

That might have been the night Jay said goodbye, in his heart, but I don't want to believe it.

Now in the car, I tell him, "I'll be right there," and hang up, because I have my own call to make.

When Jordan was born, we didn't even try the conditioning—third time's a charm, they say, but we were exhausted. They instituted One Child only five months after I gave birth to her, so I was just feeling lucky, so undeservedly special. Immediately upon entering school, Jordan wanted to play sports. She tried out for all the teams. I ferried her from practice to practice, game to game, my chest tightening with hope. But then the fights started, and the school gave us the ultimatum—start her on drugs or she's out—and we didn't know what to do. I didn't know what to do. We argued. What's best for her, what's worse? Any kind of psychiatric diagnosis increases probability of selection by twenty percent. Twenty percent! We reasoned, though, that with her behavior under control she could excel at sports. They labeled her with Oppositional Defiant Disorder, gave her a bouquet of little orange bottles I had to refill every few months, and I watched, helplessly, as her enthusiasm for anything other than quarreling with me quickly leaked away from her.

I fish around in my purse for the business card. Someone behind me flashes their lights and beeps a little; they want my metered parking space. I wave them around, single-finger-style.

When Jason was passed up his first year of camp eligibility, we were ecstatic. Maybe we'd done it. Jay and I celebrated. I was half-afraid we might accidentally conceive again, so I slipped our pharmacist a few extra twenties for that morning-after pill. Then Jeremy's year was up and passed unnoticed, and another year gone, and another. Each time, Jay was so happy, but I started to worry; what if this year, or this year, or this one? Until finally it happened, and all at once, and we weren't ready, not one fucking bit.

Our fight before the Liaison's first visit was pathetic. Jay just couldn't—wouldn't—see that our fortune had run dry.

I remember it was late, I was tossing dress after pantsuit after skirt onto the bed, trying to find the right combination that said, Please don't pick my kids, look at the kind of upstanding citizens they will become if they take after their mother, please, reconsider. Jay came in and closed the door, looked at me with this irritated scowl.

"Hon, what are you doing?" He kicked his shoes off into the corner and undid his belt. "All that shit on the bed, I got to get some sleep."

"Our Liaison comes tomorrow," I told him, as if it couldn't be any clearer what I was doing, how important it was to make an impression.

He sighed, dropping trough and unbuttoning his flannel. "It's just the first visit, don't worry about it."

"Are you serious? Are you standing there and actually telling me not to worry about one of those people coming into my home and appraising my kids? Did you get hit with a shovel out there in the field today or something?"

"Calm down, Junebug." He started to push my tossed-about clothes to one side and pull back his corner of the covers. "I'm only saying it's stage one, long way to go before—"

"It's mighty fucking close to me, Jay," I hollered at him, which shut him up fast because my temper is one thing I can usually control, at least around him. "I watch these soulless monsters take children from my hospital every day, every day, like it's just another job, like picking out the best sow for the slaughter."

"June—"

"And now one of them is coming *here*, and I don't know what to *do*, Jay." I piled my discarded outfits together and chucked them at him, threw them on the floor, all around the room. "Tell me what to do to save them, Jay. If your only idea is to wait, then help me pick a color combination because goddammit at least I'm doing *something*."

He threw a salmon blouse right back at me and laughed. "You're deluding yourself."

"I'm what?"

"You really think the Liaison makes any kind of decision? They're pawns, June! They're….they're little more than fucking robots. If the kids are going, they're already on a list somewhere, they're already—"

"Jason, Jeremy, and Jordan."

"What—"

"Jason, Jeremy and Jordan. If you're going to condemn them so easily at least call them by the names you fucking gave them."

"I'm not condemning anyone."

"You're not doing much of any goddamn thing—"

"What do you want me to—"

"—except standing there in your underwear like some—"

"—if I could do something I'd do it—"

"—fucking idiot ready to just let them take our babies—"

"—no one's taking anyone, goddammit June—"

"—goddammit Jay, I'm scared!"

"I'm scared too!"

His voice stole my own straight from my throat, the way it boomed and broke, like a gunshot, like a bomb. The room vibrated with percussive silence.

After a time, he said, "We can send them away."

Eileen and Ben Stockton tried that with their kids two years ago. One day the whole family is in church and the next their thirteen-year-old twin boys are gone, reported missing, posters up all over town. Except someone found out, somehow; a distant relative of Eileen's had them in his basement for two weeks before the police showed up and arrested him. The parents didn't want to admit to what they'd done, so they pressed kidnapping charges and the kids went to the camps anyway. When they didn't come back, Eileen and Ben confessed to the entire plot.

"We'll be smart about it," my husband told me, reading the look so easily behind my vulnerable eyes. "Keep 'em moving, in one place no more than a week, maybe not even together."

"I don't have enough family...."

"We have plenty of friends who—"

"What kind of life is it, though? The risk to everyone else—"

"You wanted ideas, that's all I have."

In this next silence, Jay bent to pick up a pair of my slacks and began folding them, placed them neatly on the bed.

"I like the blue top," he said finally.

"I'll kill for them," I told him.

"June—"

"I'll kill to keep them, I swear to god I will."

I would have gone on like that, except his hands touched my face and his lips stopped mine. I cried into him until I wasn't sure which were his tears and which came from my eyes. I wanted to push him away but he was all I had in that moment, and he is all I have now, and I resent it, I regret it.

I will change it.

Omalis picks up on the second ring. I don't know how to begin. "Miss Omalis, this is June Fontaine, I...."

"You saw the news," she guesses.

"Yes, it was...it's..."

"It's a lot to take in right now, Mrs. Fontaine, of course it is." She's so irritatingly professional. "I can assure you that this incident will in no way affect the safety and well being of your children. Should you need further assurance—"

"I need further assurance."

"Would you like to meet?"

A sudden, asphyxiating gravity blooms inside my chest. I'm nodding, shutting my eyes against this new, foreign pain.

"Mrs. Fontaine, are you still there?"

"Y-yes." I swallow. "Yes, I'd like to meet."

"I can be at your house in—"

"No, no. Not there. The house is…it's a mess. Completely trashed. Been a little, um, preoccupied. A restaurant, or maybe, let's see, a park or…some place public."

"I understand. I'll text you an address, meet you in thirty minutes." She hangs up in a single breath. Seconds later, my phone alerts me of a new text. I would call Jay and tell him I'd be late but I don't know how late I'll be, or if I will be back at all.

The jerk behind me bleats his horn again. Guess he doesn't understand sign language. I pull out of the space and wave him in, smiling.

Omalis chose the lobby bar of some ritzy upscale hotel twenty miles outside of town near the airport, the kind of place whose clients are too well-groomed to express emotion over the day's events, the staff too well-trained. It's hard to even tell if anyone's heard anything—it's like a warm bubble of afternoon champagne and business trip dalliances. I feel on edge; I feel like a needle.

Of course I'm early. No—check my watch—right on time. Why do I always forget she plays these games too. Even her business card, writing her personal number on the back—that's a game, too, and I'm not the only player.

I scan the lobby bar, the red leather booths empty save for me, in a corner, red-shaded lamp an inch above my head, beaming its dim light down on my seltzer water. There's a trio of suits at the bar, a TV on but as far away from breaking news as you can get—a prerecorded airing of last year's sports highlights. The bartender, a woman about my age, wipes out glasses and stacks them under the counter. Faceless people pass by beyond the porthole windows of the bar's double doors but I try not to look that way. I don't want to see her coming, I just want her to appear. The difference between dying by a cancer or by a bullet.

I can't stop seeing their faces in my mind. Can't stop hearing their voices. Only what I'm seeing and what I'm hearing isn't fond, isn't even pleasantly indifferent—it's the last time I saw them. That damned last day. Jordan's welt a condemnation, Jeremy's tears a reminder, Jason's stoicism a burial. How could I let them be taken away from me? How could any of us let this happen?

When I read the names of the countless dead from today's massacre in tomorrows newspaper, I guess I'll have my answer. In the meanwhile, fuck this seltzer; I order a Tom Collins.

Fifteen minutes late, Omalis sashays in on her cell phone, speaking in hushed tones, hangs up before she reaches me. She's wearing black slacks, a plain white top, subtle makeup. I'm still wearing my errand-running yoga pants, track jacket top. She signals the bartender and the woman meets us at the table.

"What's your drink?"

I eye Omalis. She eyes the drink. She tells the bartender, "Another Tom Collins."

I'm tempted to slow-clap her small deductive feat, but the impulse calls to mind Jordan's face, her trigger-happy palms whenever Jeremy painted by the numbers completely in the lines—so proud of himself—and her there, slow-clapping him back into perspective. Now I'm tempted to cry.

Omalis sits across from me, our knees miles apart beneath the table. She folds her hands atop the marble as if I should be reassured by her transparency.

"What can I do to get them back?"

"There is nothing you can do, Mrs. Fontaine. You have to wait—"

"Bullshit. Don't pretend like you don't strike deals—"

"I don't strike deals."

"—all the time, behind closed doors, for the rich, or someone who has something you need. What the Over need."

"I do not wish to indulge you."

"For fuck's sake, will you speak to me like a person? Like a god-fucking-damn human being?"

The others in the bar turn to look. She's unflappable, almost smug.

"You are still human, aren't you?"

"Mrs. Fontaine, your children are safe—"

"I think you have the wrong definition of that word."

"I understand you're upset, but if you insist on interrupting—"

"I insist."

We stare through the silence at each other. Her drink is delivered, and she slides it next to mine with the back of her hand.

"You think I don't know anything about you, Miss Omalis. You think you're as a ghost in this. The Holy Spirit, delivering souls to Heaven."

"No."

"No? Right. You don't believe that shit. Because you're a smart lady, intelligent. You haven't been brainwashed. By fear, maybe—we all have—but not by belief." I take a long drink, dribbling a little on my chin, not bothering to wipe it away. "You survived the war."

"Is that a question?"

I shake my head. "Bet I know how."

"You're a lot like your daughter, Mrs. Fontaine." She raises an eyebrow, quirks her mouth annoyingly. "She's quite inquisitive herself. Strong-willed, as well."

I ignore this, that she could know anything about my child, who she is or how alike we are. Instead, I push out the things I know about her in a barely-contained fury.

"You bargained for your life, or someone did. You couldn't have been very old—" I look her over "—maybe eleven, twelve. So someone bargained for you. Someone begged the Over for your life and they gave it to you—or some semblance of it. Because they're willing to deal, even if you aren't. So... Take me to them. I'll negotiate face to...in person, if you refuse to do it."

She sits so still, but I can tell she is thinking about all I've said. There's a shift, not in her face or her eyes, but in her entire being. It's a quaking not seen but only felt, separating the air around us, pulling all oxygen closer to her and exhaling it in measured shards, cutting her as it escapes. I can't see it, but she bleeds.

"Yes," she says. Her voice is changed, more raw yet somehow more guarded. "My life was bargained for."

"Then you can understand."

"Yes."

"And you'll take me to one of them?"

"No."

I nearly dive at her, my elbow grazing the glasses on the table, upsetting them. "If I strike at you, they'll come, they'll—" She grabs my wrist, eases it down to the safety of the table top.

"I will take your offer to them," she says. "But, June, you cannot think of this as hope. Do you understand? Whatever it is I can give to you, it will not be that."

"I believe you."

God help me, I believe.

# E L E V E N
## J O R D A N

OMALIS. God fucking dammit.

A week ago, hundreds of people die, thousands, just like that, like you blink and there's a corpse, there're a hundred corpses, and more to come. Not even enough time to scream. Here at the camp, we have plenty of time, six long weeks—down to two now— to scream our throats raw if we want to, if we want to make that kind of trouble for ourselves, very well. But those clueless people, all those average Janes and Joes never did anything worth the end they got. They only had time to think, I should run, and then, nothing. Not one fucking thing.

We watched it on TV, all of us in the dining hall. Our counselors wheeled in this huge television and switched on the news before anything had even happened yet, because they knew, they knew what was going to happen. Just when I think these people can't get any sicker. What were we supposed to do after we saw that? Go back to our arts and crafts projects? We cried, or we hugged each other, or pleaded to talk to our parents. We screamed. Well, I didn't.

They herded us back to our cabins after the showing, where I went straight for the bathroom and pried up the loose tile. No thoughts for the razor, but I'd stashed my pills there, and if I ever needed what good ol' American psychiatric science could give me, now was the time. I took three, just to make sure they'd work. Calm me down, keep my head on straight, my mouth shut tight. No need to stir things up, at least this week.

It was hard that day and night, with all the noise, all those girls talking under around and over each other, cycling from anger to despair and back again. How gravely pointless. Taylor spent the night in my bed, just kind of curled against me and stony silent. I'd like to say it was welcome and warm, but really it was just kind of nothing, kind of a cold, hard nothing. And the next day, all these girls with their bloodshot eyes and puffy cheeks were led right out to the flagpole to start their day like nothing had changed, like we should forget what we saw and continue on because what choice do we have. Except that things had changed, and the counselors knew it, and the guards knew it, that was why they had handguns now.

The guns were handcuffed to the guards' wrists through the trigger guard. These I call guards because they are not our counselors, they're new. They wear riot gear, helmets with bulletproof visors, and lead-plated body suits. A few of the girls resumed their crying at the mere sight of these new people, who slowly took up their positions, surrounding us. One of the counselors took up a bullhorn and called for attention. No pledge of allegiance this morning.

"Campers," shouted the bullhorn. "In response to yesterday's unfortunate events, the Over have instituted several policy changes effective immediately. Their authority has been disrespected, and in turn, ours, as your caregivers and mentors during your stay here, has also been undermined. In a show of solidarity expressing your willingness to continue your respectful cooperation with the Over during all camp procedures, we hereby order all of you to surrender any and all personal possessions."

Puzzlement enshrouded the group. We looked around, clearly missing something, as all our personal possessions were confiscated on the bus we took to get here.

Our gracious host clarified, "This means your attire."

It's not like we all hadn't been naked in front of each other before—like when we first met, exchanging our civvies for our prison uniforms under duress—but this was different. Purposely cruel instead of going through the motions. I scanned the crowd for Taylor; somehow we got separated on the trek out here and I lost her. All around the field, the girls started to react, breaking free of their shocked stasis in a fit of collective denial. And at the edge of it all, in our periphery and at our shoulders, the guards with their guns. It was almost welcoming, certainly fitting. Finally not hiding anymore.

"If you do not comply immediately," the counselor calmly explained, and a clicking like a thousand beetles thundering their mandibles swallowed us—the guards thumbing back their hammers. They took aim at the outer rim of girls. "Measures will be taken."

Just do it, I thought, just come right out and murder us already. End this waiting around bullshit, just—

"Oh Jesus oh shit."

It was Taylor, right beside me as if she'd been there all along, pressing her shoulder into mine and grabbing for my fingers, which I realized as she touched my knuckles had been balled into tight fists. Her skin was slack and pale, the shadows under her eyes like bruises, courtesy of the sleep she couldn't chase down.

"Now!" shouted the bullhorn, and shrieks erupted, thinking this was the call for the guards to open fire. But they held fast, and the outer rim of girls tried to push into the middle, and I thought, this must be what fear smells like, sweat made potent with desperation, thick streaks of saline on plump and reddened cheeks. So sharp and so sweet. No wonder the Over love us so much.

Now everyone was pushing, elbows jabbed there, knees stabbing here, and there were a lot of screaming voices, until, finally, someone started undressing and everyone stopped to watch her. She took her clothes off slowly, kind of defiant but really just crying away the whole time, shaking so much I thought she'd fall down, but she stripped herself to nothing and walked right up to a guard and held her pile of clothes for him. When he didn't take it, she laid it gently at his feet and stepped, calmly as she could manage through the sobbing, back into the circle. And just like that, the other girls fell in line, following her stoic example.

Taylor let my hand go and slipped her thumbs under the waistband of her sweats. "Jordan, don't look at me, okay?"

We stood back to back and undressed.

Soon there was a jumble of clothes on the ground and everyone was too scared or too ashamed to look at anyone or anything other than the pistols still pointed at their faces. Even though the counselors eyed us, there were too many bodies, too much pink and brown and tan and white flesh to see through to our scars. Mine, I didn't care so much about, they already knew it was there, but I felt some anxiety for Taylor's, so small yet so glaring on the outside of her hip. I hoped she had the presence of mind to at least try to cover it with her hand.

A kind of angry yet resigned silence descended upon us. The guards lowered their guns. You could almost hear the birds gabbing away in the distant trees.

The counselor raised the bullhorn. "Thank you," she said. "That wasn't so hard. You see, things do not have to be so difficult. We're all here to get through this. It can be easy and as painless as possible, or it can be like this. Please get dressed."

Silently, we complied.

As we dressed, the bullhorn continued to bleat out: "Tonight, we will enact one of our new policies. A lottery that is to be repeated each night for the duration of your stay. In addition, nutrition will now only be provided every other day, on reduced rations, until we, and the Over, feel you fully understand how important is your obedience. Until this evening, you are to report to your group mentor who will dole out your examination assignments for the afternoon. Dismissed."

At first no one moved. Then, slowly, as the guards cautiously turned their backs to us and marched away, our crowd began to disperse in all directions, heading for their group buildings as instructed.

I wanted to vomit. I reached my hand out behind me to try for Taylor's but all I got was air. She was gone, and I caught sight of the back of her plodding off to catch up with her group. I watched her until she disappeared around the dining hall. And then I found my group and followed them.

Later, after a late morning track and field session with my fellow group mates—a solemn affair, although Thirty-three did clock her best sprint time which usually sends her and her friends into mutual masturbatory giggles of admiration, but only got a polite perfunctory clap this time—my legs on fire and my stomach beginning to feel its emptiness, I caught up with Taylor outside the boathouse. I saw her bum a cigarette from her favorite counselor and duck inside, while the counselor moved off toward the lake. There was a guard patrolling around the shore, handcuffed gun rattling against his thigh, but he was heading away from the boathouse and the counselor joined him. I waited for them to get a little further along the shoreline before I followed after Taylor.

She was leaning her back against a wall, flicking ash onto a fallen bird's nest at her feet. On the floorboards right beside it were the three little swallows, their scraggly necks broken or their internal organs burst from the fall, or maybe starved if their mother couldn't find them, I don't know, but anyway, they were dead. It was such a pitiful thing to see, I couldn't even breathe.

"Why didn't you do something?" Taylor's voice was low, directed at the tiny bird corpses, so that I thought she was talking to them until she actually looked up at me.

"What do you mean?"

"Earlier today, at the flagpole." She pulled at the cigarette and held in the smoke.

"I...I don't know. Nobody did anything. There wasn't anything anyone could do."

She let the smoke out in a haphazard billow. "Yeah, there hasn't been anything anyone can do since we got here, but you still did something. On the bus, when you just tossed your shoes out the window like it was nothing—"

I almost gasped but tightened my jaw. I didn't know she'd been there for that, or the humiliation that followed.

"—and confronting your bitch mentor during group—one of the other girls told me about that. And *this*—" She took two broad steps toward me and lifted my shirt to reveal my name. I jerked away from her instinctively.

"See?" She went on. "You're always doing something, some small 'fuck you,' even if it doesn't change anything, even if you know it won't save you because nothing can. But today. You just stood there, like everyone else."

I can't really say exactly what I felt right then after she said all that, but it was somewhere in the vicinity of how I felt that time Mom found one of Jason's joints in my sock drawer and wouldn't let up about it for, like, a week. It wasn't really my fault but I took the blame because she was so mad, and not just mad, I mean, I'd never heard her like that, like really overcome, like she just couldn't believe it, how stupid I could be or how callous. She just kept saying, "What about your brother? What if Jeremy had found this?" Like he'd even know what to do with it, but whatever. Yeah, she was upset and, I guess the term is, beside herself, and it made me feel, I don't even know, responsible or something. Culpable. Even though the joint wasn't even mine. Anyway, when Taylor said that to me, I just, I felt the same way, or somewhere close, and I didn't know how to respond to her.

She kept her eyes on me as she finished her cigarette and stubbed it out on the floorboards. I sighed, saying finally, "Taylor... Those guys had guns. It was too much, you know?"

"Yeah. Yeah, it's all too much, it's all been too much." She turned away from me and bent down near the bird's nest. Extending an index finger, she slowly stroked the dead swallow's spine.

"You read any science fiction?"

The change of subject threw me and I lost my voice. She went on, "Well, there's this story I read once a long time ago. I remember I liked it a lot back then."

As she talked, she scooped up the swallow in one hand, flipped the nest right side up with the other, and gently placed the bird back inside the nest. "The part I liked best was when these guys, these space explorers, discovered a new planet inhabited by these cow-like creatures. They were really docile and complacent, so much so that when these other creatures attacked them, they just lay down—literally—and let it happen."

She scooped up the second swallow and placed it beside its twin. "So these explorers, they're like appalled, they're like, What is this? You just let yourselves die? They just can't believe it, one guy in particular. He makes it his personal mission to teach these docile creatures how to take up arms and fight back. He convinces them, and then the next time the attackers come for them, they counterattack."

The final swallow laid in the nest, Taylor picked up the whole thing and held it in front of her, talking to it. "And these docile cow-like creatures, they're decimated, just completely annihilated, never had a chance. If they hadn't resisted only a few would've died, but fighting back, starting a war, wiped out almost their entire population."

She looked up at me. "Needless to say, the explorer guy was thoroughly embarrassed."

I laughed at her deadpan delivery, and she laughed, but then she turned sad again. "Will you help me bury this?"

We took the birds outside and dug in the soft earth near the shore, along the far side of the boathouse, out of sight of the patrolling guard and his counselor friend, but not the ever-watchful eye of the black orb hanging from an exposed rafter. Dirt caked beneath our fingernails and filled the cracks in the skin of our palms. We placed the birds in the shallow hole and covered them with the loose dirt, stamping it tightly over them until you could barely tell the grave was there. We sat next to each other with our legs crossed, our knees touching, looking at the dirt.

"I guess it gave me some hope," Taylor said. "Whenever you'd go against them." She shrugged. "That's all."

Anyone else I'd probably say something like, There is no hope, but for Taylor, four weeks ago hope was a razor blade smuggled inside her vagina, and now it's me, so instead I said, "There's a good chance you won't be picked for any of the programs. One of the lucky thirty-three percent who get to go home."

She shook her head. "No, not me. I'm probably one of the few girls here who still has a fully functioning uterus."

I hadn't thought about it before, but she was probably right. To avoid being chosen for Breeding, a lot of girls' parents would elect to have them undergo illegal and not altogether safe hysterectomies, supposing they could find a trusted surgeon who didn't charge too much. Since being here at camp, I've overheard quite a few stories of girls dying under scalpels wielded by their own mothers who couldn't afford or find a willing surgeon and refused to risk their daughters' fate. Some parents fed their kids anti-growth hormones or testosterone injections to delay their menstruation; you could spot these girls easily enough because they were usually short and not even into training bras by fourteen. And then there were girls like me, whose biology dictated a late start.

"Plus, I'm wicked hot." Taylor bopped me lightly on the knee with her fist and laughed. "It's Breed for me, for sure."

"Don't say that."

"No worries, I have my back-up plan."

"Okay, don't say that either."

We sat in comfortable silence for a minute. Birds made plaintive or furtive calls all around us. I imagined one must belong to the mother of the swallows we just buried. Calling for them, or calling for another mate to start again.

Taylor poked at my stomach. "Can I see it?"

"Why?"

She shrugged. "I want to see how it's healing."

I rolled up my shirt. The scar was fainter, not as red, starting to scab over at its thicker angles.

Taylor started to trace the scar with her fingers but I felt it someplace else entirely and quickly shoved my shirt back down.

"Want to see mine?"

Before I could say no, she shifted her knees underneath her and rolled down the top of her sweats. She'd cut the letters of her name much smaller than she did mine, all in lowercase and not deep at all; it was faded and barely raised from the skin anymore.

"Here, feel." She grabbed my wrist and touched my hand to her flesh before I could protest. I felt her warmth and thought of Omalis: her thighs closed around my waist, fingers putting pressure on my wrists as I squirmed beneath her, peppermint breath burning not unwelcome against my cheek. I blushed but Taylor wouldn't let me pull my hand away.

"Do you like me, Jordan?"

"What?"

The memory is somewhat of a blur now, even though everything happened so slowly when she did it. She closed her eyes and pressed her lips against mine, and pushed her tongue into my mouth. My first kiss and I was so under-prepared. I didn't know at all what to do so I think I kind of just went limp. Taylor held my face in her hands and kept at it until I finally stopped worrying about what the hell I was supposed to be doing and concentrated on what she was doing, and copied her. That seemed to work, and I think I got the hang of it. I remember the wetness of her, how unexpected it was, how indescribable. Most of all I remember how, the whole time, I was never fully in the moment; I wasted the entirety of our first kiss on thoughts of Omalis, on what her mouth might taste like and what miraculous situation might lead to me being able to find out.

When the kiss ended, Taylor asked me if that was okay. I don't remember if I nodded or just said yes or even if I said no, but she kissed me again. She laid me back on the grass and ran her hands over me, under my shirt and over my scar. I felt the dirt from her hands slip into the creases of my skin. She whispered something breathily into my ear, something like "you're beautiful" or "you're wonderful," but I was back on the side of the road near that sound barrier, and hearing only, "Calm down, Jordan. Calm down."

Eventually, the loudspeaker interrupted us with its bellowing announcement that groups were to meet in five minutes. We stood up and Taylor looked at me for the first time as if she were shy.

"You're the only good thing about all this shit," she said, and walked away.

I didn't know what to think. Now, here in this suffocating space of hindsight, I hate myself for not thinking more about Taylor and what kissing me meant to her, or what it might mean to me. I'm in this windowless, endlessly bright room, completely empty except for the hard cot I'm sitting on, and I'm trying hard as hell to remember what Taylor's tongue felt like or what her hands were doing or how she smelled, but I'm coming up all peppermint, peppermint, peppermint.

Nothing else significant happened that day, until the evening, when they drew our numbers in the lottery. I still have the bruises but it has only been a few days, I think.

They gathered all of us into the dining hall, only the tables and chairs and everything had been removed, replaced by a make-shift wrestling ring comprised of a rubber mat cordoned off by rough ropes wrapped around four upright punching bags. The lady with the bullhorn was back, Bertha I've decided, and a couple of guards to round out the evening. The counselors ushered us all into the room until we surrounded the ring, some of us with better views than the shorter girls. I don't know about anyone else but I could tell what all this new equipment meant before Bertha broke it down for us.

"As previously stated, we are adopting several new practices here, and one of those is this lottery." Another counselor handed her a bucket filled to the brim with folded scraps of paper. "We will draw two of your numbers every night for the remainder of your stay, and if you don't want to go immediately to the Feed Program—" sharp intakes of startled breath all around "—you *will* enter this ring and box each other."

Some "What the hells," a few scattered "I can't believes."

"You will box, bare knuckle, for two minutes. Bear in mind that your performance is under scrutiny and will play a large role in determining your placement at the end of the Summer Program."

And there was no further ado. She plumbed deep into the bucket, dislodging a handful of paper slips, and read out two numbers. Ninety-six, and Fifteen.

The crowds parted accusatorially, opening up for the contenders to make their way to the stage. Ninety-six reached it first, a lanky girl with blond hair and eyes red from crying. She stood in a corner and rubbed her palms compulsively against her thighs.

I found Taylor in the crowd, on the opposite side of the ring, not moving even though a path had opened for her. Some of the girls closest to her patted her shoulders, offering whispered assurances while trying to push her closer to the ring. Her eyes were wide and unblinking, her mouth open.

"Fifteen, you will now enter the ring," instructed Bertha. "Or be immediately escorted to the Feed Program."

Taylor didn't even blink at this, just stood there, her face betraying nothing. I couldn't understand what she was doing, if she really was scared into a sort of paralysis at the thought of being forced to fight this other girl, or if she was making a stand, or... waiting for me to do something. My chest tightened. Okay.

"I'll do it," I yelled, raising my hand enthusiastically and practically bouncing up to the ring. "Pick me, I'll do it, I want to."

Bertha stuttered into her bullhorn, "You-your number was not drawn."

"Make an exception," I said.

"Remove yourself from the ring at once or I will instruct the guards to open fire—"

Or she said something equally threatening like that, but I'm not too sure because I was no longer listening. I was striding across the mat, staring a frightened, waif-thin stranger two years older than me in her bloodshot eyes and pulling my elbow back, readying my right hook. She took the punch well, better than Jeremy can take a friendly stiff-arm even, didn't fall or anything, but of course I'd thrown it soft, just trying to get things going. I barely registered any sounds around me, or registered it all in bursts, like fireworks popping all around me, and then she came at me—hard. I must've torn the scab off her emotional scarring because she just let loose, crying and screaming and pummeling and kicking. Her form was shit but she had me on the ropes in no time, arms up to protect my face, bent forward to shield my precious internal organs. Perhaps I hadn't thought this through.

I was certain she'd drop me well under the two-minute time limit, but it was a bullet from behind that did it. The small of my back burst open and my knees hit the mat, wet with my own urine. I'd never felt pain like that, thought I was dying, but still alive enough to feel ashamed that I'd just pissed myself in front of so many people, in front of Taylor. When the second bullet splintered my shoulder I had a split second to feel grateful before my head hit the mat and I blacked out.

I came to in the infirmary tent, half expecting to see that strange woman again, the resistance fighter. I didn't really realize how much I'd wanted to see her until a real nurse came in instead. She told me I wasn't dying, that in fact those bullets were rubber, like the kind the police used to shoot at rioters back when anyone bothered to protest anything. I'd be bruised and pissing blood for awhile, and in quite a bit of pain because she said she couldn't give me anything for it, but at least nothing was broken. She wouldn't tell me anything else, just let me lie there, feeling the throbbing degrees of my pain as it fluctuated between a manageable dullness and nausea-swelling acuteness, depending on how I breathed. I didn't even know if my intervention had helped Taylor at all, or if they made her fight anyway, or if she didn't fight and was taken away, or if now I'd be taken away, although that didn't really concern me because I figured they wouldn't bother with an infirmary stint if that were the case.

After one night spent in the tent, sleeping fitfully and peeing with a catheter, they let me go the next day because I had a visitor. At the time, I was grateful for being out of bed, even though it hurt slightly to walk, but they let me use an actual bathroom on the way to the meeting rooms and there was only a moderate amount of blood in my urine. Five minutes alone in that room with Omalis, though, and I wanted to go back to that tent, to that ring, to anywhere but there.

But, of course, I was happy to see her.

She looked different, dressed down in a red v-neck t-shirt and dark blue jeans, no makeup or discernible perfume, her hair up in a ponytail that barely managed to keep all the hair in. She was standing beside the table when I came in, her arms crossed, and she didn't invite me to sit. Her naked lips frowned at the corners, her eyes narrowed.

"I'm quite disappointed in you," she said.

"Funny how much I don't care," I shot back, even as my heart started up with its annoying racing. I could feel my neck heat up with the tentative beginnings of a blush, and I realized how gross I must look, in two-day-old unlaundered sweats (though someone had changed out my pants while I was passed out); my tangled hair; unwashed, doughy skin swelling with fresh bruises. I couldn't smell myself but that didn't mean I didn't reek, especially without her usual combo of scents to mask my odor.

"Sit down," she said.

"It kind of hurts to sit."

"Funny how much I don't care," she mimicked, but she didn't say it angrily and she couldn't even get through it without faltering into a smirk. Which, goddammit, made me smile too.

She shook her head. "You are unbelievably stubborn."

I shrugged, trying to fix my face back into some indifferent expression.

"Well, I suppose there's no need to ask you how everything is going."

I could sense that laughing was only going to hurt my kidneys so I swallowed instead, which wasn't much better.

"I'm compiling quite an impressive file of your reckless theatrics," she said. No matter how her voice changed as she spoke to me, a higher inflection or a throaty down-swing, her eyes stayed steady on me. I can't say whether or not she even blinked because I was trying real hard not to look *her* in the eye, but without being obvious about it. "There's actually a pool going among the mentors to guess what sort of disruption you'll cause next. No one bet on this latest, I might add."

Gambling folk, my kind of people. Something in common with my captors after all. Was this the onset of that Stockholm thing Taylor was talking about the other night?

"I suppose I shouldn't refer to your stunts as 'theatrics,' or even as 'stunts,' really. In truth, I find them quite brave."

Thump thump thump thump. Every vein in my body started goddamn thump-thump-thumping.

"It isn't much of a morale boost for the others, but it is something. It means something for them to see someone, one of their own, still fighting, in whatever way she can. But you aren't really doing it for them, are you?"

My scar itched. All my bruises ached and my mouth filled with the memory of Taylor, and I became aware of having to pee again.

"Parents visit next week," she said, her jump in topic so surprising I almost voided right there. "Don't suppose you will be giving them too many details of your days, hm?"

The words struggled thickly out of my wet mouth, "Isn't that your job?"

"Your secrets are safe with me."

More thumping. What could she know about my secrets? I wished I'd been able to get to my pills that day, calmed down my head spinning all sorts of scenarios, my body reacting to them.

"Are you even going to inquire about your friend?"

My brow knit a dubious line, my mouth forming the word but no sound escaping before she clarified: "Taylor Reed. You two are…."

She paused just long enough to drop her arms nonchalantly to her sides and lean in with her a head a bit more, arching one delicately tweezed eyebrow.

"…close."

"I don't want to talk about Taylor." My palms started to sweat. I wiped them on my pants, where I hoped they didn't leave a dark streak on the gray.

Then something changed in Omalis, something shifted. She seemed to decide something, straightening up and closing her eyes, only a second longer than a calculating blink, and when she opened them—there, there it was, the change. Somehow. Something. She took a step forward, edging around the table that separated us.

"She's rather pretty." Her voice was different, deeper, further away. It sounded almost familiar. "Older than you, but you like them older."

"I don't know what—"

"It's all right. It's natural, especially in a place like this, under these circumstances, to seek comfort in someone else. Someone…warm."

I could feel the heat crawling over my entire body, the ceaseless thumping now in my ears as they filled with the rushing sound of blood. She continued to step forward, and I matched her pace, stepping back.

"I am happy for you. Though, truthfully, I must confess, I am also disappointed. I thought you had a crush on me."

Oh god. I hit a wall, nowhere to go. All that heat, all that noise inside my head, snapped away. Just cold, just silence, except she was still talking.

"You made me that bracelet and all."

"S-stop it."

I closed my eyes but I couldn't disappear. She could still see me. Fuck, she could still see me.

"And how you tried to flirt, playing coy. It was…precious. Though as much as I will miss it, I should say I am also grateful. I feared one day, had it kept up, I would be forced to turn you down."

Breathing got hard, stopped all together. There was red behind the blackness of my eyelids. I tried to push into the wall, but there was nowhere to hide. She wouldn't shut up.

"Gently, of course. Perhaps if you were a mite older, somewhere around Taylor's age, I could consider an affair. But you, Jordan…you are only a child."

I couldn't stop it. She was right in front of me, right there. I could feel the moisture of her breath on my closed eyes and she wouldn't stop talking, she was even—oh god—laughing a little, she wouldn't shut up and I couldn't—I wouldn't—listen, didn't want to listen, had to make her stop stop stop—

"—Stop!"

I launched myself from the wall, hands out and grabbing her shirt, pulling, twisting around—how great her look of surprise, the force of the wall as I slammed her into it, and the heat of her throat beneath my hands as I gripped and pressed pressed pressed.

"Shut up." The words spit out between my teeth. Crying, always crying. "I hate you. Shut up shut up—"

Faster than I've ever seen anyone move, even in the movies, she took hold of both my wrists and twisted, the pain electric and sure. She thrust one hand against my shoulder, the one that had already been shot, spinning me around while still keeping hold of my wrist, forcing me to the floor. A knee in my back and my stretched arm on fire until she got the zip-tie secure around my wrists. She went to the intercom on the wall and spoke into it, not even out of breath, as I lay there, trying to bury my face in the linoleum.

So now I'm here, in "detention," and I'm unsure how long it's been. They keep the lights in the twenty-foot-high ceiling burning full power around the clock; it's all the same day to me, and none of it really matters anymore anyway.

I sit upright in bed when I hear a jingle of keys at the door. No one's been to see me since some burly old lady tossed me in here. I haven't eaten in…let me count the grumbles….feels like weeks. I stand up when the woman enters my room and places a thin sheet of paper between the door and the jamb so it won't lock us both in here. It's the woman from the infirmary tent, the resistance fighter. Marla.

"Sorry it's been so—Oh my god—" Her face contorts into worry mid-sentence as she turns toward me.

The words swell in my throat but I choke them out anyway. "Okay, I want to do it. I'm in. I'll join your mission."

"What happened to your face?" She steps a little closer, hands outstretched to examine my bruises.

"Didn't you hear me?"

"Who did this to you?" A shadow passes over her eyes. "Did your Liaison do this?"

"What? No. Who cares. Look, I'm saying I'm in, I'll do it, be your puppet or whatever. Aren't you hearing me?"

"Yes, I'm hearing you, but I'm also seeing you. What have they been doing to you? Have you received any medical treatment at all? If I'd known—"

"How would you have known?" She has no answer for me. "Anyway, didn't you see a bunch of brand spankin' new guards as you snuck in? With their shiny new toy guns. I acted up and they shot me down."

"They *shot* you?"

"Rubber bullets." Painfully, I rotate my shoulder. "I'll live. Now, can we talk about what you came here to talk about?"

She thinks for a minute, shakes her head to process what I told her, to make it jibe with whatever image she's been holding inside of what goes on in these camps. Finally, she motions me to the spare cot. "Let's sit down. We'll get to why I came here, but first I'd like to hear about what's been happening in here."

"Why?" I ask as I comply with her hand gesture. She sits next to me. "Things have gotten worse. But what can you do about it?"

"You're right, I can't do anything. I just thought—"

"How is it out there, in the world? They let us—forced us, more like—watch the carnage on TV when it happened, but we haven't heard anything else. What's going on?"

"It's chaos, but it's a sort of controlled chaos. The Over have us at a distinct disadvantage, they always have. But it certainly brings down morale when we're reminded of this. No one has done anything stupid, no counterattacks, no threats. Everyone is afraid but that's nothing new."

"How many people died?"

She swallows, makes like she is going to avoid my eye by delivering the number to the threadbare sheet, then looks back up at me. "Thirty-two hundred and twelve."

"Jesus...." My eyes fill up. It's such a large number, I have trouble picturing it. Marla lets the silence go on for a moment, then says, "It gets worse. Three of the mentors thought to be the prime instigators of the attack on those Liaisons were released from the Feed Program into the custody of the U.N. There were several riots, hypocritically peaceful rallies calling for justice, for blood. The people wanted the three individuals to hang. The U.N. decided to grant the people their wish, more or less. The mentors were given lethal injections yesterday afternoon. It was entirely public. Local news stations rebroadcast the segment throughout the day."

I look at the thin bed linen, the empty space between us. I think about my counselors here, the twisted face of Bullhorn Bertha with a needle in her arm, death in her eyes, not talking now. And all those people dead in the streets of Japan, filling it up like a flood.

"Makes sense," I say.

"If you think that, maybe I shouldn't be here."

"I'm not saying it was right, it wasn't right, but what's right anymore? No one can do what's right, we're too weak, they're too strong."

"No. We've forgotten what is right. We've allowed ourselves to forget."

In the following silence, Marla looks down at her hands folded in her lap. Her thumb absently scratches at the wrist of her sleeve, pushing it up to reveal the edges of her faded tattoo. *This too shall pass.*

"Tell me the story," I say, pointing at the ink.

"Oh. Right." She rolls down her sleeve and holds her arm up to examine the tattoo, as if she hasn't seen it before.

"You know, Jordan, there is a lot of human history you will never have the opportunity to learn, even if you decide against joining the Resistance. I regret that."

"So teach me something."

Marla smiles, drops her arm back into her lap and sighs. "I'm afraid neither of us has the time for a proper lesson right now. The abridged answer is that it's a phrase with multiple meanings, each applying to a separate yet interconnected piece of who I am, historically, culturally, and biologically."

I give her a quizzical stare. She laughs.

"They had these camps when I was growing up, too, you know. They'd been around for several years by then; statistics were becoming very popular. I was one of the lucky ones in that I made it out, but was unfortunate enough to have gone through one in the first place. I'm sure their tactics have advanced in the intervening years, become more…efficient. But it was plenty unpleasant. No one left that place unscarred, one way or another. I was fifteen when I went through, sixteen several weeks later when I was released, and I didn't know how to deal. I saw a psychologist or two and they concluded I was suffering from survivor's guilt; why me? Why didn't I die too? What makes me so special?

"Eventually, I figured out the answer. Nothing. My suffering is no different from anyone else's, except that it is mine. And it doesn't have to be meaningless. To get yourself through the worst of any situation you have to convince yourself it will end, and that you will see it through to that end.

"So these words are inked into my skin, which will decompose and become dust or soil or whatever after I die. My body will pass, if you will. The tattoo is a symbol, or a reminder, that there is something greater than me or my own suffering out there, something beyond the physical."

"God?"

She nods. "Or another world, or an entire universe, or anything, really. I can't prove it, no one can, but I believe."

"You believe that there will be an end?" I wave at her tattoo again. "That this will pass, life, everything."

"Everything."

"Then why fight?"

"Some things require a bit of push to get to that end."

She turns to me, swinging one leg up onto the cot, bent at the knee so she can look directly at me. Her voice drops into serious minor tones.

"Are you positive you want to join the Resistance and carry out this objective for us?"

"Yes." She waits, just staring intensely at me. I stammer. "Yeah, right, it's like you're saying, someone has to end it."

"Why should that person be you?"

"What? You came to me, remember."

"Right. Why are you willing to lay down your life for this fight?"

"I want to kill the Over. You said that's what we'd be doing."

"Perhaps I was too vague. What you will be doing is a suicide mission, as you've termed it. You will go in with the knowledge that your life is the price for meeting your objective."

"Which is to kill the Over."

"Which is to bring about the eventual demise of the Over, yes."

"Eventual?"

"I am going to administer to you a virus that targets the unique genetic make-up of these creatures. This species—they're akin to pack animals, not only socially but on a molecular level. The process by which they reproduce essentially makes them all one organism; in essence, they can be viewed individually as limbs of one collective entity."

"Marla," I say. "I got a C on my last science quiz, and I'd never even heard of genetics until you recruited me the other week."

"Right. I'm sorry. I'm unsure exactly how to simplify this for you."

"You're gonna infect these things, using a virus that you first infect me with."

"Close. The virus will not infect you. It will lie dormant in your blood until they feed off of you."

"Wait—I thought I was getting out of the Feed Program."

"Their reproductive process involves feeding off of their human vessel—"

"I have to *mate* with one of them?"

"Okay, I am clearly not explaining this right. Let me try again." She talks with her hands, sometimes pointing to things that aren't there, or demonstrating things I can't see, or lightly touching my knee, or her own knees. "The intel we've gathered from studying our specimen, as well as other sources, has provided us a fairly solid picture of how these creatures reproduce, which is known to us humans as the Seed Program. Are you following me?"

"Yeah...."

"The specifics are not entirely clear, but what is evident is that an exchange of fluids takes place—"

"Ew."

"—involving the transference of your blood into their systems, and vice versa. How long this process takes or how many times it is repeated is inconclusive, but once the process is complete, you will, in effect, be dead. At the very least, you will no longer be human. You will be one of the Over."

"Holy fuck."

"I know. Everyone is given a cursory break-down of the three programs—Breed, Feed, and Seed—when they enter middle school, if not before, but the specifics are left to your imaginations. But, Jordan, it isn't... As far as we can tell, this process, it isn't as though you necessarily *become* one of them. It's more akin to a parasitic relationship: your body is the host, but eventually, the parasite takes over completely. There's no... there's no *you* left."

My pulse has accelerated and I can feel a flush creeping up to my face, but I can tell it's anger and not anything stupid like embarrassment or whatever. All these things attacking us, tormenting us, practically enslaving us—they were once human. And now she's asking me to become one of them, however softly she tries to phrase it. It's really too much to even absorb— right now, or maybe ever. It's like those numbers; it's like thirty-two hundred and twelve new pieces of information I can't possibly fit inside my mouth to swallow all at once.

Marla shifts and reaches into the pocket of her sweats, pulls out an old pocket watch, glances at its face, and shoves it back inside her pocket.

"Listen, I don't have much time here, very little in fact. We have to wrap this up. I'm not going to let you decide definitively to join us yet; you'll have another week to be certain. But if you're inclined, then there are a few things I need you to do.

"You have to ensure that you are selected for Seed. They probably will not select you for Breed but if—"

"I can't," I say. "I mean, really. My period hasn't started."

She looks at me and nods, almost sympathetically. "Good, one less thing to worry about. We also have to keep you out of Feed and reduce your chances, however small, of being sent home entirely. Candidates for Feed are, statistically, imbalanced individuals who demonstrate an irrefutable lack of cooperative social intelligence coupled with a diminutive desire to contribute meaningfully to a community."

"Uh-oh."

"Don't be glib, this is important. You're not too far gone but you are dangerously straddling that edge and you need to be more discerning. Pick your battles. Carving your name into yourself and standing up to your mentor in group were probably beneficial actions; they demonstrate an awareness of your inferior position and a desire to elevate yourself to common ground. But whatever you did to earn those bruises, not that this forgives those who inflicted them, but whatever it was certainly demonstrated a stubborn disobedience and desperation that the Over will not wish to tolerate."

She stands up and walks toward the door, still talking.

"You need to show them your strength and your individuality, but only to a point. After all, if they take you for Seed it's because they want you to join their collective. So setting yourself too far apart will only alienate them. You have to show your intelligence, your awareness not only of your situation but of your limitations within that situation, and then you have to push those limits—within reason."

"Yeah," I say, standing up and following her to the door, as if it's my house and she's some guest who dropped by and I'm just being casually polite. "Sure, right. Push limits, don't break them. Cake."

"I know it sounds impossible."

"It does." We stand there in silence for a second. She looks like she wants to say something reassuring but she can't find the words because there aren't any. "I guess you chose me for a reason, right? So, I'll try." I shrug.

She smiles. "Jordan, you are a remarkable person. Thank you for your trust in me. I am forever in your debt."

"Yeah, well, if everything goes like you're planning, I won't be around long enough for you to pay up."

Without so much as a sigh or lingering look to give me some warning of what's to come, Marla throws herself around me and squeezes tight. A hug. My arms hang at my sides. She smells like spices and fresh baked bread. I pat her shoulder a little.

"I'll return next week, sometime after your parents visit. If you still want to go through with everything, I'll administer the virus then." She smiles one final time and goes, locking the door again behind her.

I'd forgotten all about the parents' visit until she mentioned it. I can't even begin to explain all the weird reactions my body has to the thought of seeing my parents again, after all this time and for the last time. Christ, I don't even want to think about it. They'll come in, all crying, at least Mom will be, and Dad will probably be all stoic and clenching his anger in his empty fists, as usual. And no one will say what they really want to say or what they really mean, even at the end, or because it is the end. And then they'll be led out and...

That's right. Someone will have to lead them in and out. It's not like a family picnic or something, no one gets to play kickball or have a barbeque. It's more like prison, locked in a room, visiting hours. And she has to be there, because, after all, she's not only *my* Liaison, she's the Liaison for the whole blessed Fontaine clan.

My pulse jumps again, the blood comes rushing back. I don't ever want to see her, I can't see her, I will not.

Omalis. God fucking dammit.

# TWELVE
## JUNE

IT'S EASIER THAN I IMAGINED, seeing them again. My boys. Maybe it's the lingering affects of the sedative—something powerful, like a horse tranquilizer, and fast-acting, knocking Jay and me out for the better part of the day, as best I can judge once we resurface—that makes me simply stand there in that small room, three feet away from Jeremy, closer than I've been in weeks, and closer than I will ever be again, with my arms hanging heavily at my sides and my eyes dry and irritating, and no words, no words, no words, for my brave, frightened, little boy. Maybe it's the steadying presence of Jay—who threw up on the helipad outside, and I looked away politely only to find my gaze crossing paths with Omalis's eyes as she, too, looked away—who walks ahead of me and, as my son rises to meet him, takes three bold strides into the room and locks Jeremy into a hug so engulfing I pray they'll both be swallowed up by it. How can I follow such a naked display of need?

What I really think it is, though, is this: Jeremy is no longer Jeremy. Whatever they have done to him in these short weeks has stained him. He looks the same, if a bit skinnier, a bit paler, but his back is straighter, his hair parted to the left instead of down the middle. But the stain is deeper than that; it leaks into the air around him, into the way he disengages from his father first, the way his hand doesn't shake when he pulls the chairs out and motions for us to sit, the way he only looks at me and smiles like he knows he's stained, he knows he's leaking, he knows that because I am his mother I will want to help him clean it up, but because I am his mother he will not let me.

"You have thirty minutes," Omalis reminds us from her customary position next to the door. She has no watch by which to keep the time, but I imagine her with one anyway, subtly clasping her left hand to her right wrist to start the stop-watch counting down, stealing glances every two and half minutes or whenever there's a long enough awkward pause in our conversation, the one she's diligently pretending not to listen to.

"How's Jason?" Jeremy asks, his eyes flitting between Jay and me as we both cautiously take our seats. "And Jordan?"

"We haven't been to see Jordan yet," Jay says. "Jason is well. He told us you don't see each other much."

Jason is being held at the opposite end of a camp so large we had to take a helicopter over to this side. The room we met him in was identical to this one, and his appearance was identical to Jeremy's—thinner, neater in a way he's never made the effort to be at home—but without a stain. He hugged his father too, or his father hugged him, and he had the heart to cry, even just a little, even if he pretended to sneeze so he could wipe his face. He hugged me, too, as we were leaving, but I let go first because if I didn't, I never would.

Jeremy doesn't say much about his brother, and like his brother, he won't divulge much about the camp program. We avoid talking about his prospects. He asks how we are, and the farm, and Jay steers around my recent transgressions and talks about the weather and the new part he had to buy for the baler and how much the price of corn has gone up since May. I sit with my hands folded into my lap and try desperately not to look at Jeremy as if I no longer know him, and not to look at him as if I hold this desperate hope inside of me that at least his father will know him, will continue to know him once my deal goes through and Jeremy comes home and I have taken his stain and made it mine.

Our time passes quickly. It's impossible to remember what we say to each other to fill the space between us. I try to tell Jeremy about a book I think he will like, but he casts his eyes to the table and scratches his shoulder in a way that makes me trail off. I don't mean to make him envious, I just want something to give him. The only sound Omalis makes to indicate our time is up is a polite clearing of her throat, the sound I imagine must escape tiny hummingbirds in the throes of mid-flight passion.

"I love you guys," Jeremy says. In that instant I can see the thing that has stained him is not anything these camps have directly done to him, but the cumulative consequence of having gone through them at all: he has already said goodbye to us, to himself. He's accepted it, and rather than asking us to accept it—either because he knows we won't or can't, or because he's afraid we will or have—he's decided not to ask us for anything at all.

"Jeremy—" But Jay's embrace silences whatever vow I was about to break. He pulls us both into his encompassing chest and breathes us in. I feel Jeremy squirming next to us, anxious to remove himself from what has become so unfamiliar. Before we part, I whisper to him, "You'll make it out. You're coming home."

In the helicopter on the way back to the airport, before Omalis ties the blindfolds back over our eyes, Jay scowls at me. "Why did you say that, June? We agreed not to make them promises."

I search for something dim to say. "I was only trying to be comforting."

"False hope isn't comforting."

I'm grateful for the blindfold when it comes, and for the sedative that follows.

Jordan's camp looks the same as the boys', what little we see of it. We're ushered, still blindfolded, from the helipad down a winding path or two, Omalis's gentle hands pressed into our respective backs. Jay wants to talk about hope, or rather he doesn't want to talk about it, because it's easier without hope, to live without hope. My reassuring words to our son are false hope, and so are Omalis's hands touching me, touching Jay. She thinks she is giving us something here, they all do, all the Powers That Be who've coordinated these brief parent-child visitations. They are the peddlers of hope, and we're spooning it up because all we have left are spoons. Omalis's touch—light as a feather, stiff as a drink—reminds me of how much she has peddled and how little she has promised and how much I have clung to both of these things.

Omalis lifts our blindfolds in the hallway. She studies us carefully. "Are you both all right?"

I look at my husband, the glaze in his eyes crusted over. He wipes at his forehead with his fingers and slaps his chin. "I'm good, yeah."

When I don't put forth a response, Omalis measures her sympathy at me and offers, "It can be a trial, I know. We can put you up for the night in a hotel, reschedule the visit for tomorrow—"

A small, mirthless laugh escapes me. "Has any mother actually ever gone in for that?"

Omalis nods briskly. "Not to my knowledge." She opens the door to the visiting room.

Jordan is sitting when we move into the room, Omalis stepping aside to allow Jay and I access. She stands quickly when she sees us, and then her eyes flick behind us. For a moment, I am afraid that she is eying the space between myself and the door, the space into the hallway, and thinking of a way to run. She'll make things worse for herself, if she hasn't already. My veins begin to burn as my thoughts race to form pictures, snapshots of Jordan's previous attempts at subterfuge: spiking a mentor's morning coffee with rat poison, acquired, naturally, from the seething black-market underbelly of any self-respecting prison; burying herself under a pile of laundry to be carted out to the cleaners; digging a hole behind her cabin with her sharpened fingernails; talking her bunkmates into starting a diversionary riot in the lunchroom while she steals into a canoe and paddles for her life. I think about these things while I watch Jordan's eyes sweep past the distant beyond and settle on something solid: Omalis. I breathe easier; the unfortunate event in that Tokyo camp could have easily happened here, or at my boys' camp, or anywhere. But here, now, that is not the thing to worry about; it is not the thing Jordan worries about.

Her skin pulls tight around her mouth and her fingers white-knuckle the edge of the table she stands partially behind. "I don't want you here."

This is the first time I notice the change in her. So much louder than Jeremy's stain, so much darker, how did it take me even ten seconds to see it? The morning she left—so willing, defiantly jubilant, sickeningly cavalier—she was just a little girl. Maybe not *my* little girl anymore, in that way, when she was still small, that she used to let me possess her—clothe her, bathe her, feed her, hold her—that way she gave up about the same time the training bra snapped on. But she was still so much a little girl, look, look at her that awful day: scuffed knees hiding under torn jeans, rough sneakers she's quickly out-growing, hair to her neck uncombed and tangled, and her hands fidgeting with the bottom of her shirt, trying to make sure it doesn't hike up in the wind, to make sure I don't see her rebellion until she reveals it, until she says, "Mom, I pierced my navel." "Navel." Such a grown-up word. A small hole in her skin, a pin-prick in her stomach and she is gone, gone, gone, lost from my possession forever, into the open and tenderless arms of the world. But she was still, even then, behind her mask of fortitude, her self-indulgent defeatism masquerading as maturity, even then she was still a little girl. That little girl has vanished.

Now she is a study in assured rigidity; this place, if it has taught her anything beyond hopelessness, has taught her to be hard. I can see that she is bruised, her skin a faded shade of purple at its softest points, and her clothes—identical sweatpants get-up as her brothers wore—drape loosely over the sharp edges of her body. She's lost weight but she's gained muscle; she's barely a girl anymore and something more than a woman. A survivor; my baby is a survivor.

She's also angry, and her entire body tenses with it. She takes a step back from us and directs her hardness at Omalis; I turn to look, to see if Omalis is hurt by this. The Liaison appears unfazed. She tries to speak, "Jordan—" but my daughter cuts her off.

"Get out, or let me out."

Jay holds a hand out to Jordan, who ignores us both, her eyes, her loathing, locked on Omalis. "What's going on?" Jay says, swiveling his questioning gaze between them both. "Did something happen?"

"No, Mr. Fontaine, I don't—"

"Stop talking." Jordan does not raise her voice but the force of it rocks me. Her words inhale the oxygen in this closed-off room and I am left gasping inside the sudden vacuum of it. I've been on the receiving end of a losing argument with Jordan but not like this; she is usually erratic in her protestations, hysterical in her excuses, maddening in her stubbornness. But she is controlled now, funneling all of her anger, her hardness, in through her eyes and out through her mouth. "Leave."

Omalis closes her mouth, smoothes an unwrinkled pleat in her skirt. Along the hairline of her unblemished forehead I think I see a droplet of sweat appear. Then she swallows, hard, the sound of it seeming to echo off the bare walls, and I know Jordan's behavior has rocked her, too.

"All right," she says, crisp and sure as ever, but her eyes drop to the floor for a fraction of a second. She backs up, her heel catching the corner of the open door so that she stumbles before turning around and closing it behind her.

"Well," I sigh deeply, exaggerating for the sake of levity. "If I'd known it was that easy to get rid of her..."

A sound from Jordan interrupts me. It seems to start in her chest, in the deepest part of her, and push up through her throat where she strains to keep it down but it forces its way out. It's animalistic, raw and scary. She screams and loses her grip on her body, and goes down heavy on her knees. The air slams out of her and back into the room, and although I want to look away, to back away and give her space, I can't. She needs me.

I practically push Jay out of the way to reach her. She's rocking back and forth slightly, her hands clasped to the hair that hangs over her ears but when I touch her shoulder she latches onto me. She gropes blindly and finds some fleshy part of me—my thigh—and digs the stubs of her fingers in, pulls me closer. Her head buries itself in my lap and her back throbs beneath my hand as she cries. I grip her just as tightly as she's gripped me.

"Oh, Jordan." I don't know what else to say. I'm afraid to say anything else. The normal parental platitudes don't apply. I can't tell her everything is going to be okay because she knows better than me that it won't be. I can't ask her what specifically is wrong because I already know the answer is everything, and I don't want specifics. So I hold her and wish for that to be enough.

Jay kneels down beside me and places his hand on her neck, massaging it. "You gotta be strong, kiddo. You just have to be strong, okay? I know how strong you are."

I want to slap him. Images of Jay massaging Jordan's shoulders before her gymnastic meets stream through my mind. "Your dismount is clumsy, kiddo." Moving his hands down to wrap his fingers around her tiny biceps. "Don't forget about these guns. Use 'em." Then facing her, smiling at her, a smile she returns only after he says, "I know how strong you are."

"It's not…" Jay struggles with his words. "It's not very much longer."

"Stop it," I rasp at him, as if I could mask our voices inches above Jordan's ears. "You're not helping."

"What?" Jay's wet eyes blink at me. "I'm just—I just want to…"

"It's not a damn meet, Jay. She doesn't need a pep talk."

Jay slaps the concrete floor with his open palm. "You don't know what the hell she needs."

My no doubt clever retort is lost to the jerky movements of Jordan as she pushes herself up and away from me. She gets to her feet and looks at both of us, still kneeling on the floor, through glistening eyes and uncut bangs. She pushes her hair back and wipes snot from her nose with the wrist of her sweatshirt. Finally, her lips smack open and she says, "Should I leave you two alone?"

Jay laughs and hangs his head, rubbing his eyebrows with his thumb and forefinger. I stand up, saying, "I'm sorry. We just want… I'm sorry." I start to ask how she is but stop myself. Instead, I say something even more empty. "They've hurt you."

Jordan nods, sucks in her bottom lip and looks like she might cry again, but swallows it down. She shrugs. "Do you want to sit?"

Instead of sitting at the table across from each other, Jay and I move our chairs to create a close triangle with Jordan's chair. We sit with our knees touching, and I close my eyes for a second, trying hard to memorize the warmth and closeness of Jordan's knee against mine. When I put out my hand to hold hers, she doesn't resist. We sit like this in silence until Jordan finally says, "How're Jason and Jeremy?"

Jay nods vigorously. "Good, good. I mean, they're fine. They're holding up."

"Are they together?"

"They're in the same camp but it's big. They don't see each other often. They send their love."

Jordan rolls her eyes. "I'm sure."

Before I can stop myself, I say, "You'll see them again."

"June—"

"Mom—"

"I just mean—"

"You know what they did to us today?" Jordan changes the subject; her hand goes cold in mine. "They took us into the woods and made us stand in a circle, and they brought out this guy, this young guy I guess, like Jason's age or a bit older, and they had him all tied up and this sack over his head and he was naked. They took the sack off and they made us stand there and look at him. He was crying, his face was dirty, he wouldn't look at us. Once they were satisfied we'd all looked at him, another guy in a mask came out and shot him."

"—Jordan!" I can't contain my gasp. Jay puts his hand on my thigh and squeezes.

"Then the masked guy walked back through the woods, and everyone was crying and hysterical, and two of the counselors dragged his body away. His eyes were still open, they were green. They dragged him off, and the counselors said—yeah, we're supposed to call them mentors, what is that? It's stupid, even stupider than counselor. Anyway they said tomorrow we get to take him apart. That's not what she said, she said we'll dissect him, like fucking—like fucking science class. We'll… I don't know why. I don't know why they do any of this to us. Why do the Over care if we suffer before they eat us?"

"They're trying to prepare you," Jay says. He scratches the stubble on his chin. "It's…not entirely designed by the Over. The government…they know what hell they're sending you to, and they want to prepare you, desensitize you. If you can't feel, if you're numb to pain and violence and death, the rest is…even if you…even when you…if you come home, the rest is easier to take. To live through."

"But it's also a test, Dad," Jordan says. "Right? One big, meaningless test. To see if we're worth killing."

"I don't know, honey." Jay shakes his head. "All I have are my theories. I don't know. I…I wish I could do something for you, I…"

"It's not entirely bad." Jordan taps Jay's foot with the toe of her shoe. "I've made friends."

"They can't do this to you," I say. "How are they allowed to do this to you?"

"It's not just me," Jordan says. She slips her hand out of my grip, crosses her arms, hugging herself. "How's the farm?"

Jay clears his throat to answer her and I can't take it. "I won't let them do this. This has to stop. We have to do something." I'm not really talking to anyone, more to the wall behind Jordan's head. I see faces in that wall, the many faces of all the hospital Liaisons I've had to hand lives over to, without hesitation, because hesitation was against the law. Fuck them, fuck this, fuck their laws, fuck it. They can't take you. They can't take any of you.

"June, calm down." Jay is on his feet because I am on my feet. I realize the moment Jay touches my arm that I've been speaking my thoughts out loud. Jordan still sits, looking up at me with eyes that have never seen me before. She's almost smiling, but in a sad way.

"Why should I calm down, Jay? Dammit, why? You can let them fuck you around, but I'm not going to do it anymore. How can you let them? She's your daughter."

Jay's voice explodes out of him. "What do you want me to do?" Then softer: "They'll kill us."

"Not all of us."

"What the fuck is that supposed to mean? Jesus, June, you're ruining...you're ruining our visit..."

"Mom," Jordan says. I look at her and hold my breath. She leans forward in her chair, squints at me. She's never been so beautiful. "Mom, what did you do?"

Jay thinks, somehow, that she's referring to my outburst at the hospital. He tries to smooth it over. "Nothing, nothing. It was...there wasn't anything. Christ, did she...did Omalis say something? Everything's okay, okay? You don't have to worry."

"Mom?"

My voice comes out a whisper. "I did it for you, baby. I did it for all of you."

In the suffocating silence, Jay finally catches on. "June?"

I grab the sleeve of his shirt and pull him closer to me, as much to steady myself as to hold onto him in case he tries to run from me, to run from what I tell him. "Jay, I made a decision. I had to. I had to do something." I nod my head as I speak, assuring myself it was right, this is right. "I offered myself in their place. Omalis confirmed the trade, she—"

"—Fucking Christ, June! You can't—"

"—She's a liar, Mom—"

"—said I might not get all of you, but even one, and I have hope—"

"—Why are you doing this? You can't do this. Nothing can change this, fuck, June, fuck—"

"—whatever she tells you, I mean, are you stupid? She's not here for you, nothing she does is for you, it's for *them*—"

"—and I just can't sit here, not like you Jay, I just can't sit and let it happen—"

"—Have you ever heard of anyone saving their kids? They can't! Fuck you, June, I want to save them, don't you think I want to save them? How can you… I'll lose all of you. I can't lose all of you—"

"—she'll use it against you, Mom, take it back."

There's a rapping on the door and then it slowly opens. Omalis's blonde head peeks into the room, as if she's shy, or trying to be polite. "You have two minutes," she says, and ducks back out.

"I've done it," I tell them both. "I'm not taking it back. Jordan, you're coming home. Okay? I'll get you home."

"Jesus," Jay breathes and slumps back down in the folding chair. I'm still gripping his shirt, stretching it out. He makes no move to pull away from me. He shields his eyes with his other hand and rubs his brow.

Jordan is crying again. I am crying. Jay won't let himself cry. Jordan shakes her head at the floor, then at me. "I'm not, though, Mom. I have to—" she sucks air in wetly through her mouth and holds it "—I have to do something, too."

Before I can respond, she throws herself at me. She's grown a few inches in these past weeks; her ear presses level against mine. She hugs me and I hug her back, pressing harder than I should, willing our bodies to fuse together, to become one, so I can carry her home with me now.

Jordan speaks into my neck, the heat of it igniting gooseflesh on my skin. "Mom, I… Mom."

"I love you." It's always been a dangerous thing to say to her, met with hurtful sarcasm or disdain, or ignored. But I can't help it; I can't help it. "I love you so fucking much."

"Yeah," she says. "Yeah."

It's enough.

Jordan lingers with me for another moment, then pulls away and bends down to her father. He's curled in on himself, so she hugs his head, nuzzling his hair with her chin. He reaches up and wraps his fingers around her wrist. They stay like that until the door opens again.

Jay gets up at the sound of the door creaking on its hinges. Omalis comes into the room but doesn't say anything, just stands with her arms held behind her, very officious.

Jay clears his throat. "Well, kiddo." He doesn't want to say goodbye but he can't bring himself to believe in "see you later."

"It's okay, Dad." Jordan backs away from us, letting us go. It's too soon, I want to reach out for her but I know she'll only push me away. Not with cruelty, but because she has to. We all do what we have to.

I walk out ahead of Jay, forcing my eyes to face forward, my knees to bend, my feet to take even steps. I can hear Jay walking steadily behind me, and then we're in the hall and Omalis has closed the door.

"I'll need you to put these on one last time," Omalis says. She hands us the blindfolds.

We walk back to the helipad in silence. Once seated, before the sedative kicks in, Jay leans in close to my ear and says, "You've killed me." I'm too tired to care.

# THIRTEEN
## OMALIS

IN THE DIMLY LIT BEDROOM of her apartment, Omalis surrounds herself with aborted memories of summers past. Spilling out of every drawer in her dresser, pushing against the door of the walk-in closet, creeping out beneath the bed, are remnants of Omalis's life, of the lives she's allowed to be taken. All of the care packages she has created in the names of the children to ease their parent's anxieties; all the letters she has promised to deliver from parent to child, each carefully handwritten mark upon the page like a stab wound driving its ink deep under her skin. The Over create this façade, this summer camp fantasy, not because it soothes the parents to think their children will get their letters, or reassures them that nothing can be so wrong if their child can send them happy sunshine cards and candy gift baskets. The Over do it because it amuses them; the Over do it because they can.

Omalis is not instructed to hang onto these lies—she can destroy the letters, eat what she wants from the gift baskets, throw away the toys. But she keeps them. She's kept them all. Hundreds of stale chocolate bars, staler greeting cards bearing forged signatures, plastic bubble-gum-machine toys, miniature travel board games, dried flowers pressed between the yellowing pages of drugstore paperbacks. The brown nondescript packaging kicked to the corners, the elements inside—the memories she never allowed to grow—clawing at her ankles. But it's the parents' letters that really cut her down.Earlier in the night, when the moon was high enough to cast its light through the blinds and remind Omalis just how much she was not sleeping, she had gotten up and walked to the closet and pulled the boxes off the shelves, ripping into their guts as if she were a beast and they her latest kill. This fantasy is so close to the truth, yet so late; most of them, she killed years ago. She doesn't look at the names on the packages; she does not have to. She remembers them all. She kept them locked away so she would not have to think of them, or only if she wanted to, just enough to make her want to feel guilty, just enough to make her ache to be hurt, just enough to make her call Marla. Tonight she felt something deeper than that ache—grown coldly familiar—something sharper. So she tore into the packages, every one, grabbed them up from the floor of the closet, the shelves, under the bed and inside the dresser drawers that have been empty of her clothes since she moved most of her things to Marla's place. She spilled them out, violently, shook out everything so she could wade through it, kick and toss and stomp it around until she felt something else. Something else. That something that has kept her going through all these summers, these memories, these murders; that something that shifted—maybe four days ago, maybe five—and slipped and fell into a place so hidden inside of her that it is lost. She knows it is lost, which is why she makes no sound as she kicks the contents of the packages. It is why she takes her bronze letter opener and slices through the seals of the parents' envelopes, opens each with careless vehemence, as if only to rip them up and add the fragments to the mess at her feet, but then she stops and stands there and reads them. Every single one, every single word. She has taken everything else from these people, why not their privacy, too? It was Jordan who did this to her. It was Jordan, the only kid through all these summers who ever looked at her with such hatred, such controlled anger, and didn't plead or bargain or threaten or break, but demanded. Commanded. Omalis responded to that kind of straightforwardness, that futile strength, with obedience. Regret came only later, after dropping the Fontaines at the runway, boarding her private jet, and promptly vomiting into the toilet. She experienced some sort of seizure, a physical sensation so completely foreign and alarming that she relished it. Cold sweat poured from her, her skin hardened and her muscles contracted in a state of paralysis that lasted maybe forty seconds before something snapped in her brain—she could literally hear the snapping, feel it, like a nerve ending being pulled apart—and she doubled over and vomited one more time before blacking out. She had thought it was the Over, punishing her for something, or retiring her. She had thought, "At last." And then she woke up in her apartment, in her bed, in a freshly laundered pantsuit and a message scratching across her frontal lobe: Take a day off. Omalis took four.

In those four days, she has not eaten, slept, showered, left the apartment, answered the phone or called Marla. Not eating hurt the most at first but she found the stomach cramping bearable if she drank a little water. She knows that her body will not let her brain control it in that way, for the simple fact that she is not the sole proprietor of her brain. If Liaisons were capable of suicide there would be no Liaisons. No, that is too hopeful. There would be fewer Liaisons. She knows she will break soon but not tonight. Tonight—or early this morning, as the sun begins to rise on other parts of the world— tonight, Omalis reads.

"Your mother and I love you very much. Don't ever forget that, no matter what they do to you. You have us, and your sisters, and grammy and grampy and even Auntie Edie though I know you two have not always gotten on. You have us, sweets, and they can never take that from you, even if it seems like they can. Remember last Christmas when we…"

"Sweets" was a twelve-year-old girl named Shauna Grimes who was selected for Breed. Omalis remembers that during their meetings Shauna refused to talk about anything that was happening at camp, or about her parents, or the life she used to have, or the future she feared. Instead, she would make up stories about faeries living in the woods, or mer-people in the lake, trolls under bridges, the usual. She went so far as to suggest that Omalis was a princess, "But a secret one," she said, "and you're not supposed to know it so forget I told you." Omalis asked, "But aren't you the princess?" To which Shauna did not reply but only poked at her thighs with her little-girl fingers and sang a nonsense song that had no words. This was six years ago. Girls in Breed last maybe ten years at the longest. If Shauna is alive, surely she is not thinking about her parents—who killed themselves three years ago, anyway, after their fourth daughter was also sent to Breed—or grammy or Auntie Edie or anything outside of her suffering and her hope, however tenuous, that she will just fucking bleed out and end it already. Omalis has tried to kill herself, in more blatant ways than starvation or alcohol poisoning or even jabbing a mysterious needle into her thigh and dreaming of air bubbles. Every year, before prepping for the camps, she wakes up, draws a bath, and takes a straight razor to the thick, pulsating blue vein in her wrist. She can't press down hard enough; whatever the Over did to her, however they wired her brain in those initial, painful connections, she is unable to leave behind much more than superficial scrapes along her skin. She figures she has to try, though. It is the least she can do.

Someone is knocking at the apartment's front door. Omalis ignores it. She's come to June Fontaine's letter. Well, she's been saving it, but now there are no other letters to distract her. It's only one page and on that page, a single line addressed not to Jordan or to one or both of her brothers, but to Omalis.

"Omalis, wake up. We all know you're their puppet, so cut the fucking strings already. Best, June."

June Fontaine is not the first parent to realize—or to openly acknowledge—the illusion Omalis is forced to create for them, but she is the first to point to the Liaison as something separate from the Over. Not that she has not received her fair share of pleas appealing to her humanity; but this, June's words, appeal to her agency.

"Yeah, right," she breathes into the stillness of the wrecked room. Whatever agency she might have had was bludgeoned by her mother's promise twenty-six years ago and buried by the Over alongside her ability to run a blade across her own arteries.

The knocking grows insistent, thundering. Omalis only looks up when there's a crash, a harsh splintering of wood and a primal scream, then a string of cursing. Marla appears outlined by the bedroom door frame, hair frazzled down her cheeks, overcoat hanging loosely, revealing the black pleather short-shorts, hot pink fishnet stockings and black tank top of her trade. She sees Omalis in her room and rushes over to her on eight-inch heels, tossing her tiny clutch purse behind. Her makeup is dry and flaking off around her eyes and lips. She stops in the doorway.

"Jesus, Heaven," she says, the two names running together like a curse.

Omalis realizes she is naked. Has been since she lay down to try to sleep, then got up to maybe shower, then felt ill, felt that sharp stabbing something, and went into the closet for the packages. She feels a light soreness on her arms and looks down to see just how carelessly she has been using that bronze letter opener to slice open the envelopes. There is no blood but bright red streaks criss-cross the skin of her forearms. She drops Mrs. Fontaine's letter and the opener into the pile at her feet.

Marla takes in the room, her irises widening and contracting, tears building up in the corners of her eyes near the small clumps of day-old mascara. The sight of those unshed tears makes Omalis's blood run hot.

"Were you worried about me?" Omalis asks. It's the first time she has spoken to anyone in four days. The words sound raw, stale, hollow.

Marla puts a hand over her mouth and Omalis imagines her biting down on the palm to keep the tears back. But they seep out of her regardless. She hugs herself with her other arm and takes a step back, out of the room, shaking her head.

"I suppose this means you won't be fucking me tonight," Omalis says.

The hand drops from her mouth. "I'm so sorry, Heaven. I'm so sorry."

"Would you do me a favor, baby, before you run off screaming into the night?"

Omalis kicks her way through the garbage, stops in front of the doorway to the bathroom. "Would you take care of this shit? I won't be needing it. You're a peach."

In the bathroom, Omalis doesn't close the door behind her because she wants Marla to follow her. She leans over and twists the faucet handles until the water is just hot enough to burn but not hot enough to make her brain tell her it's harmful to stay under too long. She flips the shower on, and turns, and Marla is there.

"Tell me what happened." The tears are gone from her, sucked back into the center of her chest where they belong. She shed her overcoat in the bedroom and now Omalis is having a hard time looking at anything but her cleavage. "What happened at the parents' visit, Heaven?"

Something inside of her tries to claw its way free, but Omalis suppresses it. "You're incredibly beautiful," she says. She steps backward over the edge of the tub and stands under the steaming water. Marla says something to her that she can't hear over the rush, and she holds her hand out, inviting Marla in. Marla hesitates, looks around the room, as if making sure they are alone, and then begins to undress.

In the shower, neither attempts to say anything. Omalis takes up most of the stream, but the excess moisture sprouts gooseflesh along Marla's collarbone and chest. Omalis covers Marla's breasts with her hands and kisses her. It takes a few stubborn seconds for Marla to part her lips for Omalis's tongue, but she does part them, and then adds her own tongue, and then kisses back harder than Omalis expected. It makes her wet.

With Marla's fingers inside her, Omalis closes her eyes and thinks about Jordan.

She thinks about Jordan's eyes, swollen and hard, unwavering accusations that burn along the frayed edges of whatever Omalis has been calling her heart these days. How her voice was like a rock curled inside unsure fingers, delivered to the base of her own skull in five swift blows—five quick syllables—"I. don't. want. you. here." How really she acquiesced not out of admiration for a flare of hatred often seen but rarely unleashed from her charges, but because Jordan ripped her open—Marla's fingers pushing deeper, her thumb parting flesh to find the clit, her teeth still not brave enough to do more than brush Omalis's neck—like she found that seam, the one loose thread, and it was so easy to pull and watch everything inside of Omalis slither its way into the light. Omalis had given her that thread the first night at the sound barrier, when she let herself believe she was doing the girl a kindness by letting her freak out, going easy on her; she let herself believe—in their subsequent meetings, through their innocent flirtation, Jordan's blushing and her own suggestive body language—she let herself believe she was a source of comfort for Jordan. She allowed Jordan to believe that there was something worth seeking within her—solace, consolation, empathy. She deceived her, and in that deception she failed her.

She failed her.

Jordan looked at Omalis the same way Marla looks at her now—her fingers quickening, Omalis's legs stiffening, skin reddening beneath the hot water. Jordan looked and she saw what Marla refuses to see. She saw the emptiness, the cowardice, the murderer.

Omalis really has become her mother.

Omalis shudders through her orgasm. Marla starts to pull her hand back but Omalis grips her wrist and holds it there. With her other hand she pulls Marla's face next to hers so that her lips are pressed against Marla's ear. She feels her body shaking as if she were cold, which is impossible. The water lashes Omalis's shoulders, back, and legs. She back-steps into the stream so that it covers them both.

"Hate me," she says into Marla's ear. But she speaks so low, the water is so loud, she is certain Marla cannot hear her. "Please."

They get out of the shower. The room is filled with steam, fogging up the mirrors, layering a film around the metal faucets, the brass doorknob. Omalis wraps a towel around herself without offering one to Marla. Marla dresses silently without drying off. Omalis leads her through the bedroom, the hall, the living room, and to the front door, which still hangs ajar from its hinges as a consequence of Marla's heroic entrance.

Liaisons are given a hefty salary, a pittance compared to the promise that any offspring of the Liaisons are safe from the Over, but certainly enough to afford a house, several, one for each season on any coast at all. Omalis has always lived in an apartment; anonymously, she has given the extra money to the families who's lives she's taken.

Omalis flicks her eyes at the door, tightens the towel above her breasts. "Thanks for stopping by."

"Shit." Marla hisses the word out like a sigh. She goes to the connecting kitchen and drops her overcoat on one of the barstool chairs at the island. She opens the fridge, and Omalis watches with amusement her reaction to the absolute nothing the appliance contains. Thwarted, Marla pulls a glass down from the cupboard and fills it from the tap.

"I don't know why we don't stay here more often," Marla says into the half-empty glass. "It's charming. Very forty-year-old bachelor."

"I'm not forty," Omalis says.

Instead of responding with the expected "You're not a bachelor, either," Marla drains the rest of the water in her glass and refills it. She sips slowly, gently. Omalis moves into the kitchen and leans against the island's marble countertop, watching her. Finally, Marla sets the glass down.

"Heaven." She struggles to meet Omalis's eye. "What happened at the parents' visit?"

"I think we should break up."

"Did you get to talk with Jordan?"

"It's not me, it's you."

"Were you able to see her at all, or—"

"We've grown apart as people."

"I'm asking you something."

"I'm ignoring you."

"Goddammit—"

"I'll move my stuff out tomorrow. I'd prefer if you weren't in."

"—Goddammit!" Marla slams her palms onto the countertop, upsetting her glass. It falls to the hardwood floor but does not break. Omalis's body tenses, but Marla breathes deep and curls her arms against her chest. "Heaven…"

She begins to count.

At "four," Omalis launches herself across the table. Her gut and hip absorb the brunt of the impact with the tabletop's edge, shooting alarms of pain up her spine. She throws her hand over Marla's mouth so fast it's like a punch. Marla recoils, bites her tongue, curses and spits blood as she backs up. Omalis pushes herself up, vaults her legs over the table, lands in front of Marla and slams her left hand over her mouth again, using a forearm across her chest to push her into the refrigerator. The lone magnet on the freezer door—a cartoon pen from her car insurance company—wobbles, tilts, and joins the glass on the floor.

"What the fuck was that?" Omalis's voice is harsh but calm. There's a steady hum at the back of her skull, the reverberations of a struck bell. Marla breathes hard through her nose, pushing hot, moist air onto Omalis's knuckles. Omalis asks again, "What the fuck are you doing to me?" She punctuates her inquiry by knocking Marla's head against the freezer door.

Marla whimpers into Omalis's hand, starts to cry. Omalis brings her knee up to Marla's pubic bone and presses. Marla closes her eyes and whines but doesn't struggle.

Omalis eases up. She says, "Talk," and pushes away from Marla. Marla folds in on herself and Omalis catches her by the shoulders before she can fall to the hardwood. She steadies her against the fridge.

"Who are you?" she asks.

She waits for an answer. Marla coughs, wipes a shaking hand across the red welts on her jaw, licks away the blood on her lip. She takes in breath, holds it, lets it out. She looks at Omalis; Omalis sees her own dark silhouette reflected in the dilated pupil.

"I never meant to hurt you," Marla says.

The humming in her skull fades. There is something she knows, but she can't hold onto it. She sees her mother's face through the splintering slats of her old kitchen floor in a house long burned to ash.

"What did you do?" Her voice is smaller than she wants it to be. Before Marla can respond, she throws a fist into the freezer door. Marla turns her head and makes an involuntary yelp. Omalis feels at least two bones in her fingers snap inward. She tenses her jaw and asks again, more forcefully, "Who are you?"

"You know who I am, Heaven—"

"Stop. No. You don't get to say my name. Stop pretending. You've lied enough. Who are you?"

"I'm…" Her eyes fly over Omalis, seeking something she won't find. See like Jordan, Omalis wills. See me. "I'm a member of the Resistance. I've been using you… to help me fight."

Omalis is not surprised because, somewhere buried deep, she already knew this. She grasps onto something else. "You're a fighter, then, are you?" She licks her lips.

Marla throws the first punch.

It doesn't have far to go before it connects with Omalis's ear. She takes the low-impact blow and sinks her own fist into Marla's unguarded stomach. Despite herself, she held back, so she is slightly surprised when Marla doubles over, until she realizes, a fraction of a second too late, that she's been played. From her crouched position, Marla tackles Omalis at her knees. Omalis's feet lose purchase, she falls back, her elbow striking the table island, followed by her head. Light explodes behind her eyes. She lands hard on her tailbone. On the verge of blacking out, she sweeps her leg out in front of her, connecting with Marla's ankle. She hears Marla bang to the floor beside her, and she kicks out without seeing, feels her heel hit against Marla's fleshy thigh; her toe catches in a cross-stitch of the fishnet stocking. Then Marla's fist knocks Omalis's lips against her teeth, and now both of their mouths are bleeding.

Omalis shuts her eyes against the pain in her head and crawls around the island on her elbows. The towel slips down her mid-section and she hastily pulls it back up, not wanting Marla to see her naked again, at least not yet. She rests her back against the dividing wall of the kitchen and living room, brings her knees to her chest, and holds her head until the throbbing tapers off enough for her to focus. She opens her eyes.

Marla is crouched directly in front of her. In her left hand, she holds a blue plastic mini flash drive; in her right, a butterfly knife. She presses the edge of the knife to Omalis throat without breaking the skin and forces the flash drive into Omalis closed fist.

"Just play this," she says through gritted teeth.

Omalis lets the drive ting to the floor and tries to hold Marla's hand but she jerks her elbow back. Omalis says, "I've never been more attracted to you."

"I know," Marla says. She backs away. Omalis is afraid she will leave, not sure what she'll do if she does, but Marla doesn't leave. She scuttles backward and sits across from Omalis on the floor, her back against the island. She does some lazy tricks with the butterfly knife, eyeing Omalis.

"Impressive," Omalis says.

"Hm." Marla holds the knife still in her lap. She just looks at Omalis, looks for what feels like minutes but is only seconds. There are footsteps in the hallway and people slamming doors in other apartments. The first light of morning peeks through the kitchen window, but the two women remain in shadow. The automatic air-conditioning system kicks on with a lurch.

"So I'm your tool," Omalis says. She scratches at a freckle on her knee. "For how long?"

"About three years," she says. "I knew who you were before you told me."

"Before you met me?"

"No." She closes her eyes, as if remembering the salt of Omalis's mouth that first night. "Soon after. The Resistance had come up with this idea, this plan, years ago. And I offered my services to help them implement it. I'm only one small part of—"

"I don't care what the big scheme is." Omalis raps the broken knuckles of her left hand against the hardwood. She feels the pain in the hollow of her bones. It keeps her going, reminds her where she is. "What have you used me for?"

"As a bridge." Marla shifts her weight from one side of her ass to the other, sniffs air through her nose, tongues her still-sore mouth, but doesn't continue.

"The syringe," Omalis prompts. "You've been doping me, and—what? Extracting information somehow."

Marla's interest is piqued. "What syringe?"

Omalis squints her eyes and tsk-tsks. "You've been careless. I found a syringe in my car the other week, before Kyoto. I thought someone had… Hm. I thought someone had attempted to murder me, or was planning to. Wishful thinking."

"No, I don't dope you," Marla says.

"Why don't you? Kill me, I mean. Wouldn't that help your cause? Don't you hate me enough?"

"You're more important alive. You're vital."

"That's funny. How do you do it? How am I a bridge?"

"Hypnosis." Marla speaks slowly, choosing her words deliberately. "I…put you under and…give you instructions."

A synapse inside Omalis's brain fires. "All good children go to Heaven."

Marla nods. "The nursery rhyme is a trigger. It puts you under and then…"

"You control me."

"I instruct you."

"You take me over. You use me. Like the Over."

Marla is clearly uncomfortable with this description. "No. I… No. I never make you do anything…harmful. I bury the suggestions deep—we've worked on this for years, perfecting it—too deep to be rooted out, there's no danger to you or—"

"Monsters dig deep," Omalis says. "You have no idea."

"You're safe from them."

Omalis laughs mirthlessly. "I'm your pawn. I've always only been your pawn."

"No." Marla rocks forward as if to get up, to go to Omalis and attempt to comfort her, as if they were still partners, as if she still had to pretend to be in love, but then she stops. "It's not exactly like that."

"Your opponent takes out the pawns before the Queen. You're risking my life." Omalis smiles, blood staining her teeth. "I approve. What have you been instructing me to do?"

"You've been…helping us attain an insider…someone who will infiltrate the Collective. You've been prepping her, and you were meant to administer the virus—"

"Who?"

"—What?"

"Who have I been prepping?"

"It isn't really important…"

Omalis pushes all of her weight into the balls of her feet and propels her body toward Marla, slamming her shoulder into the other woman's neck, striking her windpipe. Startled, her fingers loosen just enough around the handle of the butterfly knife for Omalis to steal it from her. She drops to one knee and grabs Marla by her hair—still damp from the shower and smelling like steam—and holds the knife an inch away from her eye. She allows Marla a minute to cough and get her breath back.

"Who?" She repeats.

"Jordan," Marla wheezes. "Jordan Fontaine."

Omalis becomes acutely aware of the pain in her body. She drops the knife. When she releases Marla's hair, Marla immediately scrambles for the knife and stands up, holding the weapon before her and the kneeling killer at her feet. Omalis looks up at her, flushed. "What did you make me do to her?"

"Nothing," Marla says. She rubs her throat with her free hand, coughs some more. "You were only supposed to agitate her enough to get her to become violent against you. You told me it wouldn't take much, that she's always angry. I just needed her alone so I could deliver—"

"When I saw her, she... She was afraid of me."

"Heav—" Marla gulps back the name. "I don't think... I don't think you hurt her. You wouldn't."

"I would," Omalis says. She narrows her eyes at the knife. "Maybe you should tie me up or something."

Marla looks at the knife then back at Omalis. She attempts a sigh, which turns into a cough. "I don't want to fucking do this." She turns at the hip and throws the knife over her shoulder. It skims against the wood of the apartment's front door on its way into the hall. Omalis hears its muffled thump on the carpet.

"You're not safe with me," Omalis says. "The Over will find you out. Whatever you do with me...they'll know."

"We've done this before," Marla says. "We've been here, right here, almost exactly like this. I thought I could...do it differently this time, I don't know. Gently."

"How many times?"

"Twice. You never...you always lasted longer, to completion. This time we...it's fucked. We'll have to try again next year."

"Marla..." Omalis lets her mouth hang open; she can't seem to close it. She looks hard at Marla, her turn to seek something out. For the first time in forever, she doesn't stop the tears from building. "What are you saying? What are you saying to me?"

"Baby," Marla can't stop herself from putting back on the girlfriend mask. It fits so well, soft and worn in all the right places. She bends down and touches Omalis's broken knuckles, a whisper of a touch, a suggestion, a promise. Omalis lets her. "Baby, I know it's hard for you. I know you think I'm…that I'm using you to do something against your will, to…to make you my puppet. I'm not. I'm not like them, Heaven. I'm not trading your soul to save myself. I am not your mother, I am not her. Do you understand me? Look at me. I am trying…to do something good. Good. I'm fighting because no one else can or will. You're fighting with me."

Omalis looks away, to the floor, to her own scarred and faded skin. "All this time, I thought you…I thought you were in love with me."

Marla crawls across the floor and picks up the flash drive that Omalis had left against the wall. She crawls back over and presses it once again into Omalis's palm. "Please, Heaven. Just watch the video."

They sit on the floor for an indeterminate amount of time. Omalis listens to Marla breathe, timing her own breaths to leapfrog Marla's, to not interrupt. Slowly, her body finds its way closer to Marla, thigh against thigh, hand on stomach, knee against back, lips against neck. Marla holds her as if none of this had ever happened, as if they had just had a spat about who left the toilet seat up or the milk out all night. She scratches her fingers lightly through Omalis's hair and makes many false starts at saying something that simply turn into lengthy, pregnant exhalations.

Finally, Omalis says, "I know you're not my mother."

"Good." Marla sighs. "You're not her either."

"Everything I've done or failed to do. I can't erase it."

"No."

"And I have to keep doing it."

"Yes."

Omalis pulls her face away from Marla's neck. Marla wipes a tear from Omalis's chin with her own reddening knuckles. Omalis says, "You'll do it again, won't you? Put me under. I won't remember any of this."

The corners of Marla's mouth twitch into a frown. "No, you won't."

"But you will."

Marla only nods.

"Then I…" Omalis presses her lips to Marla's forehead and holds her there, crying into her bangs. She pulls back. "I love you. I don't want to. Normally, I don't—" Marla laughs wetly, and Omalis smiles. "—but you're…not the person I thought you were."

"If I could believe you…"

"But I've said all this before?"

"More or less."

"Take it on faith?"

Marla looks at Omalis, sees what she wants to see, and kisses her.

# F O U R T E E N
## J O R D A N

It's the last day of camp; they've been taking girls since this morning. I would say "since before breakfast," but today is a ration day meaning we don't get any. Not even a last meal.

We've been confined to our cabins. Every couple of hours—or minutes, who knows? No clocks, no watches, just this plastic yellow-orange-green bracelet some stupid kid made back when she was allowed to be some stupid kid snapping against my wrist to the ticking we're forbidden to hear. So who knows, but anyway, every now and then, the cabin door opens and a counselor comes in with wet eyes and a pointing finger, and two Beef Bots—that's the term Taylor coined, Beef Bots, because the guys with the rubber-bullet guns are all muscle and robotic, just carrying out orders, just doing what they can to save themselves, who can blame them, who. The Beef Bots follow the counselor's finger and take whatever girl she points out by her quivering arms and lead her out the door until we can't hear her crying anymore, can't hear the questions she's desperate enough to believe someone might actually answer now that it's really the end.

That's the worst part. It's so hard to choose just one but I guess that's it. That we still don't get anything from these people, our captors, the Gestapo, Taylor calls them. She says it's just another way for them to distance themselves from their actions, to convince themselves there are no consequences for calling a person by a number instead of a name, for dragging someone from their bed in their prison uniform and ushering them to a fate they have no control over, honest, not them, the pawns, the foot soldiers, honest, honest. What do we want, anyway? Do we want them to end up like those counselors in Tokyo? Do we want another Kyoto massacre, right here in—wherever the hell we are?

Yes. I've thought it to myself every night since my parents left. Yes, more massacres, more carnage, more blood in our faces to wake us the fuck up.

So the counselors, they don't answer our questions, stony silence like when I caught Jason in the bathroom and he covered up quick, and afterward I bugged him about what he'd been doing like I didn't know he was masturbating. I was eleven, not an idiot. I doubt these old counselor bitches masturbate. Or they masturbate all the time. Well, anyway, they won't tell us what it means when one of us gets escorted from the cabin. Where we're going or if we'll be back. They haven't even officially said it's the last day but we know.

Taylor's been my shadow all morning. I woke up to her next to me in my bed. It was okay. It was nice. We just lay there, trying not to breathe. She touched me. I don't know. It felt all right. I started crying anyway. Not real crying, like there wasn't any noise, like when one of our collies died when I was seven, or when I watched my dad try to hide his face at my grandpa's funeral. I didn't even know I was doing it until Taylor kissed my cheek and her lips came away wet. She got upset. Stony silent. But she won't leave my side, she won't leave my bed. She asks me things but I think I've lost the will to speak.

"What's wrong, Jordan? Are you scared? Why won't you look at me? Stop doing that."

She pokes a finger under the worn-down string of my bracelet. My skin is red and raw from snapping it all day. Taylor caresses my skin. I don't know.

She was supposed to come back. Marla, the resistance fighter. I can't stop thinking about her, the things she said to me, the promises she made me. I really need to stop counting on promises. It's good that I think about her, her face when she saw how hurt I was; her eyes when she told me how brave I am. It's good. Takes my mind off Omalis for a few minutes at a time; takes my mind off Taylor's body, pressed shoulder to shoulder with mine.

The thing is, I'm ready. Every time I see another girl walk out that damn door— they've taken three of us so far; seven to go—my bones ache with it; my blood runs hot with it; my nerves itch with it. I am ready. So where the fuck is Marla? Maybe she thinks she has more time. Maybe it's only been four weeks, maybe five, certainly not the six they promised. There's that silly concept again, that silly fucking faith. Promises.

The bracelet strikes the vein in my wrist, turning blue to red.

"Here's your fucking promise," I tell my skin. Here, here. Take it.

"Stop doing that," Taylor says. She curls her fingers around my wrist. "Why do you keep doing that?"

"What else should I do?" I ask her.

Across the room, three girls huddle together, their hands folded in their laps and their eyes closed. Sometimes their lips move, sometimes a sob crawls down their spines. Praying. Two beds down on this side, nearest the door, another girl repeatedly makes her bed, sharp hotel corners, sneakers together underneath, pillow nice and fluffed. Unmakes it, remakes it, talks to herself as she goes. The last girl in our cabin stands at the front window and blinks at the waning sun. She's the first to alert us when the counselors are coming. The first to incite panic. It's a tough job, somebody's gotta do it.

"I don't know," Taylor says. She speaks in whispers. Her breath smells like my breath. Every so often she pushes closer to me, like she's trying to get inside me but she can't. I'm full up. "Something else. Anything. This can't be…you know, it just. It can't be over. Like this?"

"How were you hoping it would happen? A cake, a party, a gold watch for your stunning performance as number Fifteen, so glad you could be here, now on to your death, pip pip."

"Why are you being so mean?"

Taylor hugs my arm and holds my hand and nuzzles her head into my neck. It's pathetic. It's pathetic that she's two years older than me and she's dated girls two years older than her and she even went all the way once, she told me, though she didn't tell me how exactly that worked when it's two girls but she would show me, if I ask her to, if I let her. She has two dads who adopted her before adoption became illegal—all unwanted kids to the mouths of the Over, please and thank you—and so she has no brothers and no sisters and she loves her fathers so much and she almost didn't let them go when they came to visit and she had to be sedated and carried back here and she hasn't left the cabin since, even though we didn't get locked in until today. She plays hockey and she's on the swim team at her high school and she's only ever gotten a B in Chemistry and that was only as a punishment for letting another kid cheat off her test. She has a best friend since preschool and she has secrets and she has dreams and she has plans and she has delusions and she has hope. But none of that is real. Only I am real enough to hold onto.

The girl at the front of the cabin turns from the window and rushes to the prayer circle. "They're coming back." The girls clasp hands and breathe heavily. The one making her bed stops and sits down on the half-made bed, facing me. We lock eyes. This girl hasn't spoken one single word to me this whole entire time—in fact, I think she was the one who sneaked a spider into my mashed potatoes the third day we were here—and now she looks for all the world like she regrets this. She looks like she would open her mouth and say something if her jaw would let her.

"Jordan?"

Taylor's grip strangles the circulation from my upper arm. I look at her and brush her bangs out of her eyes. "If they're for you, I'll stall them." Long enough for her to run into the bathroom to get the razor and slit her wrists or throat with it. But I don't have to say that. We're beyond saying that.

She swallows hard. "Okay," she says. I don't know if she would stall them for me. I think she wouldn't, no matter how real I might be.

The cabin door swings inward, and all the other girls stand up, it's automatic. Facing our executioners, like good little sisters and daughters.

But there isn't a counselor standing there, or a gun-toting Beef Bot. There's one of them, an Over.

It blocks out the sun. It takes all the light of the sun into itself. It consumes the sun. It consumes our air; we choke on its presence. We burn, we burn inside out looking at it, at its eyes, viscera red, red with our own burning. It takes everything inside of us and outside of us and around us and all over, all of it, forever. It takes everything into itself and holds it there and taunts us with it and threatens us with it and murders us with it.

There is screaming. It takes their screams. There is a flurry of movement. It takes their limbs. There is a burning, there is a yearning, there is a death, more than one. It takes it takes it takes.

None of this is happening. All of this is in my head. No one has screamed and no one has moved. Except me. I've stood up. Taylor pulls on my shirt, cowering. The visceral eyes take me, take all of me. I am ready. I am ready.

Something steps out from the blackness of the Over's consuming form. Something steps around it and into the light in front of it. Half its size, blonde, thin, a regular t-shirt, regular jeans, boots, blue eyes that consume nothing and give away everything.

Omalis. She says, "Jordan, we need to talk."

Taylor pulls me, pulls on my shirt until she's pulled me back to the bed. She whispers harshly, spitting into my ear. "The razor. Go, go!" She pushes me off the bed and I stumble forward, crash into the bathroom, slam the door behind me. I don't have much time. I don't have enough time.

The yellow floor blinks in and out of blackness, everything hazy. I drop to my knees and run my fingers over the tiles. I can't remember which one it's under. I peel flakes from unmoving tiles until my fingers bleed. Any second now, or now, or now.

The pressure on my back comes from hands, not talons, or anything worse, anything unimaginable. Omalis lifts me up and turns me around. I didn't even hear her come in.

"I didn't hear you come in," I say. Or I want to say it, but my mouth won't let me. The only thing my mouth will let me be rid of is a scream, not a frightened scream, a real scream, a true one, full of rage as red as the Over's eyes, full of me, full of everything I've never been and won't ever get to be. It catches Omalis right between the eyes. She holds onto it. She holds onto it for me. But she can't hold me up. I slip back to the floor and everything's gone hazy again, hazy and wet, and her arms are around me and she feels like my mother, which can't be right, which is not right, which is something I will never feel again so okay, okay, let it be like that, let her arms be my mother's arms, sure, okay.

We seem to sit like this for too long, long after I should be dead. Omalis presses her hands to the sides of my face but I won't open my eyes. Why is she doing it like this? How sick is she, that she has to see it happen, that she has to kiss me goodbye.

"Jordan," she says, with her calming balm of a voice; her scratching, clawing voice. "Marla sent me."

The room fills with ice; my body fills with ice. I push her back from me; I kick out with my legs so she'll stay away from me. My back hits the wall and my left hand disrupts a loose tile at my side. When I look at Omalis, she's holding something out to me.

"I need you to see this," she says. It's a portable video player, like the one Marla had. Maybe it is Marla's. I scan it for blood stains.

When I don't go to take it from her, she sets it on the floor and flips it up and presses play. She isn't wearing any makeup today, her hair isn't done. She doesn't smell like anything, but she's kneeling very far away from me.

The sound of Marla's voice reaches me from the vid player. I flick my eyes to the small screen:

First there's just static, a wobbly grayness, then a blurry pink ball, ridged and cracked like asphalt. It pulls back—Omalis's thumb covering the viewfinder; the rest of her fades into view. She's immaculate. White blouse cut just low enough to tease but not low enough to embarrass you for looking too long at it; white skirt that reveals those dimpled knees, coquettish in their tan stockings, a color just a shade too dark for her skin. The video doesn't reveal her shoes. Her hair is curled and pinned up with those chopstick hair things; her earrings are diamonds, or glint like diamonds; she wears a silver tennis bracelet on one wrist and her nails are painted a delicate red. Her eyes look above the viewfinder, to Marla's voice, off camera.

"Step back a little more," Marla says. Her voice is close to the mic, too loud. "A little more."

It's hard to tell where they are; so little of it is captured in the small screen. It's a patio, I think; there's a light wooden railing behind Omalis, and grass beyond. The shadow of a tree; it's bright like they're outside. Ambient sounds like wind rustling leaves, like birds or ducks or something.

Omalis asks, "Okay?" My stomach clenches. Omalis is asking permission. There's this…this familiarity in her tone. I mean, she's only saying one word, but she is begging. I've heard so many girls beg in these last few weeks, heard it even when they were only talking with their eyes, and that is what is in that "okay," that's what's feeding it. Omalis is standing there, in her Sunday best, like my mother, but she's begging, like me.

The camera remains steady—it must be set up on a tripod—and there's no verbal response from Marla. Omalis's eyes focus on the viewfinder—on me—and she clears her throat.

"My name is Heaven Omalis," she begins. "For all intents and purposes, I've been a Liaison for the Over since I was eleven, for twenty-three years. Whatever choice I had then, I—" She looks down abruptly, smoothes her unwrinkled skirt with her hands, fiddles with her bracelet. I touch the beads of my own bracelet. "I never had that privilege. But I'm invoking it now. My choice."

She straightens her shoulders a bit, turns her chin up. Her eyes flick off camera again. In a lower voice, Marla whispers, "Good, baby. Good." Omalis smiles shyly—I don't know how else to describe it. She's never smiled like that at me. She pulls her face together and refocuses on the viewfinder.

"Under my own volition, under absolutely no duress or coercion from any external force, I volunteer my services to the Resistance. I understand the risks to my life. I understand—Marla, can we stop this?"

Again, she's like another person when she asks these things of Marla. Like a kid, in need of approvals and assurances and someone to hold her and tell her, "Calm down, calm down."

Marla's voice says, "What's wrong?"

Omalis wipes her brow with a knuckle. "Nothing. I don't know. It's…" She wipes her mouth, she brushes nonexistent bangs from her forehead. In this brief pause, I look up from the video player to see the Omalis sitting here in this room with me. Her eyes are closed, her head is turned away, facing the shower. She sits on her hands. The Omalis on the screen starts speaking again so I look back down. "Do I really talk like this?"

Marla laughs, eliciting another shy smile from Omalis. "You can say whatever you want to, however you want to say it. This is for you, remember. What words would you believe?"

Omalis casts her eyes down while she thinks. She clasps her hands behind her back. Something blows across the screen behind her, a leaf or a small bird. She looks back up and says, "I'd want to see you."

In a second, Marla is in view, standing beside Omalis. It's like having the breath knocked out of me, seeing them together. It's like being slapped, back-handed by some lie, some little tiny half-truth or omission that was so cute and small when it was born all pink and naked and ugly, but then it got big and sprouted limbs and wings and teeth and thorns and a will of its own and this hunger, this hunger to hurt you. It hurts, it physically hurts to see them together—Marla, in a floral print dress, like she just stepped out to get the sun tea that's been brewing all day, her hair longer then, flowing lazily over her bare shoulders, her bare shoulder that touches Omalis's shoulder so casually, so familiarly. I dig the tears out of my eyes with my fingers, and make some sort of awful sound, some sort of dying sound.

Marla takes Omalis's hands in hers, and kisses her knuckles. Omalis grimaces. She says, "Well, I wouldn't believe *that*, certainly."

"What? Why not?"

"It looks manipulative."

Marla grabs Omalis's body and tilts her into a tango-like dip, and kisses her, kisses her deep, so deep I feel it in my own throat, dry and hard against the core of me. On screen, Omalis struggles away but she's laughing.

"I'm attempting a level of decorum here, darling."

"See, there." Marla puts a hand to her stomach to catch her breath. "You do talk like that."

Omalis finds Marla's hand again and looks into the viewfinder. Marla watches Omalis speak.

"I'm Heaven Omalis and I am a member of the Resistance. I understand the risks to my body and to my mind. I understand them and I accept them." She looks back to Marla. "Okay?"

Marla only nods and brings the back of Omalis's hand to her lips once more.

The video stops, the screen is empty. My skin jumps when Omalis—here in this bathroom, here in this reality—clicks the player shut and pulls it into her lap. With her other hand, she gets a folded piece of paper out of her pocket and holds it out to me.

"I need you to do something for me." Her voice is so loud in this small room. It makes my ears bleed. I feel like I'm bleeding all over. "It's very important. Before we leave this bathroom, I need you to read to me the words on this paper. You'll be saving my life. You'll be saving Marla's life. Okay?"

She breaks me with that "okay," she fucking skewers me, god. It's hot in here, it's hot all over, inside and outside of me, it's my own blood making me so hot, it's my own body that won't stop shaking and leaking and betraying me. Shouldn't I be used to betrayal by now? Shouldn't I know how to handle it, how to suck it back down and hold it and crush it with my thick skin and stiff upper lip?

"Jordan. Please."

Some perverse role-reversal has her begging me now. I take the paper just so she'll stop asking me for things.

She slumps back against the closed door and looks down at her knees. Her jeans are loose on her, comfortable, her stay-at-home jeans. I can't stop crying, silently, but I can't stop looking at her either.

"That woman in the video…" Omalis shakes her head. Her hair obscures her eyes. "That was three years ago. I don't even know who that woman is. She's meant to be me but I can't remember her. Did you hear that laugh? When have I ever laughed like that? When will I again? And Marla…" Slowly, she spins the video player on the tiles next to her. "She's different, too. She's someone else. We all are. We all have to be. Someone else."

Omalis sucks in air loudly; my chest tightens as if she's taken the air directly from my lungs. She drops her knees so she's sitting cross-legged now. She stuffs the vid player in her front pocket and straightens her back against the door. It's like a yoga position, the lotus or something, like my mom used to attempt before she got too busy or lazy or whatever. Omalis looks at me, and I'm too worn out to look away.

"I don't remember myself in that moment, or anything about that moment, because Marla wiped it from me. *Phht*—" She blows air through her teeth like the sound of carbonation escaping a can of fresh-popped soda. "—Like a wizard, a spell. Gone. Never happened. She uses me to get messages to girls like you, Jordan. To put them into positions to receive her messages. After, she goes in with her magic wand like a scalpel and carves the memory out of me, so the Over can't find it. She's been hard at work for three years, and she'll keep at it for as long as it takes. Until they're dead or until she is. Whatever else Marla is… she's a fighter. She is that."

Marla is a fighter. I knew that. I could have told you that. But I never would have, because you're the enemy. You're supposed to be the enemy. Omalis, the Liaison, the cold-hearted bitch Taker of Children, whore to the Over, hated hated hated for everything you do to me, everything you make me think of doing to you. Why can't I say these things? Why can't I make more than these desperate sounds? It's the Over out there, the one mere feet away, swallowing up all the words, swallowing everything up except my blood, which burns up everything except my tears, which the Over is saving for later.

Omalis moves into a kneeling position and rocks forward on her knees. She wraps her fingers partially around my shin. I can't push into this wall far enough.

"Jordan, please look at me." She's crying. How can I sit here breathing when Omalis is crying? "Jordan, I am so, so sorry for hurting you. I never wanted that. You were...you are so strong. I admire you. I have nothing but admiration for you. I know I ask too much of you, and I'm sorry for that. Please say something."

But it's all cry cry cry. If I open my mouth, I'll start a flood. Omalis pulls me into an awkward hug, my knees stabbing into her abdomen, her fingers raking the sweat from my hair. She doesn't say anything, which is good, but this holding-me thing, this holding-me thing like my goddamn mother, like my goddamn mother who would gladly feed her left leg—hell, both her legs, the legs of my father too—to the Over like caviar at a fancy cocktail party just to fucking hold me like this—this holding-me thing has got to stop.

Trembling, I stand up. I use Omalis to steady myself as I rise. My body feels heavier than it did before. I thought I'd leaked everything out but it's still there, gaining weight. I go to the sink and run the faucet and splash my face. I rub at my cheeks until it hurts, until it hurts so much I stop crying. I turn the faucet off. Careful not to look into the mirror. To myself, I read the piece of paper Omalis gave me.

Behind me, Omalis has stood up. She says, "It's a trigger. That phrase. After you read it to me I won't remember anything that happened in here. Which means...you can say anything. If there's anything. Anything you want to say to me, you can."

Her pause waits for me to fill it. I turn around to face her. Her eyes are as wet and raw as mine feel. I say, "What now?"

She blinks, like she's trying to remember the reason for coming here in the first place. She wipes snot from her nose with the underside of her bare wrist. Like a lady.

"Right," she says. She's trying to get back something, something she feels naked without, something that separates her from me, something that elevates her. She reaches into her back pocket and it turns out the thing that separates us is a hypodermic needle.

"This is the virus." She uncaps the needle and tosses the cap in the toilet bowl. She squirts out a little fluid and gives the syringe three quick taps. It's filled up with about an inch of something innocuously clear. "If you still want to fight, I'll inject you with this and we'll go back out there and the Over will take you away. But I can't let you make that decision yet."

"I've already made it," I say. This is the calmest I've ever spoken to anyone without my medication. Because it's true. Whoever Omalis is, whatever she's done, it doesn't matter. Marla laid it out for me, and at least I know she didn't lie about that part, the part where I deliver some sort of genetic bomb straight to the collective vein of the Over and won't live to tell the tale. But Omalis has never heard me say it, so I say it now. "I'm ready."

Omalis smiles in a way that looks like a frown. "I know you are. I know you would do this in a heartbeat because you want your death to mean something. And it will. But…your life could mean something, too. Your mother, she asked me to bring a deal to the Over—"

"And they rejected it," I finish for her. "She told me. I told her it was stupid, all the parents probably do it."

"You're right," Omalis says. "Most of the parents do it. And sometimes, a fraction of the time, the Over accept. With conditions. Jordan, they've agreed to allow your mother to take the place of one of her children. They want me to decide who gets to go home. If you wanted to go home, I would celebrate that decision. Marla would celebrate it."

I'm dangerously close to losing control of my legs, my blood, my heart. All I get out is a choked, "Why?"

"Because they are truly monsters, the Over. They have the bodies of animals but the minds of…of us. And they put these minds to cruel and sadistic things, for your torment, for their pleasure. They—"

"Why would you tell me?" I shout it, then rein it back in. "Jesus, you didn't…you shouldn't… I was ready. I'm ready. Don't tell me I can live. Don't tell me my mom…that she's dying for me. Don't tell me that. Please. Just let me do this. Just let me—"

Omalis steps to me and grips my hair from the back, tugging on it painfully, keeping me standing and bent back slightly over the sink. The pain stops my mouth from saying things. She pulls my hair hard and looks at me hard and speaks to me hard: "I've never lied to you. You deserve the truth because you can take the truth. You have a mother who cares enough to give her life for you and you deserve to know that. What you don't have is the luxury of time, Jordan, you just don't. Do you want to go home?" Like a flame winking out in a sudden breeze, she softens. Her grip softens but doesn't let go, her eyes soften but also do not let go. She says, "Jordan, do you want to go home?"

I want to wake up at five a.m. to slop last night's dinner in the pig trough and grab a pail and milk the cows before the sun comes up and the chickens get restless and their eggs are still warm when I gather them. I want to make hot chocolate and watch my dad out the kitchen window, combing out the horse's mane with a tenderness he doesn't think I know he has. I want to chase Jeremy through the wheat fields and tag his shoulder and laugh as he chases me back. I want to ask Jason what it feels like to kiss someone you really want to kiss, to hold a girl's hand and have it feel right. I want to go to one of Taylor's hockey games and cheer her on and meet her friends and eat pancakes with them after the game at some retro diner that only serves coffee and beer and none of the waitresses are under forty. I want to give my mother a hard time about the way she dresses, the way she combs her hair, chews her food, drives, talks to me, lives.

I want so many things. But going home won't give them to me. Maybe someone else can have them. Maybe someone else.

"Can it be Jeremy?" Omalis has to lean in close to hear me. Her grip on my hair turns into a caress on my neck. "Can you take Jeremy home? Jason's stronger, you know. He won't be as afraid to be alone, or to…to die. Jeremy's emotional and, and he's like an artist, like Mozart, and he…and my dad will need that. They'll both need that."

Omalis presses her lips to my forehead. Amazingly, I'm not crying. But I'm shaking like I'm cold when really I'm hot all over, especially on my forehead. Matching my low tone, Omalis says, "Yes. Jeremy can go home."

She moves her hand from my neck and runs it down my left arm, stopping to press her thumb into the crook of my elbow. "Make a fist," she says.

I ball my fingers into a fist for her. She flicks the vein in my elbow until it rises to the surface of my skin. She touches the needle to it. She says, "Thank you."

The needle goes in smooth. I don't even feel it. I watch the fluid enter me as she presses down on the plunger. It's a ghost, it's a phantom. It's a promise.

She retracts the needle and throws it into the toilet bowl, *plop*. There's a little blood but she swipes it with her thumb. She curls my arm so my fingers are touching my shoulder. She holds it there. It's so silent in this room; there is only the sound of my blood, pumping softer now, pumping steady.

Omalis picks something up off the counter and puts it in my other hand. "Will you read this now?"

I'd forgotten about this part. The part where Omalis doesn't remember any of this. The part where I have to erase it all from her. The part where I can say anything.

"Omalis—"

"Heaven," she says. "Please call me Heaven."

"Heaven." It feels strange in my mouth. It feels forbidden to me. It feels like only Marla should be allowed to call her that. "Is it okay if I... Can you..." But I swallow it, I bury it. I say instead, "Can you tell me what's going to happen to Taylor?"

She looks at me with that smile-frown again. "She's going to Breed."

I knew this. Of course. But maybe I'll have time to get her the razor before the Over take me. I go to the loose tile I'd bumped earlier, pry it up, and scoop up the baggie. Omalis takes it from me.

"You can't make her go there," I tell her.

"No." She tosses the baggie into the toilet bowl and flushes it. I can't even move. From the same pocket with the vid player, she pulls out a small orange vial. She screws off the cap and spills a single white pill onto the palm of her hand. "Cyanide," she says. "So it can be quick."

"And quite painless," I breathe.

"Put it in your cheek. You'll have a second to say goodbye, but if they catch you passing anything to her..."

"Okay." I take the pill from her and stuff it down between my teeth and bottom lip.

"The phrase," Omalis prods.

"Okay," I say again. Everything is speeding back up. I unfold the paper again, hold it in front of me, and read: *Here is a candle to light you to bed, here comes a chopper to chop off your head.*

I've barely got the last word out before Omalis makes a choking sound and I look up to see her eyes roll back in her head and she collapses. I don't move fast enough to catch her. I kneel beside her while her body spasms, I don't know what to do. Did I say it wrong? She thrashes for a second, and when I go to touch her, she stops. Her eyes open and they look glassy, distant. She scrambles up and looks around and almost bowls me over diving at the sink. There, she vomits, like arch-your-back, hold-the-rest-of-your-guts-in vomits. She runs the faucet and wipes her mouth, avoiding the mirror. Finally, she seems to remember something, and turns around to face me.

"Jordan." Her voice is the same but there's a quiver in her cheek, near her lip, that suggests she's forgotten something. "I...I have to take you away now. Do you...do you understand?"

Behind my back, I rip the paper into tiny squares and let them fall into the toilet bowl. I tell her, "I'm ready."

Omalis holds her hand out to me. I take it, which surprises her; her skin jumps and she swallows harder than usual. She looks at me oddly. I hold her hand tighter.

"Jordan, I want you to know…how brave you are."

"You're brave, too."

She squints her eyes at me but doesn't say anything. She leads me out of the bathroom.

I feel the Over's dark, thick presence without looking in its direction. Taylor is still on my bed, knees pulled up to her chest and her face buried in the space where they connect. I break free from Omalis's grip and run to her. When I pull at her face with both hands she is startled; she's been crying and her pupils are small, like dots, and the skin around them is doughy and pink. Her mouth drops open to say something, and I fill it with my own mouth. With my tongue, I push the cyanide pill from against my teeth to against her cheek, and break the kiss.

"Bite and swallow," I tell her. I hope she knows what I mean. I hope she knows it's the only thing I have to give her.

The Over rips me open from behind; at the base of my neck, under my arms, between my shoulder blades. I shriek, a raw, animal sound, a sound that travels from the Over into me through my skin and screeches out my mouth. Taylor screams and pulls at my arms. The Over pulls at me, too, pulls me away from her, shrieking all the time, shrieking so loud maybe I'm the only one who hears it. My arm spasms out toward Taylor. She tries one more time to keep me but her fingers snag on my bracelet. As I'm pulled in the opposite direction, the string grows taut and snaps, and the beads fall like rain. As the shrieking gets louder, as the pain becomes a darkness that forces its way into my vision, I watch those beads fall, one-two-three, they nick my groping fingers and fall all the way down, into nothing.

✣

I REMEMBER ONLY THE COLD. Some sort of freezer, I thought when my eyes opened. I thought I was inside the Over, that it had swallowed me up, bones and all. Of course, it was not after my bones. Blood is the thing. It feeds us. It binds us. It cannot keep out the cold.

I've since been moved from that place, wherever it was. The cold has hollowed me out, left me paralyzed, unable even to shiver. All I am is blood, which for some reason I thought would be warm; isn't blood supposed to be warm? Where did I get that notion?

Where was I before? Where am I now? Where am I going?

Here's something: There is more than just me. It's a vast room, as hollow as me, except for the low hum of the machines. I don't know exactly what they are; they feel slimy and sharp, pricking my skin, burrowing in and out and over and under me, encasing me. I think maybe the Over took my eyes. Put them someplace dark, where I can only see a pinprick of light in the distance, like the end of a tunnel. I know there are others in the room because that is what the machines do: they bind us by blood.

I'm on a hard table, or the ground. Arms rigid at my sides. My feet angle toward each other, toes groping for comfort from each other. I can curl my fingers but only slightly. The machine's sharp points have penetrated the backs of my hands, the underside of both wrists, the clefts of my elbows and knees, the base of my spine, my temples, the heel of each foot, four along my sides spaced a couple of inches apart. The machines hum, but they aren't always doing anything, or at least I can't feel them doing anything. When the transfusion starts, they become louder, their gears roar into place, and they scream.

A smell precedes this. The Over smell. I always imagined they would stink, must stink, because they live in the earth, they should stink of the earth. But they smell of blood, a sweet bronze odor, like the water fountains at the library. I don't remember the library, but sometimes I can smell the pages of musty books. Sometimes I can smell the remains of a hot dinner, butter and salt, something baking, fresh. These are phantoms. The only smell is blood, mine and theirs and all of ours.

The Over cluster around me when the machine kicks up. It used to be painful. The blood goes in, the blood goes out. It lasts for a while. During this time, I start to remember things, things I never knew but know now. I remember sleeping in the earth, sleeping for a very long time, my brothers and sisters heaped around me, all of us sleeping, sleeping. Then we woke up. We fought for the light. We fought for the air, the sky we always dreamt of, the sky our ancestors promised us while we were asleep. The fight was long; we made it look easy because we knew that would frighten them. I feel their fingernails under my skin; I feel their bullets in my teeth. They made the earth hot; they set it on fire. They killed themselves. It was easy after all.

We knew these humans before they knew us. This was our advantage. Fear. Fear, and faith in our prophecies.

This knowledge blinks into existence, burns its way across my brain, and flames out. Every time. I know how many we are. I know how many are in this room, becoming as I am becoming. We know each other. Soon, we will speak, but not with our mouths. Those will be gone.

Something is wrong, though. There is a hiccup. My mother used to say that when something was wrong. It is just a hiccup, she would say. No worries. This was maybe my mother and maybe not my mother. I have so many mothers now. We all have so many mothers, but very few memories of any of them. Soon, none.

This hiccup. It's in the blood. Mine, and theirs. They take it every day, all the time. Are there days here? They take it. It binds us. It has a hiccup. It hurts us. They don't feel it yet. I feel it because it comes from me. They don't know this yet, because they keep taking it, and giving it, back and forth, weaving this deadly tapestry. It's okay. Somehow I know this. I know it is okay.

The light grows brighter all the time. Sometime soon I will be able to see them. Sometime soon they will unhook me from the machines and I will see what I've become, and I will forget having been anything else. I will forget about our hiccuping blood. I will forget about the cold.

It will be heavenly.

# EPILOGUE

OUTSIDE ON THE VERANDA, JUNE Fontaine and Heaven Omalis sip tea. The courtyard flutters with activity: a group of women in pink polos and white tennis shorts struggle to play croquet with foam mallets and large hollow plastic balls that keep getting swept up in the afternoon breeze; a few ladies, dressed in bright pastels, dirty up their checkered aprons by kneeling to weed out the flower beds; some are merely shuttled along the pristine walkways in their wheelchairs, conveyed by older women with graying or white hair to complement their plain white uniforms. These June thinks of as orderlies but she is certain they do not think of themselves this way.

"Jeremy's semester started Monday," Omalis says. She stirs her Earl Grey with a miniature plastic spoon. Even the teacups are plastic. The utensil makes no sound as it scrapes along the cup's edge. "They're doing block classes now. He seems to be adjusting, though."

"Hm."

June is usually monosyllabic on their visits. They sit at one of several two-person tables seemingly reserved for them (it's always available, even when all the others are taken; in light of this June is almost certain Omalis has reserved it, by whatever means one might do such a thing here). They meet once a week, on Thursday afternoons, and have tea or coffee. Omalis stays until June has finished her cup. Sometimes this is an hour, sometimes only minutes. Today, the tea in June's cup is as cold as the waning autumn breeze, and they've been sitting for at least two hours.

"He's getting better about doing his chores on time," Omalis continues. She sips at her cup. She's had it refilled with fresh tea three times. She takes it plain, not even a drop of honey. "Time management will be important, especially now with school starting. Jay's been good about instilling this in him."

Omalis always opens these visits by asking after June's health, but June, confident that there is a meticulous report kept somewhere, ignores these inquiries. Omalis then moves on with a report about how the farm is keeping up, how profits are moving or not moving, or how the neighbor's farms are doing, or how the town is doing. She segues from these less personal reports into accounts of how Jay is doing, how he's keeping himself and Jeremy busy with the day-to-day. She visits them once a week as well, and probably does the same thing, except it must be a far briefer report, as June doesn't feel she does anything, or she does the same thing, most every day until there's a delivery. She hopes—she prays—Omalis does not tell them about those days.

"Do you know," Omalis's tone grows lighter, almost playful, "Jeremy taught your husband to play 'Heart and Soul' with him on the piano? Jeremy does the more difficult part, of course, but Jay holds his own, though his larger fingers often press two of the keys at once—"

"Don't you have to pee?" June says.

"I'm sorry?"

"You've had three cups."

Omalis looks down at her half-full cup. She pushes it aside, folds her hands in her lap. She is the only one in this place who is not wearing bright colors; a midnight-blue peasant blouse, a lengthy maroon skirt, casual dark flats. She has the courtesy not to wear makeup here—it would make the women and the girls jealous—but she can't help her wardrobe.

"I'm sorry, June." She brushes her fingers over her temple. Her haircut is shorter now, there's no longer hair to brush back but she makes this move at least once during every visit. "Shall I... Shall we stop now?"

Before June can answer, one of the wheelchair-bound women is pushed almost into June's legs. "Pardon me," the woman says. No, she's one of the younger ones, a girl no older than Jordan. Her name is Stacy Lee; June is not her usual doctor—if she can call herself that, in this place, but then what else?—but she sat in on one of her sonograms several weeks ago. The girl looks behind her at the graying orderly pushing her. "Samantha, geez. Eyes open, right?"

Samantha smiles sheepishly and looks away. Back to June, Stacy says, "Doctor

Fontaine, my doc's with someone else today, and I know I don't have an appointment, but." She rubs her palms over her swollen belly. Seven months along and close to bed rest. The young ones invariably get bed rest. "Something's wrong. I can just feel it, you know? Can you help me?"

June pats the girl's knee. "Of course." She tries on a smile. All she can see when she looks at these girls is their red and crying faces as they fight so hard to deliver their babies, the babies they never get to see or smell or touch before the Over take them. All she imagines when she looks at these girls is their red and crying faces as they fight so hard to escape the boys—whose faces may also be red and crying—who are forced to come inside them to create life for the Over. It's difficult to smile for them, but their struggles are much worse. "Have Samantha take you to my office. I'll be right up."

"Thank you, thank you so much." And Stacy Lee is wheeled back inside.

Although the estate is large—four floors, two massive wings stretching from the main house—most of the women prefer to spend their days, whenever possible, outside on the grounds. Even though wherever they may wander on the grounds they are always within eyesight of the thick iron fence and the armed guard towers, which can become oppressive. But inside, stationed three to a floor in the center of each wing and the main room, stand the Over. Still as pillars, as if they were holding up the very house, which they may well do. Their eyes never seem to close, their bodies never seem to move, not an inch. They seem to make no sound but after two months June can hear them breathing as easily as she can hear herself breathing.

There are no Over outside the maternity house. The women in varying degrees of their pregnancies prefer this. Though there is always—always—one of them present at the birth.

June stands up from the table. Their neighbors to the right are playing a board game. One of them cries out—"Yahtzee!"—and laughs in a displeasing manner. June says to Omalis, "Thanks for coming by."

Omalis stands up, smooths out her skirt. She reaches a hand to shake June's, smiling. When June takes her hand, the smile drops, and Omalis's grip tightens like a vise. She pulls June close. Her eyes have changed color—or only deepened to a startling near-black.

"They're dying, June." She says this low, mouth barely moving, the words rumbling from her throat like thunder. "Jordan is killing them. She will kill them. Just wait. Wait."

She lets go of June's hand and falls hard to her chair. June stumbles back and rubs at her palm. Omalis sits for a second or two, a hand pressed to her throat, looking at the tablecloth. Then she looks up, blinking. "Oh," she says. She stands. "I'm sorry. You have to go, don't you? Don't want to keep that kind girl waiting."

June forces her mouth closed. She squints at Omalis, then holds a hand above her eyes to pretend it's only the sun. She nods. "Mm, yes. Duty calls."

"You're doing a good thing here, June," Omalis tells her, stepping around the table. "Jeremy and Jay—it's not the best of circumstances, but they're happy. They'll find a kind of happiness again. And all these girls, what you're doing for them. Your loss is great, but…it means something. I do hope you know that."

June looks at Omalis. Her eyes have faded back to their sky blue. "I miss them," she says.

Omalis squeezes June's shoulder with so much compassion June almost weeps. Omalis smiles again, sad, picks up her purse from the table and adjusts it over her shoulder. "I'll come back next week. Behave until then."

June had never invited Omalis here; she only showed up that first week and June never told her to leave. Breathlessly, June waves goodbye, watches her round to the front of the main house and disappear.

A near-weightless croquet ball rolls across June's feet. Beverley Niece—eighteen, three months along for the second time—jogs over to retrieve it, stringing soft apologies behind her. June pays her no attention. She is looking in through the slightly open French doors, to the just-visible side of one of the Over standing around the corner.

It just stands there, night and day, unmoving. If Omalis can be believed, some day—maybe soon—it will cease to breathe.

And June will be there to hear it.

# ACKNOWLEDGEMENTS

I would like to thank my earliest and most loyal reader: my incredible wombmate, Erin. Thank you also to everyone who read and offered feedback on drafts or portions of this novel, especially Mike Fanning, Daniella Yimenez and ;;Joyce Siedler;;.

Special thanks to my creative writing cohort at SFSU: I may not be good at remembering names but I kept all your workshop notes so that has to count for something. Thank you especially to Maxine Chernoff for your support and guidance, to Peter Orner for your generous encouragement, and to Matthew Clark Davison for your insightful and challenging writing exercises.

The most special of thank yous to Dani, whose excellent feedback is marred only by her lapse in judgement in agreeing to marry me.

Finally, thank you to Steve Berman and Alex Jeffers for your editing wizardry and continued support and belief in my work.